LINDA BARNES

Edgar Award Nominee for
A Trouble of Fools
Shamus Award Nominee for
Best P.I. Short Story for *Lucky Penny*

Also by Linda Barnes
Published by Fawcett Crest Books:

BLOOD WILL HAVE BLOOD

BITTER FINISH

DEAD HEAT

CITIES OF THE DEAD

A TROUBLE OF FOOLS

Linda Barnes

FAWCETT CREST • NEW YORK

A Fawcett Crest Book
Published by Ballantine Books
Copyright © 1987 by Linda Appelblatt Barnes

Library of Congress Catalog Card Number: 87-16147

ISBN 0-449-21640-3

This edition published by arrangement with St. Martin's Press, Inc.

Grateful acknowledgment is made for permission to quote from the following:

"Three Marching Songs." Reprinted with permission of Macmillan Publishing Company from *The Collected Poems of W.B. Yeats*. Copyright 1940 by Georgie Yeats, renewed by Georgie Yeats, Michael Butler Yeats and Anne Yeats.

"No Second Troy." Reprinted with permission of Macmillan Publishing Company from *The Collected Poems of W.B. Yeats*. Copyright 1912 by Macmillan Publishing Company, renewed 1940 by Bertha Georgie Yeats.

"That Song About the Midway" by Joni Mitchell © 1968, 1974 Siquomb Publishing Corp. All Rights Reserved. Used by permission.

"Angels from Montgomery." Words and music by John Prine. Copyright © 1971 Walden Music, Inc., and Sour Grapes Music (ASCAP). Used by permission. All rights reserved.

Manufactured in the United States of America

First Ballantine Books Edition: December 1988
Third Printing: April 1990

In loving memory of
Bertha and Jacob Grodman,
my *bubbe* and *zaide*

Remember all those renowned generations,
They left their bodies to fatten the wolves,
They left their homesteads to fatten the foxes,
Fled to far countries, or sheltered themselves
In cavern, crevice, or hole,
Defending Ireland's soul.

> *Be still, be still, what can be said?*
> *My father sang that song,*
> *But time amends old wrong,*
> *All that is finished, let it fade.*

Remember all those renowned generations,
Remember all that have sunk in their blood,
Remember all that have died on the scaffold,
Remember all that have fled, that have stood,
Stood, took death like a tune
On an old tambourine.

> *Be still, be still, what can be said?*
> *My father sang that song,*
> *But time amends old wrong,*
> *And all that is finished, let it fade.*

Fail, and that history turns into rubbish,
All that great past to a trouble of fools;
Those that come after shall mock at O'Donnell,
mock at the memory of both O'Neills,
Mock Emmet, mock Parnell,
All the renown that fell.

> *Be still, be still, what can be said?*
> *My father sang that song,*
> *But time amends old wrong,*
> *And all that is finished, let it fade.*

> —William Butler Yeats
> from "Three Marching Songs"
> 1939

I'd like to thank my reading committee: James Morrow, Karen Motylewski, Richard Barnes, Bonnie Sunstein, Steve Appelblatt, Amy Sims, and Susan Linn. The ladies who lunch—Bonnie Sunstein, Joan Dunfey, and Gail Leclerc—helped with their support and friendship. I'd also like to acknowledge Matthew Bruccoli and Richard Layman, editors of *A Matter of Crime*, for their enthusiastic response to "Lucky Penny"; my editor, Michael Denneny, for his valued insight; and especially my agent, Gina Maccoby, for taking such good care of Carlotta and me.

Chapter 1

If Margaret Devens had told me the truth right off the bat, things might have turned out differently. Or as my mom used to say, in Yiddish or English depending on the situation, "If your grandmother had wheels, she would have been a truck."

I never met my *bubbe*, my grandma, the source of all my mother's Yiddish proverbs, but thinking about it now, I guess I wouldn't mind if she'd been a ringer for Margaret Devens—stubborn, smart, and crafty behind the sweet-old-lady facade.

"CONGRATULATIONS, Mr. & Mrs. Thomas C. Carlyle," the letter began cheerily. The stationery was thick and creamy, sharply creased, names typed in boldface, the way they are in those "personal" computer-generated mailings.

No such couple existed. I read on.

The vacuum cleaner hummed pleasantly. If you've never considered your Hoover's voice soothing, you've probably been shoving it across a high-pile carpet. From the right distance, propelled by other hands—in this case the paint-smeared hands of Roz, my tenant cum new-wave artist cum sometime assistant—vacuum cleaner buzz could make the lullaby obsolete.

Roz gets reduced rent in exchange for basic household chores. As a cleaner, she's a great artist. My spice rack is color-coded, my knickknacks adroitly arranged. Books and papers are stacked in tidy piles at attractive oblique angles. My floors have never been filthier, but then Roz doesn't have

1

much time for nitty-gritty cleaning. She dyes her hair a new color every three days and that takes up the hours. I like Roz.

A firm of Omaha lawyers was pleased to inform me that the above-mentioned Mr. and Mrs. Carlyle were the lucky recipients in their *GRAND GIVEAWAY*. After a courteous tour of a "luxurious time-sharing condominium resort," located someplace I'd never want to visit, much less live, I—or rather Mr. and Mrs. Carlyle—could claim the *GRAND GIVEAWAY FIRST PRIZE* of, take your pick, a trip to Italy for the entire family, all expenses paid—or twenty thousand bucks.

I searched for the fine print that said "valid until yesterday," or "provided you make a thirty-thousand-dollar donation to the United Church of Holy Poverty." I didn't find it. I read the whole thing again. It said trip to Italy, all expenses, twenty thousand dollars.

Claiming the prize was going to be a problem.

I know Mr. T.C. Carlyle pretty damn well. The T.C. stands for Thomas Cat, aka Tom Cat. Right. A good sort, Mr. Carlyle, but definitely of the feline persuasion. Sleek and black, with a right forepaw so white that it looks like he dipped it in a dish of cream, Thomas Cat has a disposition you could describe as independent, which I prefer, or surly, which is closer to the truth. He is not your eager three-piece-suit-and-tie type. I have trouble getting him to wear a bell around his neck, a necessary indignity that keeps him from dumping dead sparrows on my carpet, which in turn prevents the parakeet from going bonkers.

I list my home phone under Thomas C. It's okay with him. He loves getting calls from admirers of the late essayist, survey takers, anyone at all. I didn't want to put my name in the book, first because women get crank calls, and second because ex-cops get crank calls. So I listed Tom, since he's the only male I share the place with regularly. And what do you know, he started getting letters. Begging letters from charitable organizations and pleas from campaigning congressmen. Credit card offers and magazine subscriptions. He

2

subscribes to the *New York Times Book Review* and *Mother Jones*.

As far as cats go, Tom's a prize, but I didn't see how I could get him married off in time to claim the trip to Italy or the cash.

The doorbell sounded over the vacuum hum, the way it does when you're wearing ratty sweatpants and have your mouth half-full of Swiss cheese and roast beef on rye. I waited, hoping for three rings. Three rings means Roz, the third-floor tenant.

The bell rang twice, stopped.

"Hang on!" I yelled, swallowing fast.

The bell rang again, twice in rapid succession.

It isn't that I have far to travel from the dining room to the hall. It's that I have about five locks on my crummy front door. Filing burglary reports has replaced baseball as my neighborhood's prime pastime.

It was slightly past noon on a late September Sunday that had no business being so cool, and I wasn't expecting anybody. I squinted my left eye shut and pressed my right one to the peephole. If I had been expecting someone, it wouldn't have been the cozy old lady who perched on my front stoop like an inquisitive bird. As I struggled with the last deadbolt, always sticky, she turned up the collar of her wooly pink coat, and got ready to hit the buzzer again. She wore white cotton gloves. I haven't seen a pair of white gloves in ages.

"Coming," I yelled, forestalling the buzzer.

She was too old for a Mormon missionary, so I steeled myself for the Jehovah's Witnesses pitch. Possibly Antivivisection. I hoped she was antivivisection. I wondered if I could keep a straight face while I asked her where to donate the parakeet for lab research.

She had sparse white hair, like powdered sugar frosting on her pink scalp, and a round face that must have been cheerful when she smiled. Her skin was crosshatched with fine lines. Deeper ridges creased her forehead and carved channels from her broad nose to her small anxious mouth.

3

Her gray eyes, unsettlingly steady, stared gravely at the peephole.

The lock gave, and I yanked open the screen, apologizing. She didn't respond like a proselytizer or a fund-raiser.

"Margaret Devens," she announced hopefully. "Miss," she added, "Miss Margaret Devens, spinster."

I smiled at the quick glint of humor in her eyes, at the outmoded term, at the clean white gloves, but the name meant nothing to me. She stretched her small mouth into a grin, and nodded as though it should.

"And you," she continued, giving me the once-over with a nice touch of disbelief, "are Miss Carlyle, the investigator?"

Now I admit I have looked better. My sweats had seen their heyday long ago, and most of my right knee was visible through a tear. My shirt was slightly more reputable, an oversized bright red pullover. I don't wear it much because, to tell the truth, it doesn't go well with my coloring. I've got red hair, really red hair, the kind that beggars adjectives like "flaming," and Mom always told me to wear blues and greens, but every once in a while I break loose. For the rest, I was barefoot, and hadn't even thought about makeup. I go barefoot a lot because I'm six one and I wear size 11 shoes. You may not realize this, but for all practical purposes, women's shoes stop dead at size 10. Much of my life is spent shoe shopping. I hoped I'd brushed my hair before I plunked it on top of my head and stuck in the hairpins.

Probably I had. I mean, I don't always remember brushing my teeth in the morning, but I do it. With my hair under control, I almost look my age, which is on a different side of thirty than most people suspect.

"I usually work by appointment only," I said, not so much to discourage her as to excuse my appearance.

"This is not a usual matter." Her voice was soft and quavery, with the hint of a brogue.

With a caseload so light I was reading the cat's mail, I figured I ought to welcome any nibble, so I ushered her inside and draped her coat on the rack in the foyer. My nose twitched with the smell of mothballs and lavender. Underneath, she wore a blue flower-print dress of such high-collared respectability that she must have come straight from church. The wooly coat had given her an illusion of bulk. Without it, she was so thin I could see the sharp shelf of bone between her shoulders.

She opened her mouth to speak, but nothing came out except a small dry cough, so she closed it again and spent some time fiddling with her gloves, rolling them together in a tight ball and depositing them in the pocket of her coat. My clients are a nervous lot, on the whole. Most of them would rather have root canals without novocaine than discuss their troubles with a stranger. I offered coffee to break the uneasy silence.

She nodded gratefully, and took her time crossing the living room. I couldn't tell if she moved slowly because of her age, which I put in the high sixties, or because she was checking out the decor. Her eyes lingered on the furnishings and she clucked and murmured as if she approved.

If she was using the living room furniture as a clue to my character, she was making a big mistake. Mostly it's the way Aunt Bea left it when she died. I even kept her dumb parakeet, but I moved the cage to one side of the bay window so it didn't block the light. Old Fluffy squawked indignantly for a week. The living room's not my style, but I don't mind it. The oriental rug's a little threadbare, but it looks terrific when the sunlight pours in, like some glistening ruby-and-sapphire brooch. The sofa velvet is worn around the wood scrollwork, and I don't polish the mahogany the way my aunt did. Neither does Roz. Her idea of cleaning is a halfhearted flick of the feather duster here and there, but then she's got her thoughts on higher things.

Margaret Devens went unerringly for Aunt Bea's favorite rocker, and settled her narrow backside against the embroidered cushion with a satisfied sigh. She fit the chair like the missing piece of a puzzle. I half expected her to yank out her

5

knitting and clatter away. I hadn't realized how much I missed that sound.

I fetched coffee, a cup for myself, too—cream and two sugars—and crammed a quick bite of sandwich into my mouth. Chewing steadily, I rolled a few chocolate chip cookies onto a plate. By the time I got back to the living room, Miss Devens was rocking steadily, staring straight ahead, chin high. She looked like a woman who'd made up her mind, bitten the bullet, and disliked the taste.

I sat on the sofa, which creaked to let me know that while it hadn't collapsed under my weight, it was only a matter of time. I steer plump clients away from the couch. No danger with Miss Devens. She touched her coffee cup to her lips, and gave the cookie plate a welcoming reception.

"You know, I'm only here because my brother's gone," she said between bites, as if we were continuing a conversation instead of starting one.

"Gone?" I wasn't sure if she was using a euphemism for "dead" or what.

"You handle that kind of thing, do you?"

I don't handle communication with the dead, so I assumed she meant just what she said. Gone, as in vanished. I wondered if she'd seen my ad in the Yellow Pages. I wondered if anyone did. I paid extra for fancy red print. "If you're talking about a missing persons investigation," I said gently, "the police are the place to start. More personnel, more clout. Step number one: file a missing persons report."

She bit her lower lip, and looked helpless. "I wouldn't like to involve the police."

"Any particular reason why not?"

She examined her hands as if she expected to see the right answer written on them. "Well, you see, I'd hate to embarrass my brother, you know. He's younger than I am, and a bit foolhardy still. But a good man, you understand, a good man." There was something almost defiant in her insistence. She started another sentence, gave it up. Her hands fluttered.

I eyed the pile of past-due bills next to the cat's mail on

6

the dining room table. Had to keep T.C. in Tender Vittles until I could figure out how to collect his twenty grand. Of course, I could always take in more tenants. I've got rooms galore, and students will kill to be within walking distance of Harvard Square.

"What's your brother's name?" I asked.

"Bless you," she said, "bless you."

"Whoa. I haven't decided anything yet, Miss Devens."

"Oh, of course." More fluttering of hands. "Well, you haven't decided against it, have you?"

"I need a little information. Like your brother's name."

My tone must have gotten sarcastic. The lady's lower lip trembled, and I felt like I'd kicked my unknown grandmother down the stairs. My tour of duty as a cop did not do much for my manners or my vocabulary. The sleazebag bastards I dealt with did not go in for "please" and "thank you."

"Take your time, Miss Devens," I muttered. "More coffee?"

"Thank you," she said, beaming as if I'd given her a present. The smile faded quickly from her eyes and she pressed her lips together, as if embarrassed that they'd been caught tilting up. "My brother is Eugene Paul Mark Devens." Again, I had the feeling that she expected more of a reaction from me than she got. I wondered if she always gave his full baptismal name.

"How long has he been missing?"

"All of ten days," she said, not trying to keep the worry out of her voice. "And he's lived with me for sixteen years, ever since his wife passed on."

"And?"

"That's it. It's hard to imagine, much less say, but one day he was there, and the next day he wasn't."

"You, uh, had some kind of quarrel?"

"I'm not much of a fighter, Miss Carlyle." She patted her white hair, and rocked gently back and forth. "Truly, I'm at my wit's end."

"What about work?" I asked. "Does your brother work?"

"Sure, he's a driver, nights mostly, for the Green and White Cab Company. That's why we don't talk as much as a brother and sister should. The hours, you know. I'm a busy woman myself, with my volunteer work and all, and our hours didn't—our hours don't coincide."

Green & White. Bingo. Light bulbs lit over my head. That's where the name Devens came from. I had only the faintest recollection of the guy's face, but I remembered those smelly cigars of his. His term at G&W had overlapped mine on both ends, but the part-time drivers, especially the ones labeled "college kid" like me, didn't mix much with the lifers.

Green & White. That answered the referral question. G&W's dispatcher, the formidable Gloria, was always good for a boost. Someday one of my old cop buddies would tip someone off to my existence. I wasn't holding my breath.

"A cabdriver." Miss Devens pursed her lips and shook her head sadly. "He could have done better for himself, no doubt about that. If ever there was a boy with all the advantages, well, that was Eugene. I can't say he was lazy, but he had a mind of his own always, and no will to follow the plans of others. Not his mother, not his wife, not his big sister, surely . . . But that's no matter now, is it? I saw my brother last on Wednesday, September tenth, before he went off to work. And then I haven't seen him since." Her hands clutched each other for support. "Should I write that down for you, now?"

"I'll remember. I have a good memory." Once it's jogged.

"I did, too," she said, "once upon a time."

I said, "What do you think happened to him?"

"I don't know."

"You said he was married . . ."

"Could have done better for himself there, too. The story of his life. Could have, should have, might have. But he married the first girl . . . his wife, Betty . . . well, she wasn't our kind of people."

"Irish?"

"Oh, she was Irish all right, I'll give her that." Miss

8

Devens used the word "Irish" the same way my Dad's relatives, lace-curtain Irish all, used it when they talked about the folks they called shanty Irish. "It wasn't what you'd call a happy marriage. I think, when she died, it was a release for him. But who am I to judge? What do I know about it, love and marriage, happy or not?" She smiled ruefully. "I could have joined the convent for all I know about it."

"Your brother have children?"

She sighed, and the smile faded. "The union wasn't blessed. In many ways."

"Could your brother be staying with a friend?"

"I'm afraid I—I don't know his friends as well as I might."

"Does he drink?" Considering cabdrivers I have known, I thought I'd better get that one out of the way.

"Some. At an Irish pub."

Ah, now I knew where to look. There are two hundred Irish pubs in Boston. Maybe another hundred in Cambridge.

"To excess?" I inquired, putting it as politely as I knew how.

"At times," she answered cautiously. "You know what men are."

I ignored that one. "Has he gone off on benders?" I asked. "At times?"

"Well, I can't say no. After Betty died, he'd go off once in a while. He'd get, well, bleak-looking, and then he'd be out a night or two. But it's been years now. And he never stayed away so long. Never."

I bit into a cookie. "Did he take things with him?"

"Things?"

"Did you check his room? Did he pack a bag?"

"If he had I wouldn't be here, would I? If he'd taken a trip, I'd know where he was. My brother and I are close, truly we are." She fumbled in her lumpy handbag. "I brought his picture," she said, and when she looked at her brother's photograph, her face melted. She tried to smile, but the corners of her mouth quivered, and tears welled up in her eyes.

"May I see it?"

She offered it with a shaky hand.

If there ever was a man with the map of Ireland on his face, Eugene Paul et cetera was it. I recognized him from the cab company, remembered him vaguely, a cheerful red-faced man with unruly hair. He looked a bit like his sister with a fuller face, minus most of the worry lines. He looked like he knew how to have a good time.

"How old is he?" I asked.

"Fifty-six. Doesn't look it, does he? Baby of the family and all. Spoiled."

He seemed a lot younger, boyish even. Charming.

When my Aunt Bea looked at you in a certain way, you knew all was lost. She knew you hadn't done your home-work. She knew you'd failed that history test. She could see clear to the back of your soul, and plumb the depths of un-worthiness lurking there. Imagine my surprise when I glanced up and found Margaret Devens peering at me with eyes like that—determined, purposeful eyes.

Quickly, she turned away, and made fluttery motions with her hands, distractions that came too late. I'd recognized her.

No, I didn't know her from some other time or place, not personally. But I have known women her age, women of steel who grew up in an era when feathers and fans and batted eyelashes were the name of the game. The smart ladies learned the score, played along. I recognized Margaret Devens's silly gestures and flowered dresses and wooly pink coats and white cotton gloves for what they were: camouflage fatigues.

She might have slipped past me if she hadn't been sitting in Aunt Bea's chair. Aunt Bea's shawls and scarves and ban-gles and hats were armor-plated, every one.

"What exactly do you want?" I asked. "To know where he is? To talk to him, to see him? Do you want him to move back?"

"I want you to find him," she said, smiling and nodding and dithering away. "That's all."

10

"Women?" I asked.

"Possibly." She blushed demurely, and for a moment I wondered if I'd imagined the whole thing. I mean, she *was*, sitting in Aunt Bea's chair. Maybe I'd had some kind of flashback. Certainly there was nothing in her demeanor now to suggest anyone but a dear old biddy come from church to set her mind at rest about her brother.

So I didn't mention the dire possibilities—the hospitals, the refrigerated drawer in the morgue—because of the blush, out of deference for her age, because of the look on her face when she saw her brother's photo. I don't have a little brother, but I've got sort of a little sister, and I have the feeling that when I look at Paolina's school photos, I get a goofy expression on my face, too.

"How much do you charge?" she asked.

I glanced down at her shoes. My full-price clients are mainly divorce lawyers with buffed cordovan Gucci loafers. Margaret Devens wore orthopedic wedgies with run-down heels, much worn, much polished, shabbily genteel. My pay scale started a downward slide.

"I'm not a charity case," she said firmly. "You tell me the same price the rich ones pay. I've plenty of money. What do the wealthy pay you?"

"Three hundred a day plus expenses," I said, knocking a hundred off the top. "But with missing persons cases, I generally take some expense money up front, and charge a flat fee on delivery. Maybe I'll find him with one phone call. Maybe I never will."

"Will a thousand do for a retainer? Or an advance, whatever you call it."

I nodded. It wasn't the cat's twenty K, but it would sure help pay the bills.

I waited for her to pull out a checkbook, but she took a fat leather change purse out of her handbag. She crowded it behind her purse, trying to block my view.

By sitting up tall, I had a perfectly clear view of a huge

11

wad of bills. She peeled off ten hundreds, squared the edges neatly, and placed them on the cookie plate.

So, don't get me wrong. I'm not saying I didn't think something was fishy right from the start.

❤️

Chapter 2

"Workers of the world, unite!" I intoned, enunciating carefully.

"Fluffy wanna drink," Red Emma chirped. Seeing she hadn't pleased me, she tried again. "Fluffy is a dirty bird," she said.

"Fluffy is a twit," I responded.

To tell the truth, I didn't rename her just because she squawked so much. "Red Emma," Emma Goldman, the infamous anarchist of the teens and twenties, was one of my mom's heroes. One of mine, too, I guess, even if I tend to see her as Maureen Stapleton in *Reds*. I grew up on my mom's glorious tales about her mom and the New York garment workers' strike. My grandma-to-be evidently bopped a scab on the head, got caught, and spent the night in the Bowery lockup. My mom made that night in jail seem like the Medal of Honor—my dad called grandma a jailbird. As I grew older I recognized those as fighting words, and I'd sit on the front stoop till the barbs and pots stopped flying through the air.

Maybe I could teach the bird to swear. She seemed to have no trouble with F words.

If I could teach her to swear intelligibly, I could put her on the phone the next time some hospital's Patient Information Department zapped me on hold before I could blurt out a protest.

As you may have gathered, I had not located Eugene Devens at the local hospitals. Unless he'd contracted that soap opera standard, amnesia, he was healthy and managing on his own.

Amnesia. Perhaps if I rapped Red Emma gently on the head, her previous existence as Fluffy would evaporate. She would return to budgie infancy, ready for me to instruct her further in what dad and I used to call The Sayings of Chairman Mom.

One good thing. I had gotten through to the morgue, and they didn't have any unclaimed corpses that matched up with Eugene Devens.

"Budgies of the world, unite!" I said to the parakeet. "You have nothing to lose but your brains."

"Fluffy wanna cracker," she replied hopefully.

Seeing that we'd reached an impasse, I said good night, stuck her back in the cage, and yanked the hood down, providing instant sunset. That bird has my late Aunt Bea's exact voice. She's just as stubborn, too. Sometimes it's like being haunted.

I fed T.C. his dinner, pulled a windbreaker over my Grateful Dead T-shirt, and checked my jeans. Both knees intact. I made sure all the lights were on before I left. That way the burglars don't trip over anything. I leave the radio blaring, too, since T.C. is not much of a watchcat.

I was going to have to do some legwork for Margaret Devens's thousand. Legwork I was looking forward to with, shall we say, mixed emotions.

My old red Toyota kicked over on the second try. I love that car, first one I ever bought, and still feisty. I indulge my passion for red in automobile ownership. Cars don't have to complement your hair.

Green & White is not one of your more prosperous cab companies. It's tucked into a block of cut-rate auto-glass dealers and used-rug shops that front on the less-than-scenic

Mass. Pike. The garage is ugly yellow brick, with an interior done in Early Oilstain. Eight cabs can park inside, as long as nobody needs to open any doors. There's one hydraulic lift, just in case the mechanic gets ambitious. The mechanic they had in my day rarely had the energy to flip the pages on the girlie calendar.

The office is the real treat. The two eight-by-four windows have never been washed. If you didn't know that, you might think they were supposed to be opaque. The lefthand Venetian blind, a blotch of black smudges trisected by strips of yellowed tape, is out-uglied only by the right-hand one, which is dirtier, and broken to boot, so that the slats list to the left. A pegboard full of car keys is the most attractive item of decor. You wouldn't want to peer in any of the corners.

I hacked part-time while I majored in sociology at U. Mass.—Boston. It taught me how to get around the city without ever being obliged to stop for a red light. It also kept me away from waitressing, which was a good thing because I've never gotten the knack of taking orders.

I worked nights. From eleven to seven the voice of the late-night dispatcher came over so smooth and fine it was a pleasure to hear the squawk box. I bet we got a lot of business from guys just dialing for the pleasure of hearing that sexy contralto say she'd pick 'em up in five minutes. I didn't meet the owner of the voice till months after I'd formed a picture of her in my mind.

I guess I'd always imagined her black. A deep huskiness in her voice, the kind I associate with gospel singers and fire-and-brimstone preachers, gave it away. In my imagination she was tall and svelte and exotic as hell, breathing heavily into the microphone, a future Motown R&B star.

Her color was the only thing I got right.

Gloria. Her immense bulk caught me totally off guard. Not to mention the wheelchair. I mean, that low sexy voice never gave a hint of anything but ease, even when the board was lit up from here to Tuesday and all the cabs were broken down and a hurricane was set to blow.

Gloria. Spinal cord injury in a car crash at nineteen. Lived in a room at the back of the garage; no steps to interfere with the motorized chair. She kept herself to herself, seemed to socialize only with her three behemoth brothers. When the cabbies joked about her—which wasn't often, and always in stifled tones coupled with quick over-the-shoulder glances in case said brothers were present—they'd say she was suicidal, eating herself to death.

I got in the habit of dropping by her office, shooting the breeze. At the beginning, I guess I went out of pity, but Gloria wasn't buying. She sat in that chair like a queen born to a throne, and she ruled the G&W kingdom with a gloved iron fist.

She never took lunch or dinner breaks, because she ate all day long, maintaining her bulk while sitting by the phones. Now I'm a snacker, but I've never seen anything like Gloria. She packs this huge handbag every morning with stuff that would make a nutritionist gag. She is Hostess's best client, bar none. If she ever goes off the deep end, she can use the Twinkie defense.

"Hey, Glory," I said. She lifted her face from a bite of cream-filled cupcake, and flashed me a grin. She looked fatter than ever, her face so smooth she seemed ageless. "Hey, babe," she said.

I parked myself in a faded orange plastic chair, first checking for roach occupation. "Thanks for sending Miss Devens by."

"Just paying off, babe."

"We're square by now."

After graduating U. Mass., I'd given up hacking and joined the Police Department. I'd been able to do Gloria a favor or two.

She grinned wider and said, "Who's counting?"

"Got a minute?"

The phone rang. She scratched a number on a pad, pressed a button on her microphone, and sang out, "Kelton Street. Who's got it?"

Static, then a tinny voice filled the room. "Scotty. Park and Beacon."

"One-eighty-five," she said. "Third floor. Guy named Booth. Got it?"

"Copy."

"Out."

"I can chat between calls, Carlotta," she said. "Sunny day like this. Warm. The folks are walking."

"Business okay?"

She held up a plump hand and waved it back and forth. Not many people know Gloria's a full partner in G&W. Sam Gianelli, the smooth-talking son of a Boston mob figure, is Gloria's other half. Sam, who specializes in running small businesses into the ground, had taken her on to save himself the embarrassment of losing another company, pumping cash from her insurance settlement into G&W's collapsing veins, building the wheelchair-accessible room in the back as part of the deal.

Possibly the smartest day's work he'd ever done.

Sam and I had history. He was the reason I looked on my visit to the garage with apprehension. I'd dated him. Even learned something from the experience: Never sleep with the boss.

"Bet you didn't come by to ask if business was okay," she said. "What's up?"

"Sam's not here, is he?"

"You care?"

Everbody wants to be a psychologist. "Eugene Devens," I said flatly. "Off on a toot?

She said, "Shit, Carlotta, I don't like this business with Gene. Didn't even bring his cab in. Left it down by the docks, and they towed it to that damn Cambridge yard."

"The one with the two Dobermans?"

"Yeah."

"Maybe he scampered so he wouldn't get stuck for the tow fee."

16

Gloria shrugged her massive shoulders. She can move fine from the waist up.

"Ever do anything like that before?" I asked.

"Reliable, on the whole."

"So what do you think?"

Gloria finished her cupcake, and carefully swept the crumbs off her desk to feed the creatures below. "Seen the sister?"

"Uh-huh."

"Maybe she made him go to church twice every Sunday. Maybe he just kicked over the traces," Gloria said. She sounded like she was trying to convince herself.

"Is he thick with anybody here? Anybody he'd move in with?"

"They're all thick," she said. "More ways than one. You remember the crowd he hung out with."

I smiled. "The Old Geezers, right? Isn't that what we called them?"

"Right. Eugene Devens, Sean Boyle, Joe Fergus, Dan O'Keefe, Pat O'Grady, all the old Irish coots. Joe Costello's in with them, but I don't know what kind of Irish name Costello is. They're tighter now, what with all the new cabbies. I mean for the Geezers, the Russian Jews were bad enough. Now they've got Haitians, and Jamaicans, and the Afghans are moving in fast. Devens and his buddies see themselves as the last American cabbies. They hang out and booze and moan about how the industry's going to hell." She smiled one of her wicked smiles. "Funny, they don't bitch much to me. I think they figure I might be prejudiced. Can you beat that?"

Nobody complains much to Gloria. First of all, she's got a tongue so caustic it ought to be registered with the Nuclear Regulatory Commission, and second, she's got those three devoted brothers, each bigger and tougher than the last. The smallest, nicest one got tossed out of the NFL for biting some guy's ear off, or so the story goes. Her brothers rigged up the room behind the garage with every electric gizmo available.

Wires and motors everyplace. There's even a network of pulleys and ladders and metal bars so she can haul herself up and get to the fridge or the stove. Walking into Gloria's high-tech room and bath, tucked behind that grimy garage, is like charging from the nineteenth century straight to the twenty-first with no pit stops.

"What about Pat?" I said. "You ask Pat where Eugene went? He used to be plugged into every little intrigue."

"Pat left, Carlotta, maybe six months ago. Cancer. Operation, chemotherapy, the works."

"Shit." Pat almost made the rest of the Old Geezers bearable with his self-deprecating humor and ready smile. "Well, you ask the guys where Eugene went? You ask Boyle?"

I waited while Gloria took another call. She frowned as she hung up. "Look, Carlotta, I hope this whole thing is a lot of smoke. It could be. I've asked all the Geezers about Gene, and I'll tell you, they're not worried. They're, I don't know, kind of weird and excited and, well, they're not saying shit. He coulda run off with some woman, somebody his sister would have hated on sight, some teenybopper, for Christ's sake. All I know is he's gone."

"He pick up his last paycheck?"

Gloria stared down at the desktop. "We owe him two days."

"I don't like that much."

"We'll hold it for him."

"He leave anything?"

The phone bleeped, and Gloria went into her spiel. I'd changed my question by the time she hung up.

"What did he leave, Gloria?"

She spent some time rooting for a cookie in her bag, removing a bag of Reese's Peanut Butter Cups, then a sack of marshmallows. I doubt she has room in there for keys or a wallet or a comb. "Well," she said finally, "I didn't tell his sister about his locker."

I just raised my eyebrows.

"Oh, I don't know, Carlotta. She looked so, hell, sort of

sweet, but, you know, white gloves and a flowered hat. I figured she'd bust it open and find stuff she could use against him for the rest of his natural life. Box of condoms or something sinful, you know?"

"I wouldn't hold it against him, Glory."

"I don't have a key."

"You got a bolt-cutter?"

"He comes back, he won't like it."

"He comes back, we'll buy him a new lock."

"Sam won't like it."

She watched me obliquely, with half-closed eyes, when she mentioned Sam's name. She always does, so I was ready. I met her with a blank stare that would have done credit to a cardsharp.

"Sam won't know," I said evenly, "will he? And if he should happen to find out, we'll snow him somehow."

"You will, babe. You're practically a one-woman blizzard."

She scribbled Gene's locker number on a scrap of paper. The phones were starting to ring in earnest now, so I left her to it. The mechanic kept a rusty bolt-cutter in a spiderwebbed corner behind the workbench. He'd flipped the calendar pages as far as April, only five months behind. Maybe the siliconed blonde straddling the red motorcycle was the stuff of his dreams.

The lockers along the back wall had collected a few more dents, but were otherwise unchanged—khaki-colored and smeared with greasy fingerprints.

No need for the bolt-cutter. The lock of 8A hung open. There was nothing inside.

I closed my eyes and rested my forehead against the cool metal door of 7A. Maybe Margaret knew about the locker after all. Maybe she'd found the key, taken Eugene Paul et cetera's extra shirt home to iron.

There were a few crumpled scraps of paper in one corner of the locker. I smoothed them out. One was a bank withdrawal slip, the kind you get from those automated tellers, for fifty bucks. The other was a receipt from an all-night grocery for a dollar and change. Big whoop. Fifty wouldn't get him far. I shoved them both in my shoulder bag, and ran my fingers around the dusty edges of the locker.

"Ouch!" The damn thing stuck me, whatever it was. I sucked the tip of my finger and put in my other hand, gingerly now, to investigate. Some rare breed of biting cockroach, no doubt.

The thing I came out with was gold, or at least gold-plated. It was kind of a pin, a collar stud. I've got one on my bulletin board at home that spells out ERA. This one said GBA, which meant nothing to me.

"Greater Boston Association? Greedy Buggers of America? Goof Balls Alliance?" Back in the office, I tried a few possibilities out on Gloria.

"Maybe it's a rock band," she said, slapping a half-empty Pepsi bottle down on the desk.

"Punk or heavy metal? Which was Eugene into?"

She laughed. When Gloria laughs, you can't help joining in. Somebody ought to record it for shut-ins.

"Well, thanks a lot," I said, even though she hadn't told me much. I guess I was thanking her for the laughter.

"Glad you came by. Do it again. Bring that little Spanish girl."

"You give her too much candy."

"So long, Carlotta."

I was halfway out the door when she yelled after me. Not yelled. Her voice just gets deeper and richer as it gets louder.

"Hey," she said, "I meant to ask, that cute guy find you?"

"Guy?"

"Somebody here asking about you, maybe three days ago. It's why you were on my mind when Miss Devens popped by."

"Give a name?"

"I don't remember."

"What did he want?"

"How long you worked here, stuff like that."

"You tell him?"

"He already had your address and phone, babe. Client, I figured."

Or maybe just a potential housebreaker.

"Looks?" I asked.

She gave it some consideration while biting into a marshmallow. "Cute, like I said. Straight, or doing a good imitation. Dark hair. Medium tall. Medium build. Thirties. White."

"If he shows again," I said, "give me a ring."

Who knows? Maybe he could play Thomas C. Carlyle when I tried to pick up my twenty K.

"How you doing with that crazy bird?" Gloria asked.

"Want it?"

My eagerness must have betrayed me.

"Hell, no," Gloria said.

Chapter 3

"Life," my grandmother reputedly used to say, "is a big headache on a noisy street."

"Hello?" I said. "Hello?"

The telephone played a syrupy version of "A Hard Day's Night" into my left ear.

"Yoo hoo."

On hold again.

"Testing," I said. "One, two."

Muzak has no charms to soothe this savage beast. I checked the sweep hand of my Timex. Thirty more seconds, I'd give them. Or else.

Seventeen, sixteen, fifteen. The recording switched to something that could have been "Raindrops Keep Falling on My Head" before it got processed into mush.

Ten, nine.

A voice that matched the canned music told me to hang on, she would switch me to blah-blah.

"What?" I said.

Raindrops kept falling on my head.

I murmured a few other things. I probably wouldn't need to teach the parakeet to swear after all. She could just pick it up around the house.

A human voice, female, nasal. "And here is our Mr. Andrews at lovely Cedar Wash Condominiums."

I inhaled. Before I could speak the music started up again, then stopped, lush strings mercifully strangled.

"To whom am I speaking?" demanded a gruff bass voice. He sounded like I'd kept him waiting.

"Carlotta Carlyle," I repeated for the umpteenth time. "Want me to spell it?"

"Ah. Wife of Thomas C. Carlyle."

"Ah," I echoed.

"You're calling about the contest," he continued.

Bingo.

"Mrs. Carlyle," he said excitedly, sounding like he was auditioning for TV game show host of the week, "could you read me the number on the top left-hand corner of your letter?"

I am not Mrs. Carlyle. Carlyle is my maiden name, which I never abandoned. I am Ms. Carlyle, sometimes Miss Carlyle, although I don't see what business my marital status should be to people who don't even know me on a first-name basis. I wasn't even Mrs. when I was married. But I don't quibble with folks who want to give me money.

The letter was tacked low on the refrigerator door, with one of those magnets that looks like a hamburger. A gift from Roz. All my plain silver disk magnets have disappeared. Roz again. She borrows various household objects with the intent of immortalizing them in acrylics. A vase here, a box of steel wool pads there. Her variations on the theme of dead Smurfs trapped in Windex bottles are impressive. Sometimes the magnet, the vase, the Windex will return as mysteriously as it flew. Sometimes substitution occurs.

I tucked the phone between my left shoulder and ear, and stooped to get a better look.

"How about A-198306?"

"Congratulations."

"This is for real? Twenty thousand dollars?"

"Or the trip to Italy. For the entire family. Up to eight individuals. Deluxe accommodations, first class all the way."

"My, my," I said.

"You'll want to make an appointment," he said firmly.

"I will? Oh—yes, I will."

"Already more than half the two-bedroom units at exciting Cedar Wash are pre-sold, but if you place your order within the next thirty days, you and your husband can select a custom-colored hot-tub."

"About the twenty thousand—"

"In order to win the grand prize, all you have to do is view the property. No obligation to buy. Would next Saturday be convenient?"

"My husband is out of town. I'd be available."

"Both you and your husband must be present."

"Like I said, my husband is out of town."

"Well, as long as the two of you collect your prize within fourteen days, we can be quite flexible."

"Flexible" probably didn't extend to cats.

"Thomas is overseas," I said gravely. "It might take me a while to contact him."

I pictured an imaginary Thomas C. Carlyle, traveling through remote and rugged mountains with a band of Afghan guerrillas, burnoose waving in the breeze. He looked like Robert Redford. Younger.

T.C. rubbed against my leg. He didn't look at all like Robert Redford.

"That is too bad," the man on the phone said. He sounded sincerely concerned.

"Any possibility of an extension on those fourteen days?" I asked.

"Well, it's very unusual. I would have to speak to my superiors."

"Why don't you do that," I said, "and I'll call back."

"Try to get in touch with your husband, Mrs. Carlyle."

"Right," I said.

I hung up and stared balefully at T.C. I mean, you can kiss a frog on the nose and have a chance at a prince, but what the hell can you do with a cat?

Chapter 4

I suppose I could have tried the direct approach, sidling up to one of the Geezers, buying him a whiskey or three in memory of our former camaraderie at Green & White, then easing in the crucial questions: So where's old Gene Devens? What's he up to these days? But I suspected that some of the old coots might remember my transformation from cabbie to cop. And if they hadn't told Gloria about Eugene's disappearance, I figured they weren't about to give me the inside scoop.

The situation called for subterfuge. Sneakiness. I live and breathe for that kind of stuff. If I thought I could possibly agree with half—well, a quarter—of their activities, I might have joined the CIA. Spying has its attractions for me. Government does not.

I knew one important fact about Eugene Devens. He drank.

I could have tried every Irish bar in Boston, beginning with the Eire Pub in Southie, grandaddy of them all, but that would have taken six months of hard drinking, and Margaret Devens didn't look like a lady who'd take kindly to footing the bill for a six-month bar tab.

Now a man might give up his home. He might stray to the arms of a thoroughly unsuitable suburban divorcée, say, or even hit the skids and forget the joys of domestic life with a devoted elderly sister. But if that man has a history of drink, and a group of buddies with whom he regularly takes a drop, odds are he will show up in their company one night.

Gloria declared she hadn't the faintest clue where Gene and the Geezers did their boozing. So starting fresh Monday night, I hung out with her—keeping away from the Reese's Peanut Butter Cups by sheer force of will—until, with a nod, her mouth too full of Twinkie for polite conversation, she informed me that a couple of Eugene's cronies were bringing their cabs in for the night.

The first time I tried to follow them, they split, and zoomed off in different directions. I took a chance and tailed old Sean Boyle, who went straight home to bed.

So did I.

The second night was more of the same, except Gloria's brother Leroy, a mere bruiser of six three, took ten bucks off me at five-card stud. When Leroy wins, I always breathe a sigh of relief. This time, I followed Joe Fergus home to his apparently blameless sheets.

The third night, Wednesday, was more promising from the start. Three of the old coots piled into a yellow Dodge Charger that looked like a graduate of a demolition derby. Now cabbies aren't easy to follow. They do the damndest things with the most righteous air, secure in the knowledge that traffic laws apply only to nonprofessionals. I'd almost forgotten the thrill of the illegal U-turn, the music of the two-wheeled corner, the joy of navigating the narrow back street.

25

These guys had a route that took them along roads no full-sized car had discovered, at speeds never intended by Chrysler. I don't think I breathed until that Dodge pulled into the parking lot of the Rebellion.

The Rebellion is *the* Irish bar in Brighton. It's on Harvard Street, in the middle of a working-class block that's experiencing Vietnamization. "Vietnam Eggrolls" reads the neon on the new take-out joint. The laundries have signs in an alphabet I can't read, and so does the Kao Palace Fish Store and Restaurant, which, by the way, is a great place for softshell crabs.

I could see that the shamrock was still the bumper sticker of choice on the beat-up Chevys and rusty Fords in the Rebellion's pocket-sized parking lot. Two G&W cabs were tucked into the lot as well, which would have given Gloria apoplexy. She wants those cabs on the road every second.

I pulled around the corner and ditched my Toyota in a loading zone, locking it carefully. The thing I miss most about being a Boston cop is that little sticker you put on your windshield that keeps you from getting a parking ticket every hour on the hour. It also has a sobering effect on potential car thieves, if they can read.

It was close to midnight. I was glad it was Wednesday, because Wednesday is not pick-up-a-date-at-a-bar-and-take-her-home-for-the-night night.

I can pass for Irish. I've got that kind of coloring, red hair, green eyes. I am part Irish, for the record. Also part Scots, and half Russian Jew. Somewhere back in the misty past, I am reputed to have had a great-grandma, on my mother's side, who stood well over six feet, accounting for my otherwise surprising height. My parents were both shorties, Mom a passionate union organizer, Dad a Scots-Irish Catholic cop, at war with himself when he wasn't doing battle with Mom.

It not being Saint Patrick's Day, I didn't wear green. I aimed for working-class chic: skinny black jeans and a blue and black lumberjack plaid shirt, belted. Shoes tell all; if I'd worn four-inch black spikes with that outfit, not that I own any four-inch black spikes, I'd have looked like a working girl. In sneakers, I was okay—as okay as any woman gets who walks into a bar solo.

Someday unescorted women will walk into bars without getting the glad eyeball from every guy who can still lift his face from his beer. But that great day has not yet arrived. Oh, I'm not making a fuss—I'm not bitter, don't get me wrong. I just hate feeling like I've got a price tag hung on my ass. There's no way to stop it. No way to win or get even. Once I spent an entire summer wolf-whistling at construction workers, reaching new heights of hollow achievement when I made some poor jerk blush.

The Rebellion's management eased my entrance by choosing a dim orangey light that made me suspect they didn't want to draw attention to their food. Baseball, the Red Sox vs. the Orioles, lit up a big TV screen over a scratched dark wood bar. Smoke laced the air, and the place smelled like they emptied the ashtrays every Easter, need it or not.

A wood partition shielded half a dozen tables from the bar. Most were square, and big enough to accommodate a four-person card game. A platform at the back of the room had space for a microphone and a folding chair. "Entertainment Weekends," a hand-lettered sign promised. "Authentic Irish music." In a rear corner, two tables had been shoved together, making a decent-sized table for eight. The table for eight had twelve chairs squeezed around it.

My three cabbies were making themselves at home at the big table, joining friends, judging from the handshakes and smiles all around. Their table was the farthest from the bar, wouldn't you know it, tucked in the corner near the restrooms.

My threesome sat together, an oddly matched trio. Sean Boyle first caught my eye, the Old Geezer I'd followed home Monday night. He had a shock of white hair and a round flabby face. Red veins stood out in his doughy nose, making him look like a cross between Santa Claus and a wino.

If I'd hailed his cab I would have demanded to smell his breath before climbing aboard. Then again, I'm not sure I'd have wanted to get that close.

To Boyle's right sat a man who still had muscle instead of fat. Maybe fifty, I guessed, his hair flecked gray, he looked like a former Hell's Angel, but maybe that was just the black leather jacket. He had a thin, sharp nose and a thin-lipped mouth. Mean-looking eyes. I thought he might be Costello, a guy who'd worked the day shift while I was at G&W. I didn't think he'd remember me.

Third was Joe Fergus, as mild-looking a little man as you might want to meet. He'd shrunk since I'd seen him last, and he couldn't have been more than five feet six then. He was wiry and wrinkled, and possessed of a legendary temper. I'd never seen him blow, but I'd heard stories. Drivers who cut Fergus off on lane changes came out the worse for wear.

Of the eleven men at the table, maybe six looked familiar. G&W drivers, no doubt, but I couldn't recall their names. They seemed to be in their fifties or sixties, except for one. He seemed younger than the rest, although I couldn't be sure because his back was toward me. He moved his hands around a lot when he talked. The old guys smiled and nodded, and apparently agreed with everything he said.

All I could hear was the Red Sox score, and that was depressing.

Four pitchers of beer, untouched, squatted along the dividing line between the two tables. There was a formality about the setting that seemed odd in view of the orange light, and the smoke, and the TV glare. Hands were solemnly shaken before the brew was poured, and the men murmured as the glasses clicked. It had the air of a toast. If there'd been a fireplace in the immediate vicinity, maybe they'd have tossed their glasses in the grate. I couldn't catch the words over the canned excitement of the sportscaster.

I'd never worked this section of town when I was a cop. I'd been a downtowner, combing the Combat Zone for strung-out hookers, trying to nab their pimps. But it took me only about two seconds to figure out that the cops were here. Not uniformed cops either, plainclothes detectives.

Ah, you say, what perception. Able to ID a cop by the smell, by the distinctive air of authority. Much as I hate to disillusion you, I knew the guys. Or one of them anyway. Mooney.

Chatting with Mooney was one of the few things I'd liked about being a cop. Moon and I got on so well together I wouldn't even consider dating him, although he is not bad-looking. Plenty of guys are good at sex, but conversation, now there's an art. Staring at him across the smoky room, his brow furrowed, his face animated with talking and listening, I wondered if it might be time to reconsider.

He was deep in discussion with two other gents at a table near the makeshift stage. He hadn't spotted me yet, and I wasn't sure discovery would be to my advantage. Did I want to be associated with cops? Would cops want to associate with me? Were they working? Just drinking? Would Mooney want to know if I was working? Margaret Devens had ordered me not to file a missing persons, not to breathe the sainted name of brother Eugene near the cops.

From my perch on a black leather barstool I couldn't see any kingpins of organized crime, but I figured I'd let Mooney make any approach. Far be it from me to blow a man's cover.

I gave up smoking years ago, but when I'm in a bar I still get the urge. It's so natural. Slide onto your barstool, light up, it's springtime. Cancer waits till autumn. My dad died of lung cancer. They should have made a Marlboro commercial out of his last few days of tubes and pain and small indignities. Still, the craving for smoke tugged at my stomach, and my hand reached automatically for my bag, as if I'd find a pack of Kools inside.

"What'll it be?" The bartender smoked and I inhaled. I know it's cheating and dangerous and all that, but hell, you can always get hit by a gold Mercedes and go out in a quick flash of glory.

I ordered Harp on tap, and earned an appreciative smile

29

for my Irish expertise. I dated an Irish guy from Boston College once. The bartender sped off and I settled back to observe my three cabbies in the mirror. They didn't seem to be waiting for a companion to fill the single empty chair. Intense discussion was taking place back there. I wished they'd raise their voices so I could hear.

The bartender came back with a foaming glass and set it before me so gently he didn't disturb the suds. He had an engaging gap-toothed grin in a youthful florid face. He looked like he sampled his own wares. He looked like he ought to arrest himself for serving somebody underage.

Never go to bars to pick up men. A few young guys in one corner were slapping each other on the back and giggling and pretty soon one of them would come over and make me an offer I could easily refuse. Maybe it was their collective leer that made me slide my license out of my wallet when I put down my money for the beer. The bartender gave it the eye.

Sometimes I'm subtle, sometimes I'm not. I figured I'd level with the guy, in case the young toughs in the corner got rowdy, or Mooney dropped by to chat. Besides, the barkeep looked like the type who'd enjoy a little intrigue.

His eyebrows slid up and he grinned. It was a nice grin, not primed with disbelief. "You want to ask me a few questions, right?" he said, like he'd been waiting for the day when somebody would come by and do just that. He looked around as if he expected TV cameras. TV has practically wrecked the investigation business. People have such unrealistic expectations.

"Eugene Devens," I said under my breath, trying to play the role.

"Gene," the bartender agreed.

"Yeah."

"In trouble?"

"No trouble."

He gave the place a quick once-over. "He's not here."

"I know."

"Oh."

"He come by often?"

"Why?"

"Pour yourself a beer," I said. "My treat."

"Why?" he repeated, reaching for a glass. He rubbed a few spots off it with a grayish dishrag.

"His sister hasn't seen him in a few days. She's worried."

"Since when's a guy that old need a permission slip to go on a field trip?"

"Got me," I said. "Did he take a field trip?"

He shrugged. "Probably just a breather. It's tough living with your sister." He spoke with feeling and I wondered about his domestic arrangements.

"You know him pretty well."

"I take an interest in my customers."

"He hang out with the group back at the big table?"

"Why?" he said, smiling brightly.

"What's your name?"

"Billy." He stared down at my photostat. "Carlotta. Does a nickname go with that?"

"Nope," I said, wondering why bartenders always have little boys' names. "Look, suppose Gene Devens decided he couldn't take living with his sister one more night, where would he go?"

"Ireland," Billy said without missing a beat. "Ireland."

"He talk about going?"

"All the time. Practically didn't talk about anything else. Hadn't seen the old country since he was a kid, you know, but he had a picture in his head. Anything wrong here must be right there. It's like, you know, in his mind Ireland stayed exactly where it was when he was a kid, while this country went to the dogs, see?"

"Yeah."

"Green fields. Pretty girls who don't mind if you call 'em girls."

"Isn't Gene getting old for that?"

"Not Gene."

"He have a woman friend? A girlfriend?"

"He wouldn't have brought her in here. You can see the old guys clucking about you. This is a pub. The men come in after work. The women stay home."

"How quaint. Gene talk about a woman? A girl?"

"Nope."

"What did he talk about?"

"The old country. The glorious rebellion. The terrible Brits. The great poets."

"Grand."

"Gene and I were tight." Billy finished off his beer and wiped foam from his lips with the back of his hand. "You'll see. Couple of days, I'll get a note from him. Dublin, maybe. Wishin' all his old buddies were there."

"He have the money for a trip like that?"

"He worked. Drove a cab."

At least we were talking about the same guy. I slid one of my cards across the bar. "Call me if you hear from him," I said.

A fellow down the bar signaled for another Scotch, and Billy made tracks. I sipped at my beer, which was strong and cold, if not my favorite.

Ireland. Does a man go off to another country without saying good-bye to his family, without packing a suitcase? If Gene was in Ireland, why were the old coots playing it so close to the vest? Why not cheer the return of the native son so loudly you could hear it clear over to Southie? Why not tell his sister, dammit?

Well, first thing in the morning, I'd check all the planes and ships bound for the Emerald Isle.

"Hiya, doll," a voice said close to my ear.

I turned, ready to disillusion the hopeful stud, and came face-to-face with Mooney. He didn't look like himself because a leer is not at home on that open, honest mug. I knew right off he didn't want me to recognize him, because Mooney knows that "hiya, doll" is not an approach I favor.

32

"Hiya, jerk," I said softly. Anybody watching from his table would think I was saying something nice.

"What are you doing here?" he said, smiling like he was telling me something else.

"Drinking."

"I have a bet going down, Carlotta. I can earn a quick hundred if you leave with me."

"What do you get if I pour beer down your crotch?"

"I can trade you something," he said.

I must have left the price tag on my ass after all.

"No bet, Moon," I said. "The lady leaves alone." I drank up, shook his hand. "Tell your friends I've got a social disease."

"I guess my line is less than irresistible."

"You catch on fast. That's what I like about you."

"I do have something to tell you."

"Tell me."

"Something important. Something worth a favor."

"So tell me."

"Somebody's asking questions about you."

"Oh, crap," I muttered. Somebody asking Mooney questions. Somebody asking Gloria questions. "Are the guys at your table cops?"

"No. And I could seriously use a good reason to get out of here."

"Then I want the hundred."

"Ten," he countered.

"Ten, hah," I said. "Eighty."

"Half! And that's robbery."

"Arrest me" I said. I added a generous tip to the price of two beers on the counter and winked at the bartender. "Let's go."

The old guys at the bar chattered like a bunch of monkeys when we left. Mooney draped his arm loosely around my shoulders. I stepped on his foot. Clumsy old me.

Chapter 5

"That'll be fifty bucks," I said cheerfully, as soon as we'd cleared the front door. The night air smelled of spilled beer and car exhaust. Faint stars struggled to compete with the city lights. A leather-jacketed teenager strutted by with a blaring boom box perched on one hunched shoulder.

Mooney kept his hand on my arm longer than strictly necessary. "Most I ever paid to squeeze somebody's shoulder," he said.

"But worth it." I smiled to take the sting out. "Hand it over."

"When I collect, you collect."

"Oh, God, Mooney. Collect from those goons you were sitting with? I can't wait that long."

"If I can wait, you can wait," Mooney said. "You're still a kid, you'll outlive me."

Mooney plays at this old guy stuff, and I guess he is starting to catch sight of the big four-oh. He's got a few gray streaks, and you can see crow's-feet when he smiles, but he keeps in shape, and it shows.

"Live hard, die young," I said. Roz has a purple T-shirt with that slogan blazed across the chest in bright gold. Roz must be twenty or so. I keep wondering how long she'll wear it.

"You got it wrong, Carlotta," Mooney said. "I learned it in school. It's 'Only the good die young.' Before they get a chance to fool around."

"What were you doing in there?" I asked.

34

"Police business."

It came across as a snub, and I took a step back to let Mooney know he'd made his point. Sometimes I think he's still pissed at me for quitting the department. "It's like that, huh? Drugs? I didn't recognize the punks at your table."

"What were you doing in there?"

"PI business."

"No kidding? You got a case?"

"It would be more flattering if you didn't look so surprised, Mooney."

"Didn't know you could see my face."

"It's the streetlamps. They cut down on crime."

"My car's over on Woodlawn."

"Let's just stroll around the block," I said.

We walked in silence for a while, the kind of silence you get on a city street, car doors slamming and horns tooting. I don't know what Mooney was thinking, but I was enjoying the stretch it took to match my stride to his. I used to love late-night walks. My ex-husband and I were great walkers. Boston's a walking town. And now—well, I haven't been for a late-night prowl in a long time.

It's not that I'm scared. I can take care of myself. I grew up in Detroit, and compared to the kids of the Motor City, most of the punks around here don't know what tough means. I'm not scared of the streets. Maybe I'm afraid of the great I-Told-You-So. You know how it goes: "Gee, Carlotta, none of this would have happened if you'd had the sense to stay indoors."

Sorry state of affairs, isn't it, when a six-foot-one-inch woman starts acting like a prisoner in her own home after dark? I inhaled the pungent smell of a Szechuan take-out stand, and vowed to start treating myself to nighttime walks again.

"Up for some ice cream?" Mooney asked.

Mooney says my sense of taste got arrested somewhere in childhood. Ice cream is my favorite food, and Boston is a mecca for the stuff. I did a quick mental survey of the local spots. "Herrell's?" I asked, not quite keeping the eagerness out of my voice.

He grinned. "Sure. We'll take it out of the fifty."

"Whose fifty?" I asked.

Herrell's has mocha ice cream to die for. Herrell is really Steve, see. He opened this place called Steve's years ago in Davis Square, Somerville, and started the ice cream revival almost single-handedly. Then he retired, and sold his successful empire, a chain of stores by then, to a guy named Joey, so Joey owned Steve's. But then Steve decided to make a comeback, except he'd sold his first name to Joey. So Steve's is Joey's and Herrell's is Steve's.

Remember that if you come to Boston.

I got a large cup of mocha with M&M moosh-ins. The real name for the goodies they blend into the ice cream is mix-ins, but, you guessed it, Steve sold the name to Joey, so now he's got moosh-ins. Makes an adult cringe to order in there, but I've gotten used to it. Mooney ordered vanilla, can you believe it? I wonder if I could ever love a guy who orders vanilla.

The accommodations at Herrell's are not lush. A few tiny round tables and some wire torture chairs lurk in a corner. Mooney and I bagged the most isolated spot we could find. A teenager with a dyed spiky blond mohawk sat at a table across the way. Her ears were pierced. That is, the right ear was pierced once and adorned with a simple safety pin. The other ear was pierced five times and had five different earrings in it, including one cascading multicolored rhinestone number that brushed her shoulder. I stared openly—I figured that's what she wanted.

She scowled. I'd have to tell Roz about the earrings. In detail.

"So how's Paolina?" Mooney asked.

I smiled, caught off guard. Paolina's my little sister. Not my blood sister. I'm an only child. While I was still a cop, I joined this group, the Big Sisters. They pair you up with a kid who could use an older female friend, a role model, you know. I lucked out. I got Paolina.

"She's ten years old," I said. "Can you imagine? Birthday last week."

"You celebrate?"

"I guess. I took her to the ballet. I asked her what she'd like to do most, and that's what she wanted, the Boston Ballet. Must have seen it on TV or something. I'd never been. I was embarrassed to tell her, so we just went. And she watched. I mean I have never seen anybody watch anything like that. A couple times I thought she'd stopped breathing. Her eyes, God, her eyes got so big. It was as if she were trying to swallow every movement, memorize it, hang on to it. For me, well, I thought it was okay, the dancing, but mostly I watched her. And then I took her out for ice cream, and home."

"Nice," Mooney said. He's divorced, too. His mom moved in with him when his dad died.

"They got Big Brothers, Mooney," I said.

"I don't need a brother, Carlotta."

I dropped my eyes and ate ice cream. I wasn't going to touch that one, not the way he said it. To tell the truth, Mooney seemed pretty attractive to me that night, but I fought it. I retired young from the man-woman business. Gave myself an honorable discharge.

"Carlotta?" I could tell from his voice, kind of gruff and deep, that I wasn't going to get off so easily. "So," he said, when I looked up, "you wanna go out sometime?"

I bit down hard on an icy M&M. "No."

"Look, Carlotta, I understood, sort of, when we were both cops. Same chain of command, and I had rank on you and all. It could have been sticky, but now—"

"No."

"I don't believe I turn you off that much."

"Don't get angry, Mooney. Please. You don't turn me off."

"So?"

37

How do you explain? Somehow I couldn't see myself telling Mooney, in a goddamn ice cream parlor, that I'd kind of come to terms with life minus sex. That if I didn't have it, I didn't miss it so much. It didn't seem the time or place to rehash the horrors of the singles bar routine I'd fallen into after Cal and I split. Retirement, abstinence, emptiness . . . *nothing* was a hell of a lot better than that. Someday, maybe, I'd get strong enough to risk waking the sleeping demons again.

"I'm not ready," I said lamely.

"You look ready. It's been a while since—"

"Besides, I need somebody to talk to."

"I can talk anyplace, Carlotta. Even on a date."

We ate ice cream for a while. The punk with the mohawk was eavesdropping, practically hanging out of her chair.

"So," I said finally, "somebody looking for me up at the station?"

Mooney said, "Right. Back to business."

"Let me guess." I repeated Gloria's description. "The guy asking questions about me was medium height, medium build, dark, kind of cute—"

"You know him?"

"Not yet."

"You in some kind of trouble?"

"Nothing I know about."

"He said he was from DSS."

I breathed a sigh of pure relief. Department of Social Services. Something about Paolina, probably. They could check from here to Tuesday on me and Paolina and find nothing but boundless affection.

"Except he didn't look like DSS," Mooney said. "Too smooth. Too well-dressed. Expensive shoes. So after he left, I dropped a dime, and they didn't have anybody by that name working for them."

"What name?"

"George Robinson. He had a business card."

"Eighteen bucks for a box of three hundred, right?"

"It looked pretty good," Mooney said.

"Shit."

"So watch your back."

"I get a crick in my neck," I said.

"Anything I can do."

"Anything?" I said.

"Got something in mind?"

"Look, how about if we forget that fifty bucks you owe me, and just call it favor for favor?"

"A fifty-buck favor sounds like trouble, Carlotta."

"I want you to find out some stuff about what could happen, legally I mean, in this hypothetical situation."

"Hypothetical," he repeated.

"Yeah."

"Go on."

"It has to do with impersonating a cat."

"Crawling around on all fours and meowing?"

"It's important, Mooney. It's about T.C."

"Somebody's impersonating your cat?"

"Mooney, if I tell you about this, you have to promise not to screw it up for me. I mean, I'd be telling you as a friend, not a cop."

"Well, that would be an improvement."

"I just want to know what kind of trouble I can get in if I have, say, you or some other guy present himself as Thomas C. Carlyle."

"Me, huh?"

"Possibly."

"Well," he said, "I guess it depends."

"On what?"

"Do I get petted?"

Chapter 6

I woke the next morning in a tangle of sheets with a sour beer aftertaste coating my tongue. Funny how neither ice cream nor toothpaste really kills that telltale beer taste. T.C., curled up on the pillow next to mine, is not too fussy, so I wasn't overly concerned about bad breath. Either I'd forgotten to set my alarm clock, or else I'd flipped it off and gone back to sleep. Just as I was about to soothe myself with a calming well-you-must-have-needed-the-rest, I realized it was Thursday morning. Which made it twenty minutes before my regular 8 A.M. volleyball game at the YWCA.

I shoved back the covers and leaped out of bed.

The Y is the only place to go when you oversleep. Nobody cares if you don't put on makeup. Lipstick before 9 A.M. is regarded with suspicion at the Y.

I spike for the Y-Birds, which says a lot fast. We play killer volleyball, not beach blanket stuff, and we do it three mornings a week. That's why my knees and elbows are unusual shades of magenta and yellow. I am intimately acquainted with the wooden gym floor at the Central Square Y, and I wouldn't miss a game for the world.

Volleyball is also why the fingernails on my right hand are clipped short and square. I always keep my left-hand nails short because I play blues guitar, not as well as I used to, but pretty damn well considering how little I practice these days. Acoustic only. The good old stuff: Lightnin' Hopkins, Son House, Reverend Gary Davis. No sweet love songs, just wailin' done-me-wrong blues.

I would like to point out that while my nose has been broken three times, accounting for a slightly off-center bump, it has never been touched during a volleyball game. The first time, I was just a kid. Ronnie Farmer, the little boy next door, banged me on the nose with a hammer, for no apparent reason other than to see how hammers and noses interacted when they met; the second time, my nose came in contact with the steering wheel of my cab. The third time was cop business.

People I like say my nose has character.

I play volleyball because I can't stand exercise for exercise's sake. I shudder at the very thought of those stationary bikes, peddling to nowhere. The symbolism is just too grim.

Volleyball, though, I love. And the women I play with are terrific: the phys ed coach from Cambridge Rindge and Latin, a couple cops, a computer jockette, some M.I.T. students. We play hard, but we treat each other kindly. You dive after a ball, give it everything you've got, and even if you miss the damn thing, you get a pat on the back and a hand up. I like that. And after the game, I swim laps to cool off.

Three days a week, that's my morning. Good healthy exercise. Makes me tingle with righteousness while I eat breakfast at Dunkin' Donuts afterwards.

I brought my Eugene Devens notebook along and flipped it open on the orange Formica countertop, next to my two glazed donuts and sugared coffee. I'd called a few more hospitals with no luck. If Gene was getting doctored, he was doing it under an alias, and while I could come up with about fifty reasons for seeking anonymous medical care, I couldn't blend any of the reasons with what I knew about Eugene Devens.

Which was not a hell of a lot.

I stared at my notebook, at the sum total of all I'd gleaned about the man, from his sister, from Gloria, from Billy the bartender, from my few remaining cop contacts.

Eugene Paul Mark Devens. No criminal record. Born, May 28, 1929. Delivered at St. Margaret's in Dublin, Ireland, second child of Mary Margaret and Patrick Joseph Devens, if you didn't count the two stillbirths and three miscarriages in between Margaret and her baby brother. What a treasured child he must have been. How do small babies, swaddled in those tiny blankets, grow up to be men who disappear without a trace?

Eugene Paul came to the States at the age of five and was educated at the usual assortment of Catholic schools. I wondered if his mom had meant her only son for the priesthood, been disappointed when he'd quit high school. I wondered if she'd been disappointed or relieved when he'd finally married at thirty-five. Married Mary Elizabeth Reilly in 1964. Wife died six years later, sixteen years ago. No kids.

Nobody had mentioned vices other than drink and ladies in connection with Gene. I hadn't found any involvement with, say, the numbers or the track, but if there were heavy loans involved, if Gene couldn't pay the sharks, that would be a hell of a reason for him to stay lost.

Eugene Devens did not own a car, which might seem strange for a cabdriver in any other city. In Boston, which has ample parking for, say, one in ten of its residents—not to mention commuters—not owning a car makes sense. You save—not only on parking tickets, but on medical expenses for mental-health-related ailments. Unfortunately, one of the best ways to trace a missing person is through automobile registration. Eugene's gain was my loss.

The Central Square Dunkin' Donuts has a phone booth at the back, one of the few real phone booths left in the world where you can talk with any privacy. By using up a lot of dimes and impersonating a dotty travel agent cursed with a missing middle-aged tourist, I learned that no Eugene Devens had traveled via Aer Lingus from Logan to either Shannon or Dublin. Aer Lingus is it as far as direct flights from Boston to Ireland. I figured anyone who felt as Eugene Devens did about the British would hardly set foot on the hated soil of Heathrow, but I checked out British Air and TWA and

Pan Am. Nothing. I even checked People Express out of Newark, in case he'd gone cattle car.

I called a genuine travel agent, and discovered that the only charters to Ireland departing within the past two weeks had consisted entirely of M.I.T. faculty members, a group with whom Gene Devens would hardly have felt at home. No, she had not heard of any travel organization with the initials GBA. Ships she eliminated in no time. Boston is not the great port it once was. Zip. Nada. No passenger ships had sailed for the Emerald Isle in the past month.

So if Gene was in jolly old Ireland, he'd traveled incognito. Walked across the water. Sailed solo. Parachuted from a secret military jet. And pretty soon, he'd send a postcard to Billy the bartender, and all would be well, except I'd feel morally obligated to refund most of Margaret Devens's thousand.

I checked my notebook again, searching for God knows what. My notes looked like an obit. Born, schooled, married. Everything but date of death.

I shook the thought away with the doughnut crumbs. It was time to speak to my client again. I needed a look at Gene's room.

My car was parked in one of those back lots off that narrow street right behind Mass. Ave., Bishop Somebody-or-Other Drive. It's the kind of street that makes you think the bishop wasn't held in high esteem. My little red Toyota was still there though, untouched. Did you know that when a woman who grew up in Detroit buys a Japanese car, it's close to treason?

Before heading to the Devens house, I swung by Paolina's housing project. It's one of those low-rise brick townhouse developments, better planned than the ghetto towers, with less concentrated poverty and hopelessness, an occasional tree, a small square of grass. It's tucked in a back pocket of East Cambridge. The steel skyscrapers of the high-tech boom have grown up around it, encircling it, blocking the sun.

It's not so bad in the daytime, but nights, I want to haul

Paolina's whole family out of there. Paolina's mom, Marta, is Colombian. She married some Puerto Rican guy over here, and he scampered after the fifth kid. There's a rotating mass of visiting cousins and uncles. Marta's a character. Put her down in the desert and she'd sell you sand. Not only would you pay through the nose for it, she'd make you enjoy the privilege. If she hadn't come down with a crippling case of rheumatoid arthritis, the family would never have wound up in the projects. Every once in a while she shows a trace of the old spark, but mostly she just goes through the paces.

Paolina would be in school for the day, but I wasn't planning on a visit.

He was sprawled on the stoop of the building next door to Paolina's, leaning against the dirty yellow bricks, staring at something only he could see. Same guy I'd been watching for three weeks, a scrawny Hispanic with unhealthy yellowish skin drawn tight across a narrow face. He had a droopy mustache, a wispy unkempt beard. Dark shadows around his eyes made him look older than he dressed. His T-shirt had sweat circles around the armpits, and his jeans were faded to the color of the pale morning sky. He hugged a worn leather satchel.

It was the satchel that interested me. More than that, what came out of it.

Drugs and housing projects go together like cops and robbers. I know that. But not drugs and Paolina. Those two are never going to be spoken of in the same breath.

I'd noticed Wispy Beard a few times when I'd come by to pick her up. I got curious. I confided in a Cambridge cop I know, a nice enough guy, but too busy to do the kind of surveillance needed for a bust. I'm not too busy. Maybe I can't clean up the world, but next door to my little sister, nobody is going to dole out little packets from an old leather satchel.

I sat in my car and took notes. Comings and goings. Two kids, one not more than twelve years old, gave something to Wispy Beard, got something in return. Full descriptions went

44

down in the notebook. As soon as I got a definite pattern, I'd give my cop friend a date and a time, and make sure the bastard got himself busted good.

His days were numbered in my mind.

Chapter 7

I'd stayed at my observation post too long, so I flew down Memorial Drive, my thoughts grimly fixed on that scumbag drug dealer. I was halfway to the Boston University Bridge before I shook myself out of it, and noticed that the elm leaves were edged with gold, and high clouds filtered the sunlight into fine visible rays. With breathtaking suddenness, the road reared up and flashed a spectacular view of Boston's church steeples, brownstones, and skyscrapers. It still gives me goosebumps after all these years.

On crisp autumn days, no city compares to Boston, especially when you sneak up on it from the Cambridge side of the Charles. It's the river that makes the magic, frames the city with a silver band. Today the Charles was flat as glass, except for two single sculls cutting the water, gliding toward the M.I.T. boathouse. The skyline is a jumble downtown, but off to the right the Hancock and Prudential towers guard the Back Bay. At the top of Beacon Hill, the gold dome of the State House caught a shaft of sunlight and beamed it back in my eyes, forcing me to look down and pay attention to the road.

They say fish swim in the Charles River these days. You no longer have to race to the doctor for a tetanus shot if you fall off your sailboat. Ever since I came to Boston to live with

45

Aunt Bea after my parents died, they've been saying people would be able to swim in the Charles in five more years. Then five more years. Then five more.

It looked like I might have to wait that long at the foot of the B. U. Bridge. Cars honked, drivers swore, but to no avail. The college kids were back in town, in sufficient numbers to take the right of way by force. When the swarm of students finally parted wide enough for my car to pass, I took the curve onto Park Drive and followed the Riverway out to where it turns into the Jamaicaway. The road traces Olmsted's chain of city parks, and it's got twists and turns enough to delight a former cabbie. I drove it too fast, but then everybody does. Unlike everybody else, I stayed in my lane.

Left at the Jamaica Pond boathouse. Right on Centre Street. I followed the tracks of a trolley line that hasn't run in God knows how many years. Jamaica Plain's a real part of Boston, a neighborhood, a nontourist section of town. I remember Centre Street lined with shoe repair shops, laundries, mom-and-pop convenience stores, and restaurants with counters where the regulars stopped for eggs, bacon, and political arguments on their way to work.

Now Centre Street has florists, at least I think they might be florists. One had two pink lilies plunked in a single vase by way of window display. Another, fearful of garish overstatement, featured a single spray of orchids. I counted three croissant bakeries, four small shuttered restaurants with hand-lettered menus, two shoe boutiques. The signs of gentrification.

Where will all those young urban professionals get their shoes resoled?

Give me an address anywhere in Boston and I can find it cold. Margaret Devens had started to babble directions over the phone, but I'd shut her down. Cabbies know.

I took a right onto a quiet residential street of big old Victorians; a few weary down-and-outers with chipped aluminum siding, some newly pastel-painted numbers with geranium-filled window boxes. Big houses for big families.

46

Most of the Boston Irish who'd escaped the Southie slums made a beeline for the elegant South Shore suburbs, but some, particularly the ones with city government ties, headed for areas of Jamaica Plain like this one. Lace-curtain Irish, it must have been once, with a lively parish church, and houses bursting with kids. Now, most of the better-decorated places looked like they'd been sliced into separate apartments, probably condos. They didn't look as luxurious as the dream townhouses my cat and I were invited to view at Cedar Wash, but I bet the price tags were pretty steep.

When I saw the white Victorian monster on the corner, I stopped wondering why Margaret and Eugene hadn't exchanged many confidences. If just the two siblings lived at number 19, they could use separate floors and never meet. They'd need two phone lines so they could call each other in case of emergency.

There must have been money in the family once, to buy that house. There'd have to be some left over, to pay the property taxes, refresh the gleaming white paint, keep the sloping lawn neatly manicured, the yews and azaleas trimmed.

Well, Margaret had a stash of crisp hundred-dollar bills.

And Eugene drove a hack.

One thing about Jamaica Plain, you never have much trouble parking. I pulled the Toyota to the curb smack in front of the Devens house.

A walkway of concrete squares and grass rectangles tempted me to hopscotch up to the porch. I controlled myself in case my client was peering from behind one of the window shades.

The front door wore a polished brass knocker in the shape of a pineapple. I ignored the doorbell for a chance to get my fingerprints on its bright surface. It clanged a bold satisfying note.

I waited awhile, humming a tune Paolina had taught me, something that named a lot of animals in Spanish, then tried

47

the bell. I could hear it buzz and echo inside. I rang again, hollered Margaret's name.

Damn. I checked my watch. Eleven-twenty. I'd spent longer than I meant to in Cambridge, but surely Margaret would have waited an extra twenty minutes.

Well, maybe she'd forgotten. She was old, after all. Maybe she was at church, or visiting some neighbor, gossiping over coffee while I shivered in the chill. Just for the hell of it, I turned the front door handle and gave the door a push. It opened easily and I stood there gaping.

City people lock their doors.

"Margaret!" I called again, yelling it loudly, as much to warn anybody in the house of my approach as to get a response. My hand reached reflexively for the gun on my service belt, the way it used to when I entered unsecured premises as a cop. As a private operator, I leave guns alone if I can help it.

I always remember what Humphrey Bogart says in that old movie when he takes the gun away from the punk: "So many guns, so few brains."

The foyer was big and cool, with wooden floorboards worn mellow. No quick sand-and-polyurethane job here. Only care, years of care—the kind my Aunt Bea had lavished on her Cambridge home—gave it that warm sheen. The wallpaper was one of those old grass-papers, in a faint beige. A worn octagonal Chinese rug colored the center of the floor. Overhead, a multiarmed chandelier hung low enough to menace.

The foyer had four escapes: three archways, the back one smaller than the right or the left, and a steep flight of beige-carpeted stairs. I turned left toward what must have been the living room, and stopped with my jaw hanging wide.

Stuffing erupted from an overturned couch. Someone had slashed three huge X's in the flowered upholstery and done his best to turn the sofa inside out. A wooden end table was cracked, baring pale wood under a dark finish. An amputated armchair leg stuck out of the shattered leaded glass door of

48

a curio cabinet. A pile of smashed crockery lay at the base of one wall. It looked like someone had hurled Margaret's treasures against the wall for the pleasure of hearing the crash and tinkle.

I swallowed and shoved my hands automatically into the pockets of my jeans so I wouldn't be tempted to right a chair, smooth a torn cushion.

Margaret.

As I opened my mouth to call her name, I heard footsteps, heavy running steps, and the slam of a screen door. Back door, side door, how the hell did I know? I ran out front, stared right and left, saw nothing, no one. I raced down the narrow walkway to the back of the house. Somewhere, a car engine roared to life and tires screeched on pavement. Through a stand of lilac bushes, I caught one glimpse of a hurtling dark van. By the time I'd vaulted Margaret's back fence, it was gone.

Margaret.

I ran back to the house, calling her name, but my voice cracked and I don't think I got much in the way of volume.

I started searching, careful where I put my feet. The destruction was even worse in the kitchen—canned goods, cereal, flour, emptied in a pile in the middle of the floor.

This didn't look like robbery. It looked like vengeance. Or war.

I found her in the dining room, crumpled in a corner, her flowered dress rucked up under her, a big white apron half covering her face. A trickle of blood oozed from one corner of her mouth. I put my ear to her chest, and felt the rise and fall of her breath. I don't think I could have heard a heartbeat. Blood was rushing in my ears, screaming.

I touched her shoulder, spoke her name, both more roughly than I intended. My hand was shaking, and I realized my teeth were clenched tight with anger. Anger at the chaos, at the broken useless dishes. Anger at myself, for not arriving moments earlier, not preventing this. Anger at my helplessness, as I knelt by my client's battered face.

"It's okay, Margaret," I said softly, once I could force the words between my dry lips "Don't try to move. I'll be right back."

The jack was ripped out of the wall, so I ran across the street and used a startled neighbor's phone. I know a number that gets a faster response than 911. Mooney's number.

"You're going to be fine," I crooned in Margaret's ear, straining to hear the wail of the ambulance. I touched her hand. It felt cool and dry. It moved, curling limply around my own, tightening. She moaned, or maybe she tried to say something. I put my head close to her lips, but I couldn't make out any words.

All I could think of was Aunt Bea, and the way her hand gripped mine in that awful hospital room just before she died. I heard a voice whispering in the still room, and it was mine, begging Margaret to hang on, hang on.

If Eugene Devens was responsible for this, I would find him. I would find him all right.

Chapter 8

Room 501 South, Boston City Hospital. In spite of the fresh white paint and the red and blue poppy-splattered curtains, I've seen prison cells a whole lot cheerier. It was a double room, the size of a large closet. Sliding curtains were ominously closed around the bed of the occupant who'd arrived first and copped the window view of the trash dumpster.

Margaret's eyes were closed, too, one of them swollen shut, purpling nicely. Breath rasped through her nostrils. An IV bag dripped colorless fluid through a thin tube connected to the veins in her left hand by needles and tape. The elevated hospital bed dwarfed her. White lab coats surrounded her. All that white, all that machinery—the combination made my stomach quake.

A broken collarbone, abrasions, contusions, probably a concussion. An impossibly young and cheerful doctor said she was lucky she hadn't broken a hip.

Hospitals and prisons both make me sweat. Maybe it's the smell. More likely, it's something about places that hold you against your will.

At least prisons don't have doctors who tell you how lucky you are.

Margaret had briefly regained consciousness in the ambulance. In a shaky voice, she'd informed the EMT that she had a mess to clear up at home, and he could just stop at the corner and she'd be on her way, thank you very much. And all the time, you could see she was hurting like hell, barely able to squeeze the words out of her swollen mouth. I hope I've got half that much spunk when I'm her age.

I waited in a dismal antiseptic-smelling hallway while two cops I didn't know tried to question her. A pimply blond teenager in hospital greens slid one of those heavy buffing machines in lazy arcs across the linoleum floor. Over the hum, I could hear the cops' voices. I couldn't hear Margaret. Every once in a while a loudspeaker would cough out a doctor's name or a room number, "Code Red" or "Code Blue," and a sudden rush of white uniforms and scuffling feet would follow. Otherwise it was just the floor-buffer man and me. We exchanged brief smiles.

When the cops came out, I introduced myself. One of them knew Mooney.

"He sends his best," the guy said. He was long and lean and wore the uniform well. "Too busy to take the squeal himself."

"Yeah," echoed the second cop. He was older, short and potbellied, with a jutting chin. Didn't do a thing for the uniform.

I nodded toward Margaret's door. "She tell you anything?"

"Too woozy," the fat cop said immediately, with a warning glance at his partner. He wasn't the type to give information to mere civilians.

"Said she fell downstairs," the lean cop said softly.

A hefty blond nurse breezed into 501 carrying a tray with a glass of chipped ice and a straw. I excused myself and followed.

The closer I got, the worse she looked, and believe me, the view from the doorway window had been bad enough. From two feet away, her skin, the part of her skin that wasn't bandaged, or raw and red, or purple from the bruises, was gray. The bandage across her forehead was neat enough, but a brownish stain was seeping through on the left side. All the tubes and drains made her look like some helpless old marionette, controlled by the huge mechanical bed and the display of instruments on the wall behind her head.

The nurse addressed her as if she were awake. I wasn't sure, but I figured the nurse ought to know.

"I hope those policemen didn't upset you," she said briskly, smoothing an offending wrinkle out of the top sheet. "They have to ask their questions, I suppose." She glanced at her wristwatch, then at me. "I'm sure your, uh, granddaughter can help you with the ice water."

I nodded obediently, and tried to look young and earnest. The beating had added years to Margaret's appearance.

The tray also held a syringe. The nurse uncapped the needle, lifted it to the light, checked something scrawled on the chart at the end of the bed.

"What's that?" Margaret was awake after all.

"It's for the pain."

"I don't want it."

"You'll feel a little pinch, Miss Devens, that's all."

"I don't—" She tried to turn away, but didn't have the strength to resist.

"There," the nurse said calmly, removing the syringe

from the vicinity of Margaret's hip. "The medication will take effect soon, so don't worry if you start feeling drowsy. Maybe your granddaughter will stay with you till you fall asleep."

I beamed her a sincere, appreciative, family-member smile. The cops got a grudging three minutes. I'd just been granted unlimited bedside time, albeit with a drugged client. Sometimes there's a benefit to not looking like your typical cop.

"She'll feel much better tomorrow, dear," the nurse promised me as she left.

I maneuvered a chair close to the head of the bed, sat down, and waited.

"Go away," Margaret whispered. I hadn't seen her open her eyes since the nurse left, but she'd turned her head in my direction, so I guess she must have peeked.

"What did he want?" I asked.

She said nothing and kept her eyes shut.

"Did you know him? Them?"

Again nothing.

"Was it Gene? Did your brother do this to you?"

That forced her good eye open. "No."

"Then why are you trying to cover it up?"

Silence. The eye closed.

"Margaret, listen to me, I'm not a cop. I'm on your side. You paid me. Maybe I can help. You didn't fall downstairs. A tornado did not strike your house."

No response.

"Did they get what they wanted?"

"No." The single syllable came out with grim satisfaction. She repeated it and her voice cracked.

"Water?"

I held the glass while she made an attempt to suck at the straw through swollen lips. She winced at the feel of it, and waved the glass away.

"Listen." Her voice was so faint I had to lean over the

53

bed. She grasped my hand, which was chilled from the icy glass. Hers was colder. "Find Gene. Please."

"I'm looking. I'll keep looking."

"If I die—"

"You're not dying, Margaret. The doctor—"

"Doctors." She practically spat the word. "Eugene . . . If I die, there's nobody else."

I thought she'd dozed off, but when I tried to release my hand, she drew me closer with surprising strength. "Hide it," she whispered. "Hide it for me. Don't tell."

Whatever they'd given her, Demerol, morphine, was starting to take hold. Her one open eye was wide and vacant, staring at the ceiling. I'm not sure she knew I was there.

"Hide what?" I said.

She gazed at me blankly, as if she'd never seen me before in her life.

"Hide what?" I repeated.

"Go . . . home," she murmured. Each word was separate, disjointed, like the beginning of a new thought. "Home . . . attic . . . toy trunk."

"A toy trunk in the attic?"

She stared at me intently, pleading out of that one wandering eye. "Home . . . behind . . . trunk . . . attic . . ." She talked the way a drunk walked, trying to toe a straight line, wavering uncontrollably. She couldn't manage to get the right words out, only the urgency. "Home . . . hide the . . . hide it. Gene . . ."

"Margaret, what does Gene have to do with it? Did you see Gene?"

She gave up, sighed deeply, closed her eye, and slept.

I sat with her a little while. The IV dripped. The second hand of the big clock described steady circles. Her breathing grew soft and even, her hand warmer.

Before I left, I tucked her hand underneath the thin blanket, and smoothed a strand of white hair off her forehead. Like I said, I never met my grandmother.

Chapter 9

I stopped at a deli on the VFW Parkway and ordered a pastrami on light rye, two half-sour pickles, and a can of Dr. Brown's cream soda. That's the kind of food I was raised on, and while Boston's delis can't compare with the Detroit of my childhood, I find them soothing in stressful times.

I gobbled a huge wedge of strawberry cheesecake for dessert. If it weren't for volleyball and a speedy metabolism, I swear I'd be as fat as Gloria.

By the time I'd patted up the last crumbs with my fingertip it was after three, which meant Paolina would be home from school. The deli has one of those minibooths Ma Bell has installed now that Superman no longer needs a place to change. I punched the buttons. Sometimes I even miss dial phones.

"Allo?" She answers the phone the way her mom does: "Allo?" instead of "Hello?" At school and with me, she speaks good old American slang. Except every once in a while, she starts a phrase with that multisyllabic "Nooooo!" which identifies a Colombiano every time.

"¿Como esta usted?" I replied.

"Carlotta!" she said immediately. "Hi!"

My high school Spanish is good for one thing. It gets a guaranteed giggle out of Paolina, who says I have an accent like a Venezuelan peasant's parrot.

You could tell she was glad to hear from me. When I was a cop I guess I never really got used to the fact that pimps and hookers were not pleased when I showed up. Even now, folks are not always delighted to invite a PI into their parlor. Paolina is my antidote, my official welcoming committee.

"How're ya' doin', Carlotta?" Sometimes she gets deliberately slangy to show off.

"You take your history exam?"

"You remember everything."

"That's not an answer."

"I got eighty-eight. But I think she's going to grade on a curve, so maybe I got an A."

"You study?"

"Yeah."

"You panic?"

"Right at the beginning, when Miss Vaneer was passing out the papers, my heart started pounding, you know, but I thought about taking deep breaths, like you said, and then I was okay. I didn't rush or anything, and I finished on time."

"You did great. Even without a curve."

"I did?"

"Terrific," I said.

"Terrific," she echoed. I could tell she was smiling, and I pictured her at the phone, sneakers untied as usual, eyes shining.

When I first met Paolina she was seven years old, going on thirty, thin and tough as whipcord, with a knuckle splay of bruises across her right cheek, courtesy of one of her visiting "uncles." Marta, Lord bless her, didn't stand for that kind of thing. The guys could slap her around— something I've never understood, something I don't want to understand—but mess with her kids and that was the end. When he wouldn't stay away, she preferred charges against the guy who'd smacked Paolina, and some kind soul at the police station suggested Big Sisters for the small scared girl with the wide eyes.

Marta doesn't offer Paolina much in the way of praise, especially for schoolwork, because she's not sure it's any use to females. I've talked to her about it, and we've sort of agreed to disagree. So I try to fill the gap. I make sure I know when the tests come, and what the grades are, and I'm extremely generous with compliments. Paolina used to be so scared of taking tests, so sure she'd fail, that she'd faint or throw up. She used to spend testing days in the nurse's office. Now she's pulling As and Bs.

Am I proud? Not so you'd notice, provided you're blind and deaf.

"Hey, about Saturday," I said.

"You can't come?" Paolina's always prepared for disappointment.

"Of course I can come." Sometimes, when I was a cop, I had to back out on our regular dates. Now I'm private, that doesn't happen anymore. Ever. When you're ten, there ought to be somebody you can rely on. "I just wanted to make sure you remembered."

"Noon, no?" she said, using the multisyllabic national marker. "I'll be ready."

"I'll honk."

"Where are we going?"

"Surprise," I said, to cover the fact that I didn't know yet. "Jeans and sneakers."

"Okay. And I want to talk to you."

"You're talking to me."

"Not on the phone. When I see you."

"Anything special?"

Her voice sounded troubled, but all she said was, "It's about volleyball."

"Can it wait till Saturday?"

"Sure," she said, but she didn't sound right.

"Any tests tomorrow?"

"Just a quiz. In Spanish."

"Better you than me," I said.

"*Es verdad*," she agreed with a giggle.

"*Adios, amiga*." I hung up. There was this guy waiting to use the phone. I hadn't even noticed him.

It used to be easier to find places to take Paolina. Puppet Showplace in Brookline was great, but now she's kind of old for that. They get so sophisticated so young, it kills me. And one of the Big Sister rules is not to spend much money. The kids come from poor families, and we're not supposed to come on like fairy godmothers. Just friends.

On the way back to Margaret's, I decided I'd drive Paolina to this wild-animal farm in New Hampshire. The trees up north would be in full fall color, and she really likes animals. She's got two scraggly cats already, and if Marta would okay the deal, I'd give her Red Emma in a flash.

Paolina calls Red Emma Esmeralda, because she's green. She's trying to teach her a few choice Spanish phrases, and says the bird's accent is better than mine.

What with having three names, the bird probably can't learn anything because she's in the middle of an identity crisis.

I cruised Margaret's block to see if any cops still lurked there. No blue-and-whites out front, no anonymous vans, no suspicious unmarked sedans with elaborately casual guys reading newspapers in the front seats. The door didn't have a police seal on it, but I could tell the lab boys had come and gone by the gritty residue on the brass pineapple door knocker. They must have gotten a great set of my prints.

Since I had the front door key in my pocket, it didn't take me long to get inside. I'd snitched it from Margaret's handbag during the ambulance ride. As an honorary granddaughter, I figured the least I could do was bring her robe and slippers to the hospital.

And as a private investigator, I could do what I'd intended to do that morning. Search Eugene's room.

Chapter 10

I tell myself I have a mind above housework, but one glance at Margaret's living room and I was sorely tempted to race to the kitchen for a broom, a mop, a bucket, Handy Andy, Spic and Span, *anything*. The memory of what the kitchen really offered—more chaos—held me back. That and the fear that maybe, God forbid, I was developing a latent house-keeping streak.

If the crime lab team had bothered to step into the living room, they hadn't righted the furniture, restuffed any cushions, vacuumed the rug, or dusted the mantle. They might have swiped a few bits of smashed china, but there was plenty still scattered on the scratched floorboards. From the foyer, the shards looked like exotic flower petals.

Paolina painted a watercolor once, for art class, of three soggy crumpled yellow Kleenexes, next to a pile of orange peels. I keep that picture in my bedroom, framed. I like it. Her teacher didn't. Her teacher asked her why she was paint-ing garbage.

Paolina told me it hadn't been garbage from far away. In the picture, the Kleenex and the orange peels, floating gently in a gutter, are magical water lilies.

It was the same with Margaret's broken plates and vases. Far away, flowers. Close up, garbage.

I tried to piece together two chunks of purple glaze, and dropped them back on the floor in disgust. Maybe I could bribe Roz to clean. Nobody should have to come home from the hospital to a house that looked like the target of a wrecking ball. And Margaret Devens, I reassured myself, would come home.

The cops had left a trail of muddy footprints on the stair carpeting. I followed them.

Four bedrooms and a tiled bath opened off the narrow hallway. I glanced in each doorway. Picking Eugene's room seemed easy. Only the left front bedroom, a largish room, maybe twelve by sixteen, lacked a pastel dust-ruffle and frilly lace curtains.

Standing in the dimly lit hallway, I tried to imagine the room before the whirlwind struck, make a few guesses about the guy who'd slept there for sixteen years' worth of nights. It didn't seem like the room of a fifty-six-year-old man. I wondered if I'd stumbled on Gene's boyhood bedroom, preserved intact as some family shrine.

I checked the other rooms again, just to make sure. Frills and lace. Scented dusting powder. Only one room smelled of cigar smoke, the one I'd singled out first.

The narrow bed's brass headboard was barred and knobbed. The mattress had been yanked onto the floor, and slit repeatedly. Coils of wire poked out of the springs like jack-in-the-box toys. Over the bed hung a giant poster of young Carl Yastrzemski, Red Sox hero.

So the searchers had been looking for something substantial, not a key, or a photo, or anything flat that could be taped behind smiling Yaz.

I took a few steps into the room, letting my eyes wander. It's hard to get to know a guy from his room when that room's been trashed by persons unknown, and possibly rifled by the cops to boot.

On surfaces not graced by old baseball posters, Eugene favored taped-up pages from girlie magazines. That was the total of his decorating pizazz, at his age, unless the previous searchers had stolen the Picasso prints off the paler rectangles on the walls. More likely Miss September had fallen into disfavor, or under the bed. Eugene read soft-porn "male adventure novels" that looked like Harlequin Romances for men. I loved the titles: *Beyond Glory, Glorious Flames, Gunrunner to Glory.* A whole lot of glory on the covers; that and big-breasted women falling out of slinky nightgowns.

The day after I covered my first homicide as a cop, I went home and scoured my bedroom. Threw out all that embarrassing junk I'd hoarded, marveling at the bizarre items I'd thoughtlessly shoved into the bottom drawer of my dresser for the cops to smirk at on that inevitable day. The gonzo Diet-Aids I'd purchased, convinced I was two pounds over the fashion limit for my latest bikini. They made me throw up, but I'd paid so much for those dumb pills, mail order, sight unseen, that I'd been too angry to toss them in the trash. So I'd heaved them in the bottom drawer instead, along with the book of illustrated religious poetry (can you believe it?) that was the very first gift my very first boyfriend gave me when I was an old maid of fourteen. I tossed out the early letters from Cal, my ex, letters I suppose could be called love letters, if you stretched the bounds. Out went the old tube of birth-control foam, along with one of those sexy uplift bras, and the torn jeans I'd worn, almost exclusively, my eighteenth summer. I found and discarded a coupon for breast enlargement cream, corny birthday cards, a mercifully brief attempt at a diary.

If the cops come and toss my room tomorrow, they won't find much of a personal nature. Pictures of my mom and dad. My wedding album, a curiously impersonal item, since the smiling bride seems a total stranger to me. Aunt Bea's oval gold locket, with its two photos of faded young men. My Aunt Bea never married. I have no idea who those men were or what they meant to her, but she treasured that locket, and I shine it up every once in a while in her memory. Probably the most personal item in my room is my old National steel guitar, and there's no way those cops will ever know what that guitar means to me.

My worst cop trait was insubordination. My best was sheer stubbornness, and I haven't lost it. Even though I knew the place had been plundered by the bad guys and the good guys both, I searched it again. I shook out the pages of those trashy novels, twisted the stupid knobs off the brass headboard, poked inside them with a wire coathanger.

Did I find any terrific clue the cops had overlooked?

Of course not.

One loose scrap of paper fluttered out of a paperback, and it made me feel a little better about brother Eugene. It was a poem, ''No Second Troy,'' by William Butler Yeats, copied on lined notebook paper, the kind you tear out of ring binders.

> Why should I blame her that she filled my days
> With misery, or that she would of late
> Have taught to ignorant men most violent ways,
> Or hurled the little streets upon the great,
> Had they but courage equal to desire?

I remembered what the bartender had said, about Gene's interest in the glorious rebellion, and the great Irish poets. It added a little depth to a character otherwise defined by sports memorabilia, *Playboy* centerfolds, and sisterly devotion. I read the rest of the poem out loud. I liked it, but I have to admit I enjoyed the contrast, too. It's not often you come across a poem by Yeats stuck in a semiporn paperback that would probably have caused the poet to puke.

Chapter 11

The attic steps were narrow, steep, and uncarpeted. They took a ninety-degree turn ten steps up, and from that point on I had to crouch to avoid the ceiling. At the top step the paneled door swung open with one of those creaky horror-movie noises I absolutely adore as long as I'm safe in the depths of my cushy cinema seat. I'm ashamed to say it had a different effect in Margaret's attic. The spit in my mouth dried up so fast my tongue felt like a prune. My ears, suddenly sharp, started to register each faint noise as a threat. Passing cars, wind-whipped branches, ratlike scamperings . . . Was that a footstep? In the house?

I swallowed, took a deep breath, and sternly ordered myself to stop behaving like the women on the covers of Eugene's hot novels. I tried to whistle, but my mouth wasn't wet enough, so I hummed a few bars of an old Lightnin' Hopkins blues tune I'm learning to pick.

The door opened into shadow, not darkness, therefore the attic had a light source somewhere, one sadly insufficient for a search. I dipped into my shoulder bag—which weighs about a ton because I keep it crammed with picklocks, my trusty Swiss army knife, MBTA tokens, and stray lipsticks—in hopes of locating a flashlight. My first find the right shape turned out to be a can of that old-style lacquery hairspray, which, believe me, is just as off-putting to muggers as a can of Mace, much cheaper, and you don't need a license for it. I never use hairspray for anything else.

After a bit more groping I came up with a flashlight. Not

quite a full-sized one, but adequate. I beamed it through the doorway, and stepped into its pool of light.

As haunted attics go, Margaret's was a real disappointment, consisting of two semifinished slant-roofed rooms, the smaller a sort of anteroom to the larger. Both had been painted beige within the past century. Pink insulation of a more recent vintage peeked out from behind an occasional unpainted joist.

They seemed to be storage rooms, containing no big items—which would never pass the bend in the staircase—but lots of small stuff. An old wire birdcage hung on a metal stand, door ajar, occupant long gone. Two china-doll figurine lamps, chipped, eyed each other from opposite ends of the smaller room. Between them was a cracked vase, sloppily glued, a pile of ratty velvet curtains, and layers of undisturbed dust, which led me to believe that neither the cops nor the robbers had lavished their attention on the attic.

In the larger room, I located a single stingy window and yanked at its stained shade, which snapped up with a bang and hit the roller so hard that it brought the whole business down in a heap. The sudden alarm made the silence eerier, and I found myself listening for footsteps again. I hummed a few more bars of the Hopkins blues. The room had a nice echo.

A pedal sewing machine sat on a mahogany case against the wall opposite the window. A dress dummy wrapped in India-print cotton gave me an uneasy moment or two. Four chairs shared a corner, set up in a square, their upholstery faded to uneven rose. I wondered where the card table had gone.

The place smelled like an attic, dry, stale, and dusty, a haven for moths. I thought about opening the window for a little ventilation, but a spiderweb bridged the frame, and I hated to disturb the pattern on the dirty glass, much less the crawly little beast who'd designed it. I am no fan of spiders. I know most of them are harmless wee creatures, the do-gooders of the insect world, but honestly, yuck.

No toy chest in the first room. No toy chest in the second room.

Talk about stubborn. I searched those two rooms, side to side, top to bottom, methodically, and probably damn close to maniacally. I played my flashlight into every cranny, got my hands filthy, and my hair full of cobwebs. I strained to shift heavy cardboard boxes, kicked the lighter ones across the floor as my frustration level soared. I kept banging my head on the sloped side of the ceiling, which gave me a headache, and did not improve my temper.

Nothing.

As the light faded in the attic window, I sank to the floor in the middle of the larger room, clasped my arms around my knees, and let my eyes and my brain do the work for a change. I pivoted slowly, dusting a small circle with the seat of my jeans, checking the floor and the walls. The attic seemed small for the house beneath it.

My first thought was that one patch of flooring was less dusty than the rest. By the time I stood up, I'd registered that the clean square was near one of the unpainted joists, that the wallboard next to the joist leaned at a slight angle. It moved easily when I wiggled it. And when I gave it a shove, it slid to one side, revealing the rest of the attic, the real unfinished attic.

I poked my flashlight in the four-by-three gap, but I didn't have to follow. A wooden arch-topped trunk sat right behind the panel. I grabbed it by one of its two brass handles and hauled it triumphantly over to the window.

It was latched, not locked, and the lid was heavy. The layer of kid's stuff on top startled me. Halloween costumes, mostly. I pulled aside a net tutu, gray with age, and tried to imagine it on an eight-year-old Margaret. A magician's hat and cloak followed, then a feathered Indian headdress. The dust made my nose itch. I gave in and sneezed loudly. It echoed. If anyone else were in the house, he'd hear it.

Stop it, Carlotta, I scolded myself. Nobody else around. Just you and the boogeyman.

I kept emptying the trunk, figuring Margaret probably hadn't been worried sick about the safety of her old tutu.

I have never seen that much money before.

It took my breath away, a lovely sight, done up in neat bundles, banded in green. Most of the bills were old, so the stash didn't have that phony TV-ransom-money-in-the-attaché-case look to it. Stacks of vintage tens and twenties lined the entire bottom of the trunk. On top, a few thinner stacks of bright, new, mint-fresh hundreds perched like candy roses on the top of the cake.

I knew where Margaret had gotten the cash to pay me.

I wasted a while staring at the loot, wondering whether there was more or less than my cat's promised twenty grand involved.

Hide it, Margaret had begged. Hide it.

To tell the truth, it seemed pretty well hidden already. I could drag the trunk back to the gap in the wall, replace the wallboard, wipe out the tracks in the dust with a kitchen broom.

But the absence of dust would be a clue. That stopped me. That and the fact that I'd found the trunk in the first place. If I could find it somebody else could too. Especially somebody who suspected it was in the house. Somebody who'd already exhausted the possibilities of the first two floors before being interrupted by a nosy red-headed private eye.

I picked up a stack of bills. I really hadn't meant to touch it, but the money drew my hand like a magnet. I riffled the edges of the hundreds, flipped the stack over to admire whichever president was pictured on the face, and that's when I noticed that the cash was not only banded, the band was initialed.

With the letters GBA.

Chapter 12

The stash would never have wound up where it did if it hadn't been for Mooney.

My favorite part of those Gothic suspense novels, aside from the climactic moment when our heroine gets a message from our hero and waltzes off to meet him at midnight in the old abandoned warehouse, is where the heroine goes outside carrying thousands of bucks belonging to some secret organization, armed only with a can of hairspray.

Granted it was barely ten o'clock when I locked Margaret's front door, balancing a suitcase and two Hefty Bags, but I sure had that dumb heroine feeling as I peered into the backseat of my Toyota and glanced furtively into the nearby bushes. A fleeing squirrel could have given me heart failure.

Once in the car, I felt more resolute. I drove like the ex-cabbie I am, and I can absolutely guarantee you that nobody followed me from Margaret's house to my own.

What I didn't count on was Mooney. He was sitting smack in the center of my front stoop, the porch light gleaming off the top of his head in a kind of halo effect. If I didn't make a habit of leaving lights on to illuminate the burglars, I might not have seen him.

Shit. I didn't want to leave that much cash in my car for five seconds, much less the time it would take me to deal with Mooney. Boston is the car-theft capital of the Western world, and Cambridge runs it a close second. Quickly, I pulled into the driveway.

I had my door open before the car actually came to a halt.

I keep my trash on the back landing, and I hurriedly swung the two Hefty Bags up to join the three already awaiting tomorrow's garbage pickup. Then I grasped the suitcase, and headed toward the front door before Mooney got the bright idea of coming around back to see what was taking so long.

"Hi, Carlotta," Mooney said, still seated in the porch light's glow. I was trying to breathe normally. Inhale. Exhale.

He indicated the suitcase. "Moving in or out?"

"Robe and slippers," I answered truthfully, "for the lady who got clobbered over in Jamaica Plain."

Mooney said, "I hear she's gonna be okay."

"Yeah," I said.

"I was hoping you'd invite me in," Mooney said.

"So, you wanna come in?" I said.

"Thanks."

"Play with the cat for a minute," I said apologetically as soon as we got as far as the living room. "I'll be right back." I turned the kitchen faucet on full blast to cover the noise of the back door opening, grabbed the two garbage bags, and hauled them into the bathroom.

The cash smelled a little the worse for wear because I'd layered a level of Margaret's kitchen trash over each batch of money, just in case, for camouflage. Maybe that's what gave me the idea.

I'd bought this new litter box for T.C., one of those plastic Rubbermaid things that I thought His Majesty might prefer to his old dilapidated box, but no way. So I took the plastic tray, filled it with the cash, shook it so the bundles were level and then plunked T.C.'s old litter tray on top of it. A perfect fit. Nobody could have guessed that the cat was doing his business over a fortune.

I flushed the toilet, and went back out to face Lieutenant Mooney.

Mooney doesn't dress like a cop, off duty or on. He wears button-down Oxford cloth shirts and tweedy jackets. Sweater vests. Blue jeans. It's a soft, comfortable look, like the image some Harvard prof might choose, except that Mooney's shirts bulge around the kind of biceps you don't get from sitting at a desk correcting exams.

He'd seated himself in the rocking chair, which was thoughtful of him because the sofa isn't up to a man his size. He was surveying the room with the same quiet, focused attention he gave to crime scenes.

"I like it," he said gravely, "but it's not what I expected."

"Disappointed?"

"No. It's just not the way I see you," he said.

"It's not me, if you want to know the truth. I didn't decorate this place. My aunt did."

"Ah," he said.

The only room in the house that I really call my own is my bedroom. I chose it for the three wide windows—they give plenty of morning sunlight for my jungle of plants. I started from scratch on that room. I sanded the floorboards. I steamed off the wallpaper. I stripped sixteen coats of paint—sixteen!—off the window moldings, until the natural wood came through. The bed is huge, king-sized, because I finally got fed up with mattresses that dangle my feet over the edge. I make my bed twice a year, so I buy good-looking sheets on sale at Filene's Basement, always solids, never pastels. I've got this fantastically warm down comforter, also bought on sale, with a charcoal gray cover. I wanted a brass headboard, but talk about expensive! So I settled for a white wicker one that's really two single-bed headboards laced together with invisible wire. The dresser and the bedside table are vaguely Chinese, picked up cheap in a Cape Cod antique shop. Plants, books, my big illuminated globe, my record and tape collection, and my guitar are the decorations. I'd like to have one really good oil painting, but so far Roz hasn't delivered. The stereo system, which is so high-tech glossy it's practically blinding, probably cost more than everything else in the room combined, even if you toss in the old black-and-white TV that I keep in the closet along with my underprivileged wardrobe.

Who knows, maybe someday Mooney will see my bedroom. I wonder if he'll think it looks like me.

He earned points by not starting out the way most cops would, barking questions about Margaret. We'd worked together long enough that he knows I'd just clam up. He's got roundabout ways, and that makes him a dangerous man in my book.

He said, "So, how are you doing collecting the cat's loot?"

For a panicky moment all I could see were the bundles of cash hidden under T.C.'s kitty litter. Then I remembered. "Oh, yeah," I said quickly, recovering, "I called the guys. They just want me to bring old Thomas along and I—or rather we—get the cash."

"Has to be the both of you?"

"Yep."

"That's the only obstacle?"

"It looms fairly large."

"If you propose nicely, say down on one knee, and maybe buy me a bunch of daisies, we could get married tonight," Mooney said.

"Takes three days for a license," I said.

"I know a JP who takes bribes. I wouldn't even hold out for an engagement ring."

"You'd change your name?" I said, letting the sarcasm flow. "Your whole name?"

"Women can take any name they want when they get married. What's wrong with that?"

"Unless it's done to defraud, Mooney."

"Hey, I'm willing to try to make the marriage work. I'm not talking about one of these quickie divorces."

"Come on, Moon. Don't tease. I've been there."

"Carlotta, not all guys turn into Mr. Hyde on their wedding night."

Right. Even Cal waited a while. Mooney met Cal once. Arrested him even. God, I was young when I married. Didn't know what the words "addictive personality" meant. Cal was a walking time bomb from day one. He didn't smoke,
70

he chain-smoked, lighting the next cigarette from the stub of the first, ignoring a hacking cough. He didn't drink beer, he guzzled six-packs. He didn't just play guitar, he led all-night marathons, grabbing the bass when the bass man dropped out, jumping and shouting, singing till the neighbors howled. He didn't make love, he . . .

Well, we might have made it through all that, the good and the bad, if he hadn't discovered cocaine, found that he loved, adored, worshipped that white powder he snorted up his nose more than he loved or needed me.

I know I'm not supposed to think about it that way. I'm supposed to think about it as a disease. Go ahead, try to control the way you think. Especially if you've been brought up by a Jewish mother whose house specialty was GUILT. Then you say to yourself, where did I go wrong, how did I fail him?

"Hey," Mooney said gently. "Come back. So you need a husband named Thomas in order to collect. What else?"

"That's it."

"These contests usually have other requirements. Like you and Tom have to earn fifty grand a year, and you need a major credit card, or stuff like that. You read the fine print?"

"There isn't any. Wait, I'll show you." I went into the kitchen and yanked the winning letter off the refrigerator door, brought it back, and held it out. He read it intently, almost without blinking, just the way he always studied police reports.

"Looks okay," he said.

"Yeah," I said, with the same lack of enthusiasm. "I should probably run it by the bunco squad. Maybe the Attorney General's Office. There's gotta be a catch, right?"

"Let me take care of it," he said, folding the letter. "You mind if I borrow this for a day or two?"

"I don't know," I said.

"Come on, Carlotta. What have you got to lose?"

"Twenty thousand," I said, going along with his smile.

"Sure."

71

"Mooney," I said, kicking off my shoes and sinking onto the creaky sofa, "thanks and all that. But don't mess this up for me. I mean, if they're broke, go ahead and arrest them. But if they've got money, even if they're illegal or something, don't you dare bust them until I figure out a way to collect T.C.'s twenty grand."

"I'll be careful," he said. "Trust me."

"Hah," I said. "Trust a cop."

So then he started in on Margaret Devens and I dodged questions for a good fifteen minutes.

I must have been awfully tired because I actually thought about spilling the whole thing in his lap. My natural wariness won. I admitted that Margaret Devens was my client, that the work involved was of a confidential nature, that, of course, I had every intention of cooperating with the police, but that I could not say whether today's attack had anything to do with the work Margaret had hired me to perform. Miss Devens was, after all, under sedation, and I had no reason to assume the attack was perpetrated by other than random thugs. I mean, aren't things getting out of hand in our fair city when decent people are attacked in their own homes—

"Carlotta, I have heard this speech before," Mooney said.

"Well, hell, I don't want to bore you."

"You don't," he said with a smile that told me he wasn't about to take my hint to leave.

"Coffee?" I said.

"No, thanks. That guy ever show up?"

"What guy?"

"You must have a lot of them around. The smoothie who said he was with the Department of Social Services. The pseudo George Robinson. Remember?"

That's when the first thud came from upstairs. Mooney was on his feet before I could speak. His size is deceptive. He can really move. He'd taken about three steps toward the stairs before I stopped him.

"Relax," I said. "It's my tenant."

"I thought you lived alone."

"I have a tenant."

"He lifts weights? And drops them?"

"*She* takes karate lessons. Her name is Roz. Her boyfriend and instructor owns the truck parked across the street. They've covered the whole third floor with tumbling mats, and sometimes they get a little loud."

They do get a little loud, particularly Roz, and not just when they practice karate. She picked that particular moment to start making the kind of noise that doesn't go with fighting, and Mooney sat back down, grinning broadly. Damn Roz, anyway. To keep the lieutenant's mind off the upstairs activity, to keep my mind off it as well, I led with the first question that sprang to my lips. I asked Mooney if he'd ever heard of an organization with the initials GBA.

"GBA," he said, and I swear the smile on his face got even wider. "God, I haven't heard that one in years."

"What, Mooney?"

"My dad used to belong. All my uncles. I think it's defunct now, has been for years. It was big in the old days, the NINA days."

"Nina?" This was getting worse by the minute.

"No Irish Need Apply. NINA. I forget you're not a Boston native. Boston natives know these things."

"Do they know what GBA means? Am I the only one who doesn't? And are you ever going to tell me?"

"Let me see, I guess it stood for the Gaelic Brotherhood Association. It was a social club. Must be dying out by now."

"Oh," I said.

"Why?"

"I just came across the initials somewhere."

"In conjunction with your private-eye work?"

"Mooney," I said, "let me put it like this. The PI business is so bad, I'm seriously thinking of going back to driving a hack."

Chapter 13

First thing the next morning, I locked myself in the down-stairs bathroom, crouched between the cat box and the toilet, and counted the cash under the kitty litter. I stopped, over-whelmed, at $12,480, with a few piles left untotaled. I mean, what the hell, what's a few hundred here or there? I rocked back on my heels, smacking my right elbow a mean one on the edge of the sink, and thought about safe-deposit boxes. The abundance of loot must have unnerved me because I actually considered mailing bundles of bills to myself in large manila envelopes, in spite of the fact that my experience of the U.S. Postal Service indicates that it would be more reli-able to flush the money down the toilet than trust it to a mailbox. If I flushed it, at least I'd know it would eventually wind up in Boston Harbor.

I decided to let the money stay put. T.C. didn't seem to mind, and Roz doesn't do cat boxes.

Friday's a volleyball morning, so I played volleyball. The Y-Birds won a resounding victory over some elite health club whose members didn't want to chip their nail polish. I swam laps, ate two jelly doughnuts, drank two cups of coffee, and staked out Paolina's neighborhood drug pusher for an hour. This time I'd brought my camera—I took candids. Wispy Beard's customers seemed so young I started wondering if he might be dealing crack.

Heroin, as in white powder injected into the veins, is ex-pensive. Cocaine, as in white powder sniffed up the nose, is expensive, which puts them both within the reach of football players, rock stars, and high-tech executives, which is okay by me, because most of them are old enough to ruin their lives if they so desire. But crack, also called rock, is cheap, smokable coke. You can cook it up in your kitchen—just add baking soda and water—wait till it hardens, and chip it into saleable chunks. No chemists needed. We're not talking sophisticated toots through rolled hundred-dollar bills. We're talking ten, fifteen bucks for a half-hour high, not to mention addiction. The users are young. Kids. Like Paolina.

I dialed Boston City Hospital from a vandalized pay phone, and was informed by a nasal voice that while Miss Devens's condition continued to improve, she could not take any calls, but would be allowed to receive two visitors, members of her immediate family only, between the hours of seven and nine that evening.

Somehow I didn't think Eugene would show up. And I needed to talk to her before then.

Hospitals are confusing places these days. They used to seem organized, back when the nurses wore caps that told where each one went to school. Nurses' uniforms used to be just that: uniform. Now, anything goes, as long as it's white, so I stopped home long enough to change into white slacks and a white cotton sweater, an outfit a bit summery for late September. I retained my scuffed, once-white Adidases. They didn't quite cut it as typical nurse footwear, but my choices were limited—sneakers or stack-heeled peekaboo sandals. I scraped my hair back into as severe a bun as I could manage, scowled into the mirror, and departed, Margaret's robe and slippers stuffed into an official-looking briefcase that I tucked under my arm.

Act like you belong and folks tend to let you be. What with nurses' strikes and part-time workers and day-night shifts, I was sure nobody would pay attention to me unless I strolled into the operating theater and started to perform brain surgery.

I took the elevator to the fifth floor, walked briskly past the nurse's station with a crisp nod at the woman on duty, stared at my watch, and plunged ahead. Clutching the briefcase and a hospital administrator's clipboard that I'd borrowed from a nearby desk, I entered Margaret's room and closed the door behind me. The bed next to hers was empty this time, but looked just as forbidding with the curtains open. I yanked the chart from the end of Margaret's bed with professional aplomb. Most of the stuff written on it was gobbledygook, but her temperature and blood pressure seemed pretty normal, which was what I wanted to know. I mean, I needed to talk to the lady, but I didn't want the shock to kill her.

The color TV suspended high on the far wall was tuned to some daytime game show. The sound was mercifully off, but a couple who looked like Barbie and Ken dolls were jumping up and down and pointing at a huge roulette wheel as if it were a holy vision.

Margaret Devens's good eye was fully open, but she wasn't paying any attention to the animated dolls on the TV screen. The area around her purpled eye had a yellowish tinge to it. At first glance, it looked even worse than yesterday, but when she turned her head, I could see that the swelling had gone down and the eye was actually open a slit. I was wondering just how severe her concussion was when she said calmly, "Well, thank God for small favors. You're not a nurse."

"How are you feeling?" I asked.

"That's what they all say," she mumbled. "Not that any of them gives a rat's tail."

I smothered a smile that seemed inappropriate to the surroundings. "Remember me?" I said.

"I know who I am," she responded fretfully, "and I know who you are. Now please, be a good girl and march over to that front desk and get me out of this place. I'll never get well here. They don't let you sleep, and the food can't be eaten. Just because I'm old and I've got Medicare doesn't give them the right to keep me. Every soul who comes in here jabs me with a needle or stuffs pills down my throat or—"

"Whoa," I said. "I want to talk about the money in the toy chest."

Her mouth snapped shut, and all the animation left her face as if it had been wiped clean with a rag. She stared at the silent TV, which now displayed a young woman surveying the triumph of her day, her freshly mopped, gleaming kitchen linoleum. The happy housewife got so excited that she whirled into a little dance. Roz would have puked.

"Miss Devens?" I got no response, so I made a production of pulling over the visitor's chair and seating myself, just to let her know I had no intention of leaving. "Margaret?"

She didn't meet my gaze, and when she spoke, her lips barely moved. "I didn't mean to say anything. It was unfair, them giving me that drug, you asking me questions—"

"You asked me to hide the money and I did. I'd say that gives me the right to a few answers."

Her hands laced themselves together across the bedclothes. The IV line was still fastened to her left hand. She fingered the tape that held it in her vein. "First you have to promise me," she said slowly.

"Promise you what?"

"You'll look for Eugene."

"I have been looking for Eugene."

She closed her eyes. Her lips were still swollen and I had to lean forward in my chair to hear her clearly. "If I answer your questions, maybe—I don't know—maybe you'll give it up, walk away."

"How can I promise before I know?"

She opened her eyes wide. No doubt about it, the stubborn Aunt Bea streak I'd noticed while she sat in the rocking chair in my living room had been real. "If you can't," she said firmly, "then I think I'm much too weak to answer any questions." Her right arm stretched out and grabbed a black box fastened to a long rubber hose. She held it so tightly her knuckles whitened. "This buzzer calls the real nurse, Miss Carlyle, and I'm sure she'll agree with me."

77

I should have quit right then. Instead I counted to ten and said, "Hey, I brought your robe and slippers."

"Thank you." Her hand poised over the call button, she was stubbornly polite.

"Is there anything else I can bring you? A book?"

"No, thank you." Just as stubborn, just as polite.

"Okay," I said. "How about a deal? I keep looking for your brother, no matter what you tell me, provided you let me file a missing persons report with the police."

She closed both her eyes. The IV tube trickled liquid into her left hand. The white sheets had more color to them than her cheeks. I felt nasty bargaining with a battered old woman. I had to remember that steely streak in her before I could make myself speak.

"Deal or no deal?" I said.

"Deal," she said, releasing her grip on the black box.

"Did you recognize the man who beat you up?"

"Man," she said scornfully. "Men. Two of them."

"Did you recognize them?"

"They had blurry faces, all bulgy. Eugene always told me keep the door on the chain, even in the daytime, but I don't know, maybe I thought it was him coming home. I didn't think, I just opened the door."

Blurry, bulgy faces sounded like stocking masks to me.

"They knew about the money?" I asked.

"They knew about it. I told them I didn't have any idea what they were blathering about."

"Why?" I asked softly.

She consulted the TV. It showed the roulette wheel again. She didn't answer.

"Just because you're stubborn?" I insisted.

"Yes," she said angrily, "just because I'm stubborn."

"The Gaelic Brotherhood Association," I said. "Tell me about it."

She stared at me for a long time, stared through me like she was seeing someone else.

"Deal or no deal?" I said.

She took a deep breath and shuddered like it hurt her somewhere inside. "It is, it was, a social organization, folks from Ireland. It's old. My parents belonged, my uncle Brian—"

"I know what it was. What is it now?"

"Maybe eight months ago, maybe a year ago, it started up again. I used to belong myself, but this time Eugene said I wouldn't enjoy the meetings, it was just a bunch of the cabbies, and they met odd hours." Her right hand tapped the edge of the bed restlessly and she murmured, almost to herself, "I should have known something was wrong."

Catholics and Jews are tied, I think, for the guilt championship of the world. Here was this old woman, beaten to a pulp, probably because of something her brother had done, blaming herself for not having the gift of second sight.

"Go on," I said. I probably sounded a little angry. I was. "That's all he told me, all I know to this day, I swear. A harmless little social club, an excuse for a few drinks. It wasn't till after Eugene disappeared that I looked in the toy chest. We used to hide things there, secret messages and such, when we were children. That's why I looked. And when I saw what was there, all that money, I didn't know what to do. I came to you."

"After you visited the cab company."

"Wouldn't you have gone? I tried to talk to some of the men, Sean Boyle, Joe Fergus. I couldn't find Pat—Patrick O'Grady. He might have told me something, but he was out sick. Oh, those men! Some of them I've known for years, and they smiled at me and said go home, don't worry. It made me so angry I can't even tell you. They gave the old biddy a pat on the head and said go on home, don't trouble yourself, it's only your one relative in the world gone missing. It'll all turn out fine—"

"Did you open Eugene's locker?"

"Locker? I didn't know—"

"Why didn't you mention the money when you came to me?"

Silence.

"Where do you think the money came from?"

She tried to shake her head, winced with the pain of the effort, and said, "I don't know."

"Where do you think it's going?"

It was a question she must have expected, but it made her hands jump as if an electric current had passed through them. She swallowed with an audible gulp. "I pray God I'm wrong, but in the old days we used to send money, the Gaelic Brotherhood Association, I mean, used to send money—to Ireland."

"The IRA," I said flatly. Oh, shit. Deep shit.

Margaret twisted her hands together, forgetting about the IV hookup. "You don't know how it was, Miss Carlyle. You're too young. I remember though, I remember. When I was still a child my mother took me to Boston Common and there must have been a hundred thousand Irish-Americans, all gathered together in protest against the British, for the Cause. It was so different back then, it was like another world. Before the troubles started again in the sixties, it was organized. The money was for food and clothes, to help the families of the men rotting in the British prisons, to help the children go to Catholic schools—"

She stopped, out of words and breath, and seemed to want me to say something. "Sure," I said. I guess I am too young. I've got some respect for the Irish; I'm part Irish after all. The music and the poetry are terrific. But then you've got the divorce laws. And the IRA . . .

Margaret seemed satisfied with my one-word contribution. She started talking again, more slowly. "The American money tapered off. The fund-raisers were desperate by 'seventy-five. Noraid contributions were way down because of the horror stories in the newspapers. Children maimed. Husbands shot in front of their wives. It was too much, too much, and there was no end to it. And the trickle of money still coming stopped dead on Saint Patrick's Day in 'seventy-seven, when the Four Horsemen said, 'No more.' "

"Four horsemen?"

"Teddy Kennedy, and Moynihan, and Tip O'Neill, and Governor Carey. They spoke out against the IRA, and we listened. The groups were disbanded. The GBA stopped meeting. The churches preached against the violence. It ended." She closed her eyes and I could tell by her pallor that I'd have to stop soon.

"Did it end for your brother?"

"I don't know." Her voice was flat and toneless. "I thought so then. He didn't have much money to give, and if he'd given to the Provos, he wouldn't have mentioned it to me. Terrorists I call them now, even if some of them are my own people."

"Do you have family in Ireland?"

"Not anymore. Not that I know of."

"If somebody said your brother went to Ireland, would you believe him?"

"Not Eugene. He might have talked about going now and again. But he was like the rest of the old men at Green and White, all talk."

"He didn't think life might be better there?"

She tried to smile, battered lips and all. "One of the things my brother believed, with all his heart and soul, was that the Irish were a terrible people, if you left them in Ireland. It was his joke, that the Irish weren't so bad once you got them away from the old sod. He used to say the trouble with Ireland is they've got too many Irish there."

The knock on the door startled me enough to bring me to my feet. It announced the entrance of an earnest young woman, who declared it time for Miss Devens to accompany her down to X-ray. A name tag was pinned to her white cardigan. Before she had a chance to continue her set speech, I said, "Nurse Hanover, this patient is a witness in a police case, and she tells me she's been bothered by unwanted visitors."

"Visiting hours aren't till seven o'clock—"

"I know when visiting hours begin. I suggest you phone

the Police Department, Area D, speak to Lieutenant Mooney, and ask him to provide a guard for Miss Devens's door."

"If you think that would be best—"

"Take care of it immediately. Personally. And until the police arrive, alert the nurse at the station to be extremely careful about who enters this room. People dressed in white tend to look alike." I pushed back my sleeve, checked my watch, made a notation on my clipboard, and nodded a quick farewell to Margaret.

I'm not sure, what with the state of her eyes, but I think she winked at me.

█▓█▓█▓█▓█▓█▓█▓█▓█▓█▓█▓█▓█▓█▓█▓█▓█▓█▓█▓

Chapter 14

"I need more time," I said.

"Let me get this straight." The voice on the line was the same gruff bellow I'd heard the last time, belonging to "our Mr. Andrews." I had a lot less trouble getting through to him this time. Either his name moved mountains, or I was finally getting my just reward for my charm school manners. I wolfed a bite of tuna sandwich while he summed up the situation. "You haven't been able to reach your husband."

"That's right," I replied truthfully enough. "I've left messages," I added, less truthfully.

"And he hasn't gotten back to you."

No doubt about it. This man had a grip on reality. I shooed fluffy Red Emma away from my potato chips. She adores potato chips, but then she has to drink about a gallon of water because she gets salted out.

"Er," the gruff voice sounded oddly hesitant. "Er, I don't

quite know how to put this, but are you and your husband having any difficulties?''

I swallowed. "Difficulties?"

"Of an, er, marital sort? You're not separated, are you?"

"Would that disqualify us?"

"Oh, er, no. Not at all. As long as he, uh, as long as both of you show up to claim your prize."

"Well, like I said, I'll keep trying."

"Where exactly is your husband?"

"Why?"

His voice got all smooth and jovial. "Oh, I just thought we might be able to phone him. Cedar Wash has operators on call twenty-four hours a day, seven days a week."

"Thomas hates to be bothered by strangers," I said, which was an out-and-out lie. T.C. will rub up against any stranger, any time, any place. "I'll get through. I just need time."

"Can you call me back in two days?"

"Sure. No problem. Don't give the money away till then."

I held the phone to my ear long after he'd hung up, because I could swear I'd heard an extra click at the beginning of our conversation. It made me wonder if someone didn't know wiretapping was illegal.

They've got this bug detector in the Sharper Image catalog, this monthly bulletin of trendy gadgetry that I get through the mail due to some computer error. Anyhow, this item only costs forty-nine bucks plus two-fifty postage, "thanks to a breakthrough in microcircuit technology." And it only weighs two ounces, so I could keep it in my shoulder bag.

Roz picked that moment to enter the kitchen. At least I thought it was Roz. Her hair was a bizarre shade of pink, and I wondered if she had done it on purpose or if this was the end result of all that dye. She yanked open the refrigerator. The seat of her skintight black stirrup pants looked like the seat of Roz's skintight black stirrup pants. When she turned around, a jar of peanut butter in one hand, I knew beyond a doubt that it was Roz and that she, at least, thought her hair had turned out fine. She had a dreamy, faraway smile

83

on her lips, in anticipation of the peanut butter, which she adores for breakfast, lunch, and dinner, and she was wearing one of her signature T-shirts.

Roz is a sweet kid, honestly, underneath the fake eyelashes, the pouty makeup, the garish jewelry, and the tough-gal, heavy-metal image. She has a fake leopard skin coat. She's only about five two, and she's really thin, except for these incredible breasts which may be why she has the best T-shirt collection in the world. The messages range from ''McGovern '72'' to ''Tofu Is Gross'' to ''Stamp Out Smurfs.'' Today she wore one of my favorites, a copy of the classic crimson T, with Psychotic U. emblazoned where Harvard ought to be. My absolute favorite comes from a shop in Harvard Square and is a wild shade of purple, imprinted with the following verse:

> Roses are red
> Violets are blue
> I'm schizophrenic
> And so am I

I never comment on Roz's appearance.

''Yo, Carlotta,'' Roz said. ''How're ya' doin'?'' She unscrewed the peanut butter jar and scooped a glob of yellowish goo onto a green-painted fingernail. We use the same refrigerator, but we buy separate supplies. Her attack on the peanut butter made me glad about that.

I wondered if her karate-instructor boyfriend was still lurking upstairs. Roz calls him Lemon. I'm not sure if that's his genuine nickname, or just Roz's special term of endearment, but his real name is Whitfield Arthur Carstairs III, I swear, and when he's not teaching karate, he's a performance artist. Some days he stands immobile, on a soapbox, for hours, in the middle of Harvard Square. I once saw him juggle four grapefruits. He also does sporadic underground theater, and has one of the most gorgeous bodies I have ever seen.

"You busy today?" I asked Roz.

"Not especially," she said. At least I think that's what she said. Her speech was slurred by the peanut butter.

"Want to earn a few bucks?"

"Today?"

She's sharp as a tack sometimes. I don't hold it against her. She's at least ten years younger than I am, and she was probably weaned on television and marijuana. When she's cleaning the house she sings TV-commercial jingles. On the other hand, she really can paint when the mood strikes her; wild abstract oils, layered with color and energy. She also does an occasional, surprisingly delicate, watercolor.

"Yeah," I said. "Today. You have other plans?"

"Lemon's coming by."

Hah, I thought, you mean Lemon's here. I'm a detective, for crying out loud. His truck is still parked across the street. I wondered if she thought I'd charge more rent for the two of them, or if she imagined I'd be scandalized by his overnight presence. The last thought kind of offended me. I mean, I'm not that ancient, and I'm not particularly righteous. I comforted myself by recalling the anguished and delighted grunts and groans of the night before. If Roz really wanted to keep Lemon a secret, surely she would have muted her ecstasy.

"If he wants to earn some dough," I said, "I can use him, too."

"Great," she mumbled through the peanut butter. "What's up?"

"Wear working clothes. And you'd better bring rubber gloves."

"Rubber gloves," she repeated. "Is this weird?"

"The job is housecleaning. At a client's house."

"Time and a half for housecleaning, if it's not this place," she said. She is sharp where money's concerned.

"Okay," I said. I had access to a lot of cash. I gave her Margaret's address, made her write it down. She's scatterbrained on addresses.

"Bring your camera," I said. "And before you touch anything, take photos. For insurance, okay?"

Roz brightened. She loves photography. She converted this old root cellar in the basement into a darkroom, and sometimes she stays down there for days, coming up only for an occasional hit of peanut butter.

"No artsy-fartsy stuff, Roz," I warned. "For a straight-arrow insurance company. And the place is a real mess. You'd better have Lemon drive his pickup so you can haul stuff away."

"Okay."

"And bring Hefty Bags."

"Hefty Bags, rubber gloves, and a camera," she said. "Lemon's gonna love it."

"Leave the Wesson Oil home," I said.

She giggled.

"Look, Roz, seriously, here's the key to the front door, and if anybody rings the doorbell, check them out before you open it. The lady who lives there is mixed up in some heavy-duty shit, and I don't want you taking any chances."

"Me and Lemon—"

"I know the two of you can kick anybody's ass around the block, Roz, but you can't kick a gun unless they let you get close enough."

"Okay," she said. "I'll be careful." She returned the peanut butter jar to the fridge. Breakfast was evidently over. I wondered what poor Lemon subsisted on. "Hey," she said, "did I tell you that guy came by again?"

"Huh?" Sometimes I don't catch on very fast either.

"That guy you went to school with."

"School," I repeated. "Where?"

"I don't know. I thought U. Mass., probably, but he looked kinda well dressed for that."

"You've seen him with me? Here?"

"No."

"He have a name?"

"Yeah. Let's see. Smith. Roger Smith. Didn't you see the note on the fridge?"

We both stared at the forest of paper on the refrigerator door. Time for a little local housecleaning, I thought.

"Oh, Roger Smith," I said finally.

"A really nice guy," she said. "You dating or what?"

"I wouldn't know," I said.

"Huh?" It was her turn to look bewildered.

"I don't know anybody named Roger Smith, and I never went to any school with anybody named Roger Smith."

"Well how was I supposed to know?"

I shook my head sadly. The phantom had struck again. According to Roz, he'd made two appearances at the front door: the first, about five days ago; the second, the day before yesterday. The first time, he'd worn a navy blazer, charcoal slacks, black loafers, a light blue shirt, and a patterned tie. The second time, he'd worn a three-piece gray suit with a faint stripe, white shirt, dark tie, wing tips. He'd been sorry to miss me, just wanted to know how I was doing. Was I still driving the Toyota? Did I have another car? Did I ever buy that place on the Cape?

Huh?

I have to say that for an artist, Roz was terrible when it came to describing the guy's face, which tickled me because she had his clothes down cold. Maybe she concentrates on bodies. Lemon is certainly evidence of that. She told me the guy had a definite mauve aura. When I questioned her closely, it sounded like he was the same man who'd chatted with Gloria, the same preppy, good-looking soul who'd passed himself off to Mooney as Mr. George Robinson of the Department of Social Services.

"Was he alone in the house, in any room, even for the briefest moment?" I asked.

"Well, I guess," Roz said reluctantly, "I mean, when I went to get a piece of paper to write his name down and all."

Shit. I was definitely going to buy that bug detector.

Chapter 15

While Roz and Lemon were over at Margaret's—cleaning, I sincerely hoped—I rescued Red Emma from T.C., who had her treed in the curtains. I fed and watered the menagerie, and tried to teach the dumb bird more Marxist propaganda. Then I hauled out the phone books, Boston and suburban, and ran my finger down the list of Carlyles, hoping to find a genuine Thomas C. of a slightly larcenous bent. There was a Thomas D. Carlyle in Brockton, and a Thomas C. in Walpole, who had the nerve to spell his last name Carlisle. There were several T. Carlyles, and I dialed them all, and sure enough, they were Thelmas and Theodoras and Tinas; females every one. I gave it up, puttered around, picked some guitar, which I found frustrating, since I don't practice enough to sound the way I used to sound, not to mention the way I'd like to sound. I gave up and fed a cassette of Rory Block's "High Heeled Blues" album into the tape deck, because she sounds the way I'd like to sound, effortless and funky. I sang along while I answered the mail—which for me means shoving unread junk mail into those postage-paid envelopes enclosed along with the other junk mail.

After making a dent in the mail pile, I began a detailed report of the Eugene Devens case thus far. Turning my chicken-scratched notes into typed sentences reminded me that I hadn't talked to old Pat, the cabbie, so I dialed Gloria's back-room number, the unlisted one, and asked for his address.

I may have woken her up. She sounded downright hostile,

but then if I were a cab dispatcher, I wouldn't even own a phone of my own, I'd get so tired of answering the damn things. It took a while, but she eventually gave me a number and street in Dorchester.

Before leaving the house, I took two precautions. Using most of a roll of wide duct tape, I neatly joined the two litter boxes in the downstairs bathroom, making a money sandwich. The ensemble looked like a slightly high-rise cat box.

I also took my gun out of its wrappings in the locked bottom drawer of my bureau, and loaded it.

You can't live in Boston without acquiring a certain awareness of the IRA—initials spray-painted on mailboxes, fundraising announcements tacked to laundromat bulletin boards, shamrock green collection cans strategically positioned beside certain cash registers in certain bars. But to judge by the Boston press, most of the juicy IRA stories—the bombings, the kidnappings, the shootings—are either foreign or ancient history, far away or long ago. The only recent local cause célèbre that came to mind was the *Valhalla* affair.

The *Valhalla* was a gunrunner, an ''alleged'' gunrunner, I should say, that allegedly steamed out of Gloucester Harbor one September morning in '85, carrying more than $1 million in alleged munitions (guns, bombs, et cetera) to the alleged Irish Republican Army. A federal grand jury had been investigating the hell out of everybody who had anything to do with the *Valhalla*, but so far, after a full year, no indictments had been handed down, which made me wonder about the ancestry of the jury members. In the meantime, one guy, an alleged informant, had disappeared under ''very mysterious circumstances which rule out the possibility of flight,'' according to the *Boston Globe*, and the rumor had duly circulated that he'd been taken out by the Boston IRA.

On the strength of that rumor, and just in case I ran into Margaret's stocking-masked thugs, there I was, staring at a .38-caliber S&W with a four-inch barrel, a ringer for standard police issue, and believe me, standard police issue revolvers have nothing but bad memories for me.

From where I stand, the whole bloody Irish carnage makes no sense. It might have made sense once, but now it seems to roll on from force of habit as much as anything else, turning into some kind of modern Hydra. Chop off one head—one British soldier, one Irish Republican, one Protestant UDR man—and ten more sprout from the bleeding wound. From the heart of Massachusetts, the "troubles" seem more mythic than real. There are too many factions, too many righteous grievances, too little hope of reconciliation. A whole generation of children has been born to violence in Northern Ireland. It's what they expect from life. For them, the Glorious Struggle is daily life. Something To Do. A Way To Pass The Time Until You Die. Or, more likely, until some passerby, who chose the wrong street at the wrong time on the wrong day, dies.

I prepared myself for any encounter with the Boston branch of the IRA by adding two pounds' worth of gun to my overcrowded, overweight shoulder bag. A lot of effect that was going to have on hundreds of years of oppression, right?

I stopped at a liquor store on the way, and made the sort of cheap-whiskey purchase that raised the young clerk's eyebrows. I remembered Pat's taste.

The old man hadn't made a fortune driving a hack. The address I hunted was in an area folks escaped from if they could. Pat's apartment was on the second floor of the skinniest, seediest triple-decker on a block that had seen better days. The outside of the place was gray, but I couldn't tell if that was the intended color or the result of years of bleaching sun and lack of care. Not a bush, not a sapling. Clumps of crabgrass made an ugly excuse for a lawn. The porches on the top two levels sagged. A single lawn chair perched on the front stoop. Faded strips of once-gaudy yellow, blue, and red webbing drooped dispiritedly. One broken strip trailed on the ground.

On the spur of the moment, I reached into the depths of my shoulder bag, and groped around until I located the gold pin with the GBA initials, the one I'd found in Eugene's locker. I held it up to the light. It was scratched and slightly bent. I stuck the pin into the collar of my blouse.

Patrick Day O'Grady was my man. There was a button to push under the crooked nameplate, but the door to the stairwell was ajar, propped open with a broken cedar shingle, so I just walked up to the second floor and rapped on the door. I could hear a TV voice, loud over organ music.

I counted to ten and knocked louder. The hallway was as attractive and well kept as the outside of the house. Either the first- or third-floor tenants had eaten something greasy last night. Bad hamburger, maybe. I tried not to breathe, and banged my fist against the door hard enough to rock it on its hinges.

I heard a shuffling on the other side of the door, mixed with a syncopated tapping sound, and then a determined and familiar old voice ordered me to go away and stop bothering an old man, you should be ashamed of yourself, all of you young kids with nothing better to do than taunt an old man who worked every day of his life and now was brought to this, and don't bother breaking in because I haven't got anything worth stealing, and the German shepherd would as soon eat you as look at you.

All uttered in one breath.

"Pat," I said for about the tenth time, trying to interrupt his speech before the curtain call. "It's a friend. From Green and White. An old friend."

"Call the cops on you, I will," continued the refrain from the other side. "And don't you think I won't. You can't scare me. Bums is what you are, bums, the lot of you."

"A friend," I hollered. "A friend with a drink." If I yelled much louder somebody *would* call the police.

Silence from behind the door, followed by a suspicious inquiry. "You're not selling anything?"

"No."

"What's your name, then?"

"Carlotta. I used to work with you, at Green and White."

"Carlotta," he repeated. "A girl." Long pause, then some more shuffling. "And what color is your hair?"

"It's red, Pat, and I don't dye it."

The first of an impressive series of locks clicked. The door creaked open to the limit of a solid three-inch chain. A single reddened eye peered out. The door closed firmly in my face, then swung open wide.

"And why has it taken you seven years to come courting?" Pat said. "Come in, girl, come in. I've got to bar the door against the Huns."

Illness had hit him hard, sucking off most of his muscle and fat, leaving a gaunt shadow behind. His face drooped as if somebody had released a valve and deflated it. His feet were encased in huge floppy slippers, which accounted for the shuffling noise. He leaned heavily on a walking stick. That was the tapping. He was wrapped in a chenille bathrobe way too large for him. The ends of the self-tie belt dangled almost to his knees. He was wearing pants under the robe. The cuffs flapped around his waxy ankles. He'd aged twenty years in seven. I'd seen healthier-looking cadavers.

"Don't bother telling me how fine I look," he said quickly, noting the expression on my face. "I know I'm gorgeous. Just give me a kiss, and slip off your clothes, and I'll die a happy man."

"Jeez," I said, "you haven't changed."

"Come in, come in. You're more beautiful than I recall. Say thank you for the compliment. A blush would be nice if you could manage it. Are you married yet or still an old maid?"

Shit. Was I going to interview him, or was he going to interview me? I breathed in a considerable amount of air and was surprised to find it sweet. The place was clean. Pat's flat was a shabby affair, Spartan, the final resting place of a fussy old flirtatious bachelor. Probably a virgin. A faded print couch anchored one wall. Blowsy off-white curtains framed the windows. A framed picture of Jesus hung on the wall over the sofa, a crucifix next to it. A threadbare easy chair

92

with a fat dented cushion faced off against a huge color TV. The furniture wasn't arranged with conversational groupings in mind. It was set up for one man watching TV alone.

Pat flicked the set off quickly, rightfully embarrassed at being caught watching some overwrought evangelist.

"Where's the German shepherd?" I asked. "The one who'll rip me limb from limb?"

"Died," he said. "Years ago. I resurrect him when the neighborhood youth come to call. You married or what?"

"How's your love life?" I asked.

"No rings on your fingers," he said.

"Nor on yours."

"I thought you said something about a drink, or I'd never have let you in."

I looked at the pasty color of his skin, and wondered if a drink would finish him off. His cheeks each boasted a dime-sized circle of color. Excitement, or maybe a flush of fever.

"Be a dear," he said, "and fetch two glasses from the drain on the kitchen sink. It'll take you less time than it would me." He sat heavily in the TV chair.

The kitchen was as barren and neat as the living room. One plate, one fork, one knife, one spoon in the drain. Two coffee cups, two glasses. I wondered if he'd entertained another guest lately. I hauled a kitchen chair into the living room, and placed it near the TV chair. It was that or sit on the floor. I noticed marks on the cheap carpeting, grooves where chairs and tables and lamps had once stood, and I wondered if Pat had given his furnishings away, paring down his possessions before he died.

"To the old days" was the toast he chose when I poured the Four Roses, his preferred label, a brand I link to foul taste and worse hangovers. He patted the bottle and said teasingly, "A pint is fine, but a quart would have been better."

"A gallon, maybe."

"An ocean," he said. He gulped his drink. His smile turned into a grimace, and he shifted uncomfortably in the

93

chair. "What do you want from me?" he asked sharply. "Nobody comes by here anymore unless they want something."

It was a sudden mood change. Pain can do that to you.

"Margaret Devens sent me."

"Margaret."

"Her brother's missing."

"Eugene's not come home?"

"No."

"How long has this been going on, with nobody saying a word about it to me?"

"Two weeks."

Pat started to pour another drink. His hand shook, and he replaced the bottle on the table. "Well, I don't know where he is. If I did, I'd tell Margaret. I admire that woman, always have."

"She's worried about him," I said.

"Every right to be," he agreed.

I let his words hang there for a minute. Then I said, "Why?"

"The way things are out there," Pat said, gesturing vaguely. "Pour me another, will you? And don't ask me whether I'll be okay, will you do me that favor? I've been drinking this stuff since before you were hatched."

"What's going on at G and W, Pat?"

"I left," he said.

"Because you were sick."

"Sick and tired," he said. "Sick and tired."

I had hoped he'd notice my lapel pin, but he didn't. "Margaret says you used to be a big shot in the GBA," I hazarded.

"The old GBA," he said. "Those were good times." He drank down the whiskey I'd poured in one practiced gulp, sucked air, and twitched in the chair. It hurt him to drink, but he was drinking defiantly. "If anything's happened to Eugene . . ."

"Why would anything happen to him?"

"I don't know."

94

"What does the GBA do, now?"

"We started meeting again, maybe a year back, harmless enough. A bunch of us old men with no better way to pass the time. We wanted to help the Cause. Everybody was down on the Provos, you know, and we thought, well, maybe we should help them out again, and it started very small. We were all cabbies and we'd just collect the donations, pick up the canisters at the bars, you know. Cabbies have a lot of loose bills and change, from tips, and sometimes we go to the bank with rolls of quarters and dimes and nickels, and the tellers know what we do, so they don't think it's odd. We'd pick up the canisters and get ten- and twenty-dollar bills instead of quarters and nickels, and pass it on, that's all. That's what we did. Small stuff, but regular. Nothing sinister about it, but secretive-like, and we enjoyed it. A little spice in your life can't hurt."

Yeah. Dimes and nickels to kill small children in Belfast. Terrific. I kept my mouth shut about the morality of the whole affair, but I shot a glance at the picture of Jesus on the wall. I wondered if Pat and I were talking about the same bunch of guys. It takes a whole lot of quarters and nickels to tote up to twelve thousand dollars.

"You said it started small," I prompted.

"Huh? Oh, yes, the GBA. Now why did you want to hear about that?"

I moved the bottle of whiskey out of his reach.

"Gaelic Brotherhood," he muttered. "Fine Gaelic Brotherhood." He swallowed another mouthful. "A young man, a man from Ireland, came to us, and he said he'd heard about us, and would we be willing to risk more."

"What was his name?"

"Jackie's all I know. From Ireland. Doesn't sound any more Irish than I do. Maybe he was born over here, and went back to fight. A few of them do, you know."

"What were you supposed to do?"

"That's when I left, and had my operation."

"But Eugene would have told you."

"Friends don't come around much when you're ill. Oh, they visit at the hospital, but then, well, you start to get the smell of death on you, and it scares the old folks off."

"Anything you remember could help."

"Memory's a funny thing with me these days. I remember you clear as a bell, with that silly hat you used to wear. But ask me what I ate for dinner yesterday, and I'm not sure I could oblige you."

He was clearly chatting for the sound of it, hesitating. "Pour me another drink," he said.

"I want your memory to stay sharp."

"Come on, why do you want to know? Why would Margaret send you?"

"She can't come herself, because two thugs beat her up."

"Holy Mother! She's okay? Margaret?"

"Barely."

"Holy Mother of God," he said under his breath. "Eugene gone and Margaret beaten up."

"It's time to talk."

"Why would I talk to you? There are police officers. Not that you can tell around here most days, with the kids smoking that stuff on the stairs."

I pulled out the photostat of my license. "I'm working for Margaret Devens."

"I can't read small print."

"I'm a licensed private investigator in the state of Massachusetts."

"Glory be, what will they think of next? No wonder she's got no time to marry me."

"Come on, Pat. You're cute as hell, but I need more than cute."

"And she swears, too. What's the world coming to?"

"Pat."

"One more shot of whiskey. I can be bribed."

One more shot, and he'd probably fall off the chair. I made it a short one.

His voice lowered to a fuzzy conspiratorial whisper. "I

96

only know what Eugene told me, you understand, and most of it he told me in the hospital, and you know, they kept me under a lot, this drug and that drug, until I thought I was half-crazy. But it seems to me that Jackie had a way for them to move a lot of money, IRA money, around the area, bring it in from Logan, and get it to sources at the air force base who could change the money into guns and ammunition. A really big deal, something to make a difference against the damned Brits, you should excuse me for mentioning them.''

"How did it work?''

"I remember how pleased Eugene was, at first. It was something poetic, I think, something having to do with the radios, maybe, the cab radios.''

I plied him with liquor. I told him the story of my life. I scrambled two eggs, and watched while he made a pathetic attempt to eat. But that was all I got out of him until the shadows were starting to darken, and I'd made my excuses, and headed for the door.

"Carlotta,'' he said blearily, "thanks for coming by, dear. The whiskey was grand.''

"Yeah,'' I said. "Likewise.''

"It was something about a woman's name, I think,'' he said. "That's what tickled Eugene. A woman's name.''

I left my card so he could call if any more pieces of the puzzle came floating back.

Chapter 16

I thought about calling the cops, spilling what I knew, and letting them take it from there. I remembered one of my mother's favorite sayings, straight from my grandmother and the old country. I wish I could say it in Yiddish, because it *sounds* so funny you don't even need the translation to get a laugh out of it. The best approximation my mom could come up with was something like: "With a stranger's hands, you can tie a string around a cat's neck." In other words: If you care about the results, do it yourself.

The best time to approach Gloria would be the quiet hour after the 11 P.M. shift change, but I hesitated, feeling increasingly uncomfortable as the time drew closer. Finally, I let myself admit why I was worried. If Green & White was involved in more than the hackney carriage trade, I had to face the fact that my pal Gloria could be deep in the shady side of things.

I tried to envision Gloria as a secret IRA powerhouse.

Failed utterly.

Possibly a sympathizer. *Comandante* Gloria of United Oppressed Peoples, or some such group. Even my imagination, which Mooney has called excessive, refused to provide a believable link between Gloria and the Provisional Branch of the IRA. Matter of fact, the image that sprang unbidden to my mind, Gloria as Grand Marshal of the Saint Patrick's Day Parade, an annual South Boston affair at which blacks are conspicuous by their absence, tickled me so much I laughed out loud, and scared T.C. under the bed.

I decided to risk Gloria. Gloria, but not her partner, not Sam. Maybe it was the memory of last night's noisy third-floor lovemaking that did it, maybe it was Pat's repeated queries about my marital state, but my face heated up when I thought about Sam. He was a Gianelli, I reminded myself, and somehow hoods in stocking masks, the kind who'd roughed up Margaret, said Gianelli. I wouldn't risk Sam. Personally or professionally, I told myself sternly. I always give myself such good advice.

I left the house at eleven, wearing jeans and a wind-breaker, my hair tucked up under the slouch cap I used to wear for driving.

Renewing my vow to take nighttime walks, I parked a half-mile from G&W, under a streetlamp to discourage car thieves. The first drops started slowly, a single leisurely splash against my cheek, another on my hand, then a heavy wet plop on the bridge of my nose. The drops ganged up quickly, and turned into an unexpected shower. A sudden gust of northeasterly wind tried to steal my hat, and the rain began battering the pavement, bouncing back inches high. I walked briskly. I ran.

Listening to the Boston weather report is a pure waste of time. In G&W's office, the phones almost drowned out the storm.

So much for quiet time at the cab company.

Gloria, erect in her wheelchair, was massaging buttons on the switchboard, playing it like a church organ, and crooning into the mike, her deep voice commanding, soothing, cajoling. A vast box of Chicken McNuggets sat within easy reach.

Ten hectic minutes later, she punched a button, and the bells abruptly halted, cut off mid-jangle. Lights still flashed and flickered, but she ignored them, and pushed the Mc-Nuggets in my direction. I eyed them suspiciously. I like my chicken in identifiable parts. Legs. Wings.

"Downpour like this, I can't pick up anybody in less than an hour," she said with a shrug. "You tell folks it'll take an hour for them to get a cab, they get downright surly. Call you names. Soon as some of the cabs get loose, I'll pick up again.''

She pressed a button on the mike and said, ''Free cabs call home, everybody. Free cabs call home. Forget those hailers out there, even the ones waving twenty-dollar bills. I got a list, so call home to Momma.''

The storm whistled and sang. I shook water off my hat, and sat in the plastic guest chair.

''See Pat?'' Gloria asked.

''Yeah. He looks bad.''

''Can't sleep?'' Gloria divided her attention between me and the honey-mustard dipping sauce.

''Nope,'' I said.

''Warm milk's good,'' she said. ''Or a man, so I hear.''

''I have nightmares.''

''Got to watch what you eat,'' she said, smiling through a mouthful of McNuggets.

''I have this recurrent dream—that your cabbies are collecting IRA cash on the side, maybe dealing for weapons.''

''Weird,'' she said.

''Not so weird, Gloria. True.''

She ate a handful of homogenized chicken things in a thoughtful manner then said ''This is a joke, right?''

''Nope.''

''Are we talking IRA, as in Individual Retirement Account? Because I don't know much about banking.''

''Irish Republican Army.''

''Whoo-eee,'' she said.

''Exactly.''

''Has this got something to do with your looking for Eugene Devens?'' she asked, plainly skeptical.

''Eugene was fund-raising,'' I said.

''Why would you think a thing like that?'' Her eyes narrowed. No dummy, Gloria.

''Trust me,'' I said. I trusted her, to a point, but I had no intention of mentioning the cash in T.C.'s litter box.

''IRA, huh?'' She made a noise that could only be described as a snort. "Whoo-eee. I tell you, I wouldn't put much past some of these old farts. I'm just glad they're not collecting for the KKK."

"Maybe they are. On the side."

She made a face and moaned, "Why me, O Lord? Why not Town Taxi? Why not Red Cab? I've got the Hackney Bureau crawling all over me. You read about those new regulations? A dress code for cabbies and all. I ask you, shirts with button-up collars, no shorts? What kind of—"

"It doesn't have to be so bad," I said quietly, before she launched into a full-blown tirade.

"Carlotta—"

"Listen to me. If I took what I've got to the police, what would happen? A mess. A couple undercover cops prancing in here to get hired. Maybe FBI. Maybe ATF."

"ATF?"

"Alcohol, Tobacco and Firearms. Everybody makes them for cops within two seconds, right, and the surveillance lasts forever."

"While I'm stuck with two cabs full of cops doing squat," Gloria said, glaring at the ceiling. "Lose me a bundle."

"Eleven," blared a voice over the loudspeaker. "I'm at Beacon and Exeter."

"Yo, eleven," Gloria said, grabbing the microphone as if it would steady her. "Comm. Ave. one-seventy-six. Guy named Ervine. That's one-seventy-six Comm. Ave." The lights were flashing like crazy on the switchboard. Gloria penciled a line through one of the top entries on a narrow pad. Her fingers, grasping the skinny stump of pencil, looked like plump sausages.

"Got it," the metallic voice said.

"Empties call home," Gloria pleaded into the mike. "Come on, folks, it's raining out there."

"So." She flipped a switch and turned her attention back to me. "Tell me how I'm gonna get out of this painlessly."

"You handle it my way," I said. "No cops, minimal revenue loss. If anything's going down, I isolate the perps, and let the cops mop up. Easy.''

"Carlotta, when you say easy, it makes me sweat.''

"Come on, Gloria.''

"Spell it out for me. ABC.''

"I want to look at your records, driver's license stuff, and all. You got anybody driving who's an Irish national?''

"Some of the old guys were born in Ireland, but they're all citizens.''

"Somebody young.''

"Nope.''

"You got people driving for you with priors?''

"What do you think?''

In Boston, there are four kinds of cabbies: the regular working stiffs; the overeducated, underemployed Ph.D.'s; the undereducated, coffee-colored gents right off the boat from Haiti or Barbados; and the guys with rap sheets.

"I want to check out your drivers. And borrow your radio log, say, for the past six months.''

"Anything else? My shoes? Shirt off my back?''

"Sarcasm goes over big with the cops, Gloria.''

"Right. Anything else?'' This time her voice was sugar and spice.

"Tell me about the radio. The equipment's new, right?''

"This year,'' she said proudly. "State of the art. Cabbie can tune in across the band and catch all the calls, or he can fine-tune, and just pick up what I give him. Most of the guys start out taking all the stuff. Gives them a headache, and they quit. It'll drive you crazy, all that yapping.''

"Maybe,'' I said, deep in thought.

Gloria was cooperating. All was going as planned. Except the storm kicked up such a fuss I didn't hear Sam Gianelli come into the office until he was practically dripping rainwater on my sneakers.

Chapter 17

I had forgotten how handsome Sam was. Repressed it entirely.

"Hi, Gloria," he said, halting three feet inside the doorway, underneath one of the swaying lamps, grinning and shaking water off his dark hair. "Busy night. Hope it rains forever." He noticed me, and the grin turned mechanical, like he'd been waiting too long for the photographer to snap the shutter. "Carlotta?"

Warm brown eyes and an easy smile have always attracted me. I find a stubborn chin a challenge. Add to the above a body both well proportioned and taller than my own, and I could see how a younger Carlotta had fallen hard.

"Sam," I said.

He was more elegant at thirty-six than he'd been at—what?—twenty-nine? Grown up. His face was still bony, broad through the cheeks, narrow at the jaw. He walked differently, his stance more erect, more—I don't know—substantial. His chest filled out a well-cut charcoal suit. He used to look like he was wearing hand-me-downs, and I was never sure if it was the clothes, or the burden of being born the youngest son of Anthony Gianelli.

Anthony Gianelli, for those outside the immediate area, is as connected as you can get. LCN, La Cosa Nostra, the Mafia, call it what you will. Everybody knows it, and nobody does much about it. Sam, the baby, is supposedly clean. He has bad business sense, which doesn't matter all that much. Your last name's Gianelli, your credit's good.

103

Sam hadn't gone running to Pop or begging for loans to keep G&W afloat. He'd partnered up with Gloria instead, and ran the company on the straight and narrow.

Maybe that helped the fit of his clothes.

"Hey," he said, adjusting his smile, "you slumming?"

"She wants—" Gloria started, ignoring my silent plea.

"I need a job, Sam," I interrupted quickly. "Driving."

"I thought you were a cop." It came out too quickly. He hesitated, and added, "Or something." Wouldn't do to let the lady know you'd kept tabs on her.

"Didn't like it."

"Law school?"

"Dropped out."

"You don't look like you're doing so badly," he said, gazing at me, top to bottom and back again, like I was some naked statue in an art museum. Normally, I *hate* that, I really do. This time I could feel my face redden because I realized I'd just done the same to him.

"I can't seem to get a handle on things," I said lamely. "I keep thinking I'll do some more grad school—"

"Do we have an opening?" he asked Gloria. He said it without looking at her, without taking his eyes off my face.

"We could use somebody nights," she said crisply. "To replace Eugene Devens."

"Imagine him taking off like that," Sam said. "After all those years."

I watched him with hawk eyes, but I couldn't see any discomfort in his eyes or hear any secret knowledge in his voice. But then Gianellis have been lying to grand juries since before I was born.

"Somebody nights," he repeated, smiling. "Well, she'll do fine. You still at the old place?"

What he was really asking was if I had the same phone number.

"My aunt died—"

"I'm sorry."

"It was a long time ago. She left me her house."

"That old Victorian in Cambridge? The big one? You live there alone?"

What he was really asking was if I was married.

"I'm the landlord," I said.

He smiled. "I can't picture that," he said.

There was one of those pauses. I could hear Gloria breathing, and I wished she'd say something, say something or disappear.

"I'm still at the same apartment," he said finally. "Same phone. Here." He reached in his pocket and brought out a slim leather billfold that was as ritzy as his apartment's Charles River Park address. He dug out a business card and passed it over. I took it, and our hands brushed for an instant. "Day or night," he said. "Anytime. Give me a call. I've got one of those machines, but leave a message and I'll definitely get back."

"I've got a machine, too," I said, kind of inanely, I admit, but I was still feeling the fine wispy hairs on the back of his hand.

I have unerring chemistry with men. If I breathe faster when they enter the room, if the hairs on the nape of my neck stand up, and my pulse races, I know, beyond the shadow of a doubt, that I have found the wrong guy for me. The kind of man I like, and the kind of man who'd be good for me, make up two nonintersecting sets.

He'd stopped by for cash and the books. Gloria passed over a tin lockbox and a black ledger. He left, and I swear, the lights in the room dimmed.

"Shit," I said, letting my breath out slowly. "You could have warned me he was coming."

"Whoo-eee," Gloria said. "Now that's better than the soaps. What's that I smell in here? Ozone? Smells like lightning hit this very spot."

"Fuck off, Glory," I said halfheartedly. I don't swear that much anymore, which I guess comes from being raised half a Jewish princess. Now when I was a cop, boy, did I cuss. When I put on the badge, I put on the mouth. I was tougher than tough. It took me a while to realize that I didn't much like the person I was turning into. Anyhow, when the spirit moves me I can still say shitass-motherfucker with the best of them, but mostly I don't.

"Temper, temper," Gloria said. "I never know exactly when Sam's going to drop by. Or who's gonna come with him."

"If you're talking about Sam's girlfriends, I couldn't care less," I lied. "If he brings his daddy around, I'm not sure I want to risk driving for you."

"Temper," Gloria repeated, but her lips twitched. "Just trying to see how big a torch you're carrying. I always thought you married that bum Cal on the rebound."

"Look, Gloria," I said. "About the records."

"The books flew the coop with Sam. You better give him a call, like he said."

"Employment applications, driver's license stuff."

I could tell she was deep in thought because she wasn't eating. "Sam is my partner, Carlotta. I should let him in on this."

Would anybody with the name Gianelli be an avid promoter of the IRA? I didn't think so, but I didn't trust Sam. He got accustomed to having his own way while he was still in the cradle. He got used to calling all the shots, and back when I knew him, he wasn't about to give up any of the God-given privileges of the Gianelli male.

"You think he lets you in on everything he's up to?" I said.

"He's not going to like this."

"He's not going to know."

"Yeah. Sure."

"If the shit hits, tell him I lied to you, Gloria. Tell him I stole the stuff."

"That's right, babe. That's what I'll do."

Somehow I didn't think she would. We exchanged frozen smiles that gradually broadened and turned into the real thing, and I accepted another one of the chicken things, taking it as a sort of peace offering. It tasted like fried dough.

"You know, it might not be a bad idea," I said.

"What?"

"Driving for you."

"*What*?"

Cab number 403 got free, and called in his location. His voice was a little scratchy and distorted, but I thought I recognized Sean Boyle. Gloria informed him that Maudie waited at 44 Audubon Court.

"Seriously," I said. "You need a replacement for Eugene, right?"

"Yeah, but—"

"If anybody asks, you just say I'm coming back for a while because I'm not making it on my own."

"Sam bought it," she said. "Anybody ever tell you you're one fine liar?"

"All the time."

"And no need to say you're not making it as a private cop."

"No need to mention it." I warmed to the idea. "From the inside, I can figure the patterns out. Who talks together, drinks together."

"A regular fly on the wall."

More like a roach in the corner, around that place. "I know the ropes, so I won't be any bother at all," I said breezily. If I had my own cab, I could listen to all the radio calls.

Cab 827 called in and got his new assignment. The list was dwindling, the console lights flashing, the rain holding steady.

While Gloria deployed her army, I slid Sam's card into my pocket. I thought I'd done it unobtrusively, but Gloria gave me one of her complacent Buddha looks. I had no intention of calling Sam. I should have tossed the card in the trash can.

It took Gloria some time to dust the cobwebs and cookie crumbs off the employment records. Then we argued about when I'd start driving, what my hours would be, whether I'd actually pick up fares, and if I did, what I should get paid. I could get flush, working two jobs, getting paid for both. Better catfood for T.C. High-class birdseed for the budgie. Steak.

Just being in Gloria's company makes me fixate on food.

■■

Chapter 18

Saturday, I picked up Paolina five minutes early, because she gets jumpy if I'm not right on time. She came charging out the door, pigtails streaming behind her, hollering good-bye to Marta and hello to me at the same time, wearing sneakers and jeans and a pink hooded sweatshirt with a double-front kangaroo pocket.

After buckling her seatbelt, she tucked her hands in the pocket pouch, and we drove out Route 2 to 128 to 3 while she filled me in on all the school gossip. Who was cute and who was "fresh," which means "cool," and who was in and who was out. Ten-year-olds these days—at least urban, street-smart ten-year-olds—have the kind of dividing lines that I don't remember showing up till high school. Remember? The jocks and the preppies and the hoods? Except Paolina calls them the fresh, the freaks, and the nerds. The week's news update was highlighted by the adventures of one Emanuel Rodriguez, a twelve-year-old dreamboat too fresh for words.

"He even told that jerky old guy where to go," Paolina said proudly.

"What jerky old guy?"

"Nobody. Just this freak who sits on the stoop all the time."

"Emanuel walked you home?"

"We walk together sometimes," she admitted, "with some of the other kids."

"T-shirt? Leather bag? The old guy have a beard?" Wispy Beard didn't seem old to me, but to a ten-year-old, everybody's ancient.

"Yeah."

I breathed, in and out. "Listen, tell Emanuel to stay away from him."

"Yeah, well, he better stay away from Emanuel."

"Paolina," I said quietly, "I mean it."

"Yeah, sure," she said.

"That guy ever bother you?"

"No."

"He talk to you?"

"No."

Her second "no" came out after a pause. I didn't say anything. It didn't sound right.

"He sells stuff," she said finally. "You know, Carlotta, drugs and stuff like that."

It's a good thing traffic wasn't heavy, because I had a moment of what people must mean when they say "blind anger." I couldn't see. I could hear, faintly, and Paolina was talking.

"I'm okay," she said. "You know that. But he goes right over to the school. You know, where there are really little kids, second-graders, dumb kids who'll do anything on a dare."

I didn't say anything. For once I wished I was still a cop. If I were a cop, that jerk would be in a cell.

"Carlotta—"

"Listen, Paolina. He ever bothers you, he ever talks to you again, you tell me. Call me."

"Okay."

"Keep away from that guy."

"No big deal. I'm sorry I said anything." She dug her hands deeper into her pocket and stared at the floor, sure she was at fault for wrecking my mood.

Damn that druggie bastard.

I reached over to pat her shoulder, and after a while she relaxed, and started seeing what was out the window.

"Hey, Paolina," I said, "I'm glad you told me about that guy. Thanks."

"No big deal," she said. It's her favorite phrase.

After that we oohed and aahed over every red and gold leaf. I didn't want to think about that damn drug pusher. It made my hands tense on the steering wheel. I thought about Paolina's crush on Emanuel Rodriguez instead. I don't talk to Paolina much about boys. I haven't got a lot to say on the subject. Sometimes I worry about her. I mean, neither Marta nor I is a terrific role model in that respect. But how many kids have that perfect role model, that perfect marriage to shelter and nurture them as they grow up? Anyway, we admired the trees, and I let my mind wander. . . .

I'd had a busy morning. I'd filed a missing persons report, bemused as always by the bureaucratic blandness with which the guardians of law and order greet a sudden disappearance. I'd spoken briefly to an overworked, ornery Mooney, who informed me that he hadn't a single extra officer to guard Margaret Devens's hospital room, and what the hell was she paying me for anyway?

Then I drove over to Boston City, to check on my client's progress and drop off an updated copy of the case report. It looked so skimpy, typed out single-spaced on plain white bond, that I was all set for Margaret to say forget the whole thing. I'd gone so far as to itemize my bill.

Her face looked bad, but I knew, from grim experience, that the most colorful bruises are not the most painful. She sported a single large bandage on her scalp, but the IV line was no longer attached, and she was sitting up, supported by a nest of pillows, knitting something the color of oatmeal. The TV was blank.

Her face was so swollen she couldn't perch her reading glasses on the bridge of her nose, so I read the report aloud. She had me read some parts twice, while she knitted and nodded her head. She didn't seem to be concentrating on my voice, but then she didn't seem to be concentrating on her knitting either, and a complicated pattern was rapidly taking shape, with the tension even and no stitches dropped.

"Working at the cab company," she said when I'd finished. "I suppose that's the best way."

"Considering what Pat said, yes."

"How's he doing, the poor man?"

"He's dying, and he knows it, and he's still making jokes."

"Ah, Patrick," she murmured. "I wish he'd never retired. He could always talk sense into Eugene." She turned her attention back to her knitting and for a moment I thought the conference was over, but then she said, "This cab driving, would it be dangerous for you?"

"Driving in Boston is always dangerous."

"Will it help you find my brother?"

"If you want me to go on, it's the only lead I've got. I suspect your brother was doing something illegal. I suspect it's connected to an organization of cabbies. I'm not saying it's guaranteed, but if I can gain the cabbies' trust, they might tell me something. Your brother could be in hiding. He may be wanted by the police for questioning. By the FBI."

I thought it far more likely that he was wanted by the IRA, not for something he'd done, but for something he hadn't done, like passing along the cash. I didn't say that because I didn't want to scare Margaret. I saw this BBC documentary once, and one scene chilled me to the bone. A parade of maybe ten IRA "soldiers," armed with machine guns, was marching through throngs of cheering civilians. Each member of the army was anonymous, a black hood tied over his head, eyeholes slit for vision. While nine of the Provos emptied their machine guns toward the sky, one calmly blew the head off an informer. I remembered wondering what the hell the filmmakers thought they were doing, and why hadn't they

111

stopped filming and done something, anything, to save the poor man's life. It was the only execution I've ever seen where the executioners wore masks instead of the condemned.

Margaret sighed. "No matter," she said softly, "we have to keep on. What they're doing, it's got to stop somewhere."

"I'll keep in touch."

"I'm tired," Margaret said fretfully. "The kind of bone-tired you get when you have to fight the battle over again, after you thought you'd won. Grinding tired, and I do wish they'd let me go home."

I lowered my voice. "What should I do with the money?"

"Keep it away from the Provos. Keep it out of their filthy, bloody hands. Is it safe where you've put it?"

I envisioned the cat box. "I think so. Yes."

"Then leave it, just leave it. I don't want it. Lord, I'm so tired." She closed her eyes, and the knitting collapsed against her chest. "I don't know what to do, but you have to go on. Certainly, go on. I can't look for him, stuck here like this, but I have a bad feeling about it. If he were nearby, he'd have heard about what happened. He'd have come to see me. He was always good like that, always good . . ."

She fell asleep while she was talking, which I found so disconcerting that I went in search of a nurse, who reassured me that this was a normal effect of the medication, that Miss Devens's concussion was minor, but that the physician in charge felt a few more days of observation would do no harm. Margaret must have had all her medical insurance paid in full.

I was glad she did. Margaret in the hospital, even unguarded, was safer than Margaret at home . . .

The Toyota, which had been on automatic pilot for some time, arrived at its destination, and Paolina tugged me back to the present. She led me around the wild-animal farm, proudly tracing the map they'd given her at the entrance. Some parts of it were fine, spacious and open and clean. Some were like those awful old zoos, with animals in metal

112

prisons so small the inmates could barely pace, back and forth, back and forth.

Paolina liked the huge fenced-in range with the Siberian tigers best. Mom and three cubs. Paolina names all the animals at the zoo. She started the game years ago, when I first took her to Franklin Park, and it's become a tradition. She's not interested in the animals' real names, and scorns those signs they sometimes put up to educate the public. All the names must be alliterative. Jeremiah Giraffe. Penelope Penguin. Since the tigers were Siberian, the three cubs became Sonia, Sasha, and Sofia. We watched them stalk and tumble, imitating mom, but too clumsy to be fierce. We ate ice cream, and cotton candy, and got our hands sticky. We picked a bouquet of colored leaves for Marta.

It wasn't until we were getting back into the sun-baked car for the drive home that I remembered our phone conversation. "You wanted to ask me something about volleyball, right?"

Her face fell. One minute she was smiling, holding the bright leaves like a trophy, the next minute grim.

"Hey" I said. "What's this?"

She pulled a grubby, folded square of newsprint out of the pocket of her jeans, and passed it over wordlessly. I unfolded it. I'd seen it myself, in the *Globe*.

"Where'd you get this?" I asked.

"Somebody brought it in for current events."

It was a combination news item and obituary. A filler, really, from the sports section, with an inch-square photo that could have been anybody. The caption said it was Flo Hyman, co-captain of the women's U.S. silver-medal-winning volleyball team. Dead. Died suddenly while playing an exhibition game in Japan. Thirty-one years old.

"I didn't play hard this week," Paolina said when I looked up after reading the brief sentences. "I wish—how old are you? I don't want you to play."

"Oh, honey." I put my arm around her and drew her

113

close. "This doesn't happen. This is a freak, a one-in-a-million shot."

"I don't want you to play," she insisted, her voice a stubborn parody of Marta's.

When I was a cop, she was always afraid I'd get shot. You take a kid when she's young, and expose her to a lot of loss and death, and either she toughens up so hard she never risks loving again, or she's scared all the time.

"Paolina," I said as gently as I could, "this is like being hit by lightning. Run over by an ice cream truck. Like getting eaten by a shark."

Like having your husband turn into a drug addict, I thought but didn't say.

"She was sick. She had a disease called Marfan's syndrome, or something like that. It hits mostly tall, thin athletes—hey, a lot taller and thinner than me, and mostly blacks. These things happen, but they happen very rarely."

"If she hadn't played so hard—"

"She might have lived longer, but I'm not sure she would have wanted to." I had vivid memories of watching Flo Hyman hurl herself across a court as if she thought she could fly. I'd hauled my old black-and-white TV out of the closet in honor of the Olympics. We'd watched the volleyball games together, Paolina and I, but I thought she'd be too young to remember. I'm always surprised at the things she remembers. And the things she forgets.

Paolina's voice was muffled by her hand. I could barely hear her, but I think she said, "I'm scared," said it in Spanish, the way she does when she's not completely sure she wants me to understand.

"That's okay. It's okay to be scared."

"It made me think about dying. I'm scared I'll die, and I'll go someplace, and nobody will tell me what to do, and I'll be all alone."

Oh, God. Let me get this one right.

"Paolina," I said slowly. "There are a lot of things that people believe about what happens when you die. Some think you go to heaven, where it's beautiful and peaceful. Some people, and I'm not one of them, think bad people go to hell and get punished. Some people think you just stop, that it's like sleeping at night, with no dreams at all. But I've never heard that you're lonely when you die."

You're lonely when you're alive, I thought but didn't say. I remembered it late that night, curled on my half of the king-sized bed I'd bought for the extra length, never mind the width that made me feel so wasteful. I couldn't get to sleep, so I played my old National steel guitar well into the night, cutting into my calluses till they bled.

When I divorced Cal, people told me I was lucky to be rid of him. I suppose so. Except the guy I was rid of wasn't Cal any longer. Acquaintances said to be glad we hadn't had kids. I wasn't. I was happy to have Paolina.

There's this old song that kept rattling through my mind. It's a Blind Lemon Jefferson tune, bluesy and upbeat, but you wouldn't think it to hear the words:

There's one kind favor I ask of you.
There's one kind favor I ask of you.
There's one kind favor I ask of you.
     Won't you see that my grave
     is kept clean, pretty momma,
Won't you see that my grave is kept clean?

I played it three times, trying to remember the order of the verses.

I turned off the light, but I couldn't sleep, and finally I got up and searched for Sam Gianelli's card. I found it tucked into the pocket of my jeans, and stood staring it down for a long time. Anytime, he'd said. Day or night.

He won't be home, I thought. I'll hang up if he answers, I thought.

I should have called Mooney, but I called Sam.

And he was home, and alone, and awake.

Chapter 19

Funny how the old moves come back when you need them.

Reporting for Sunday's graveyard shift at G&W gave me a genuine shiver of déjà vu. Because I was the new kid on the block, I got stuck with one of the worst of the vintage Fords. Gloria, blank-faced, handed me the key to Eugene's locker—now, temporarily, mine. I had nothing to store, but I chugged on back and tugged the door open, pretending to make sure the lock worked. I was really spying on a group of cabbies gathered near the bench, talking Red Sox, talking Bruins, talking Celtics.

Usually you don't have to follow the Sox to comment on them. Their autumn slide to box-score oblivion is sadly predictable. This year was different. They seemed unbeatable, but the loyal fans were waiting for them to fold.

I went through the motions, bitching about the high salaries those bastards get for striking out three times in game, but all the time I was watching the other drivers, and how they reacted to me, to the fact that I'd appropriated Eugene's locker, to the GBA pin sparkling on my lapel. I felt like an undercover cop, and I didn't like the sensation. It's too weird. First you join up with the baddies, identify with them, and then you betray them. If you don't keep a part of yourself separate, shut off, you wind up bonkers.

I recognized a few members of the pack. One middle-aged woman, who'd been hacking for all eternity, was named Rosie, or Happy, or some cheerful name completely at odds with her forbidding face and dim view of the sports world. I

116

said hi to her first, and she either vaguely remembered me, or politely faked it. Then Sean Boyle said hello, and a couple of the others. Rosie—that was her name—took charge of introductions. I nodded and smiled and tried to match the names to the employee records, which was difficult because intros were strictly on a first-name basis. A lot of the drivers had nicknames, like Red Light, and Speedy, and Mad Dog.

I'd have to run the *noms de cab* by Gloria.

Cab number 223. It had a ding in the right front fender and smelled like the inside of an old shoe. I made an immediate detour to buy air freshener. 223's supposedly bulletproof plastic shield, required equipment on all Boston cabs, was so scratched and cloudy that the rearview mirror was useless.

Tucking my license into the slot on the sun visor, I felt like a TV actor caught in a rerun. Just walking into that grimy garage, dressed in jeans, work shirt, and driving cap, made me think about who I'd been when last I'd hacked for a living—and who I am now.

And Sam Gianelli.

Funny how the old moves come back . . .

He'd wanted to drive over at two in the morning, as soon as he'd recognized my voice on the phone. I'd backed off. We'd compromised on Sunday brunch at a small North Cambridge restaurant. It was a place we used to visit, jammed with closely packed tables for two, and probably a choice I should have vetoed. Too many memories of ravenous afternoon breakfasts, delayed by hours of lazy lovemaking.

At ten-thirty, a guy banged on my front door, and presented a bunch of flowers. Not one of those awful dyed-carnation-in-a-pot things, but a bouquet of iris, alstroemeria, and freesia. Freesia's my favorite for its apricot smell. That's the kind of thing you can hustle up on a Sunday morning if your name is Gianelli.

I dressed casually, maybe to show Sam I set no great store by our meeting—lie number one—and wasn't impressed with the flowers—lie number two. I chose white jeans and a hot

117

turquoise knit top that's a perfect match for my malachite beads. I wear necklaces. No rings or bracelets, on account of volleyball. I never wear earrings. They bother me, the whole idea of earrings bothers me, not to mention the pressure on my earlobes. And I can't stand the thought of poking holes through my ears. It seems, I don't know, barbaric or something. Earrings and nail polish, I can't stand. I wear makeup though, so try to sort that out.

I wore sexy silk underwear, so I won't pretend I was shocked by the outcome of the afternoon.

Of course, he wanted to see the house. And, of course, the area of the house that is really mine, that I'm proud of, is my bedroom. And that's where the stereo sounds best. Sam and I don't share a common taste in music. He's more into jazz. But we agree that Billie Holliday makes everyone else sound mediocre, so I stuffed a tape in the tape deck, and soon we wound up just where I knew we'd wind up when I saw him shake water off his hair under the light bulb in Gloria's office.

"I remember you," he said. "You're the one who likes to climb on top."

"You look like you could hold your own weight, Sam," I said, turning over, obligingly prone. He did. He could. He looked like he'd been lifting weights, sculptured and sweaty.

We took turns on top, and it was great. I found myself making noises that would put Roz to shame, and I secretly hoped she and Lemon were upstairs, ears glued to the floor in astonishment at the landlady's afternoon antics.

Funny how the old moves come back . . .

A beat-up VW bus charged out of an alley masquerading as a street, and I had to yank the wheel over to the right to avoid a collision. My tires screeched a protest.

Back to work.

Downtown traffic was faster paced, more tightly packed than I remembered. Aggressive driving is the Boston norm, but things seemed to have taken a turn for the worse. Rudeness reached new heights. People leaned on their horns, really leaned on them.

All the way down Storrow Drive, the crush of cars got in the way of my three objectives. Number one was the radio. I intended to listen in on every call and note it down. Later, I'd see if I could figure any code, any pattern. Number two was to match names with faces and voices, to figure out who was piloting which cab. Number three: follow one of the Old Geezers each night. See if anybody's dumb enough to do something openly suspicious.

My candidate for the evening was my old pal Sean Boyle, driving number 403. Now I couldn't have done it in sunlight. A one-on-one tail job is ridiculous enough, but in the daytime it's impossible. At night, in order to be just another set of anonymous headlights, all I had to do was shut off the roof lights. By hard-won arrangement with Gloria, I had to pick up fares only if every other cab in the city was busy. I hoped we'd have no more typhoons.

Late-night cabbing is alive and well in Boston, mainly because the T, public transit, shuts down at twelve-thirty in order to discourage the citizens from staying out late and indulging in wild revelry. If you revel in Boston, be prepared to stumble home or flag a cab. The best places to score fares are the areas devoted to revelry, like Kenmore Square, home of the college student, the disco, and the punk bar; and the Combat Zone, home of the lowlifes, the strip show, and the XXX movie.

Sean Boyle cruised the Zone, sandwiched between Chinatown and the struggling theater district. It's a place I'd just as soon avoid. My cab smelled bad enough. The Zone is one reason I quit being a cop. They kept sticking me in that damn stinkhole, and pretty soon I thought the world was composed of nothing but creeps. All I saw was the gutter, and I couldn't take my eyes off it for fear something would crawl up out of the depths flashing a straight razor. At first, I felt a kind of awed fascination, sharpened by unadmitted fear. Life's cheap in the Zone. It's where people peel off that thin veneer and get right down to bone. Thirteen-year-old runaways trick for ten bucks a throw. Respectable suburban daddies screw kids younger than their daughters. "Working late at the office, honey, sorry I can't make Sally's band concert." You've got your choice of alcoholic derelicts and drug-fogged former beauty queens. It's a place that breaks your heart, or turns it into granite. Mine must have been seven-eighths petrified before I threw away my badge.

I reached under the seat of the cab and, sure enough, felt a reassuring hunk of lead pipe. Cabbies aren't allowed to carry guns in Boston. Mine was within arm's reach, resting on a layer of junk in my bag, but I haven't used a gun since one of my last cop days. A bad day in a bad place, not far from the corner of Washington and Boylston.

Boyle hung a right on Tremont, then a couple of lefts, and drifted over to the Pussy Cat Lounge. A blond male hooker semaphored his desire to use my cab as his traveling boudoir. I drove by quickly, wondering if there was any long-term denizen of the Zone with sufficient brain cells intact to remember Carlotta, the cop.

I followed Boyle all night. He ferried lost souls out to the suburbs. Once he had to wait in the cab while this guy went inside and found some dough. Poor bastard probably got rolled by some hooker, and was too embarrassed to report it to the cops. Boyle dropped by several bars. Either he had to drink a lot, pee a lot, or pick up the dimes and quarters from those green canisters.

I wrote it all down; time, place, everything. If other cabs were in the area, I noted the license plates. I collected a hell of a lot of data. I could toss them up in the air, and see how they came down. That was the best organizational scheme that came to mind.

By 7 A.M., when Boyle turned his cab in, my ass was numb, an occupational hazard I'd forgotten. I hung around by the lockers, but nobody talked about anything more significant than Wade Boggs's batting average, so I waited until the office was clear.

120

Gloria tore herself away from a bag of chocolate-covered peanuts long enough to answer a call. Then she glanced up at me with arched eyebrows.

"Comfy cab," I said, rubbing the seat of my jeans.

"How long's this going to go on?"

"I just started, Gloria. Give me a break."

She snorted M&Ms.

"Gloria, one of these records is—" I was going to say "nothing but a piece of shit." That's how far I'd retreated into undercover cop mentality. I stopped myself. "One of the records is incomplete."

"Oh, yeah?"

"You hired a guy named John Flaherty a year and a half ago, and all you've got on him is an address."

"So?" Gloria was in a talky mood.

"So on everybody else you've got an employment history."

"Maybe it's his first job."

"At thirty-one? He a slow learner?"

"Look, he drives his cab. He shows up. He's okay."

"He shows up out of the blue without even a Social Security card, and you hire him? Come on."

"Leave this one alone, Carlotta. It's got nothing to do with Eugene Devens."

"Convince me."

She pursed her lips, then bit down on them until they disappeared. "If you want to know more about Flaherty—"

"Yeah?"

"Talk to Sam."

I tried to keep my face as blank as hers. "Gianelli recommend this guy?"

"Talk to Sam, that's all I can say, and I shouldn't have said that much. You coming in tonight?"

"Yeah. See if you can give me a car that drives."

I shouldn't have said it so angrily, because my ire had nothing to do with Gloria. She looked at me in a kind of speculative way, and raised both eyebrows. Sometimes I think

121

she can see my thoughts in the air, floating inside a cartoon balloon.

Chapter 20

I was exhausted, and my butt ached. Maybe I'd have fallen asleep if I'd gone right home, but then I would have missed volleyball, which might not have been a bad thing considering that Caitlin, our best center setter, was down with the flu, and all the women were trying to make up for her absence, crashing into each other as well as the floor. I took a flying elbow in the ribs that knocked me breathless. After winning three out of five from a team we should have beaten three straight, I did my twenty laps, and finished up with an adrenaline overload. Ah well, I read somewhere that it's easier to adjust to a new shift if you stay awake extra hours instead of forcing yourself to sleep when you're not tired.

I jaywalked to Dunkin' Donuts out of force of habit. My stomach wasn't sure if it wanted dinner or breakfast. I ordered a lone cinnamon cruller and black coffee. If I stayed at Dunkin' Donuts, I didn't have to go home. If I didn't go home, I didn't have to check my answering machine. If I didn't check my answering machine, I wouldn't have to respond to any messages left by Sam Gianelli. If I didn't talk to Sam, I wouldn't have to figure out a discreet way to question him about John Flaherty, the man with no employment history.

I could hear myself casually tossing probes about Flaherty into our pillow talk. "So, Sam, I been meaning to ask, you hire anybody at the cab company, say, in the past year and a half?''

I burned my tongue on the coffee, and set the cup down so fast that it teetered in the saucer and almost spilled all over the counter. Why do simple things always get so mixed up? I'd seen the man, and liked what I saw. I was ready for a little uncomplicated coupling. I should have known better. Sex without strings attached is a rare commodity.

I called Missing Persons at Area D, and harassed some poor sergeant. Nothing on Eugene Devens. I called my client, in the hope that the wayward brother had suddenly seen the light and come to visit his ailing sister. No such luck.

I'd parked the Toyota in its usual Bishop Richard Allen Drive slot, and since I was close to the project, I kind of gravitated to Paolina's school, ugly yellow brick with bars on the windows, just like a prison.

The kids were outdoors, although it seemed early for recess, divided boys and girls, just the way we used to be back in my Detroit elementary school, not by decree, but by custom. A red-faced male teacher with a silver whistle on a chain around his neck supervised an intense game of late-season baseball among the boys. The girls played halfhearted unsupervised volleyball, which made me angry. I mean, why teach girls to play, right? They're never going to make millions in the big leagues, right? As if all the tubby little boys on the field were hot prospects. I wanted to join the girls' game. Take it over.

I yawned and stretched, and told myself to stop being so bad-tempered. It was easy to shift moods. All you had to do was watch the kids. They wore bright colors, and they moved fast. Spots of yellow and blue and red flowed over the playground. I felt like I was staring through a huge kaleidoscope at a swirl of color come to life.

I tried to sort through the color spots to see if I could find Paolina. The kids seemed about the right age.

One white and brown blob stood out. I swear the hairs on the back of my neck stiffened.

He was behind the high fence, half hidden by a brick wall, but I picked him out. I knew him. Old Wispy Beard with his satchel, selling dope by the schoolyard.

I had the car door open before I realized I'd moved, and I had to force myself to stick my legs back inside and cool off. What was I going to do anyway? Assault the guy in front of fifty young witnesses?

I wanted to. God, I wanted to.

Instead I breathed deeply for a count of ten. I took my Canon SLR out of the locked dash compartment, and took several long-lens shots. I breathed for another count of ten.

I located my little sister on the volleyball court. I was glad to see her involved in the game. She was holding back, you could see that, letting a taller girl on her right smash most of the shots. But she was playing.

No doubt about it, I was going to have to teach her a few finer points of volleyball.

I waved, even though she didn't see me. I drove off.

I didn't go far. Just over to the police station.

Chapter 21

The lone parking space at the curb, smack in front of a PO-LICE BUSINESS ONLY sign, was a tight one. I wedged the Toyota in, rubbing bumpers with two cruisers, and trotted up the front steps.

I'd been dealing with a Cambridge detective named Schultz—a guy I knew from my police academy days—on the Wispy Beard business. While I waited for him to answer the desk sergeant's call, I wondered if he'd be clued into IRA activities in his fair city. I've never heard of an Irishman named Schultz, so I figured he wouldn't be likely to lie if I asked him outright. On the other hand, you can't always tell by the name. I mean, with a tag like Carlotta, wouldn't you expect a trace of Spanish blood on my family tree? Not a drop. Dad named me for some starlet who was eclipsed the day after her movie debut.

Even if Schultz turned out to be a whiz on Cambridge crime, that didn't mean he'd know squat about Boston. Cambridge and Boston don't cooperate. As a Boston cabbie, I couldn't even pick up a hailer in Cambridge, which makes cabs in both cities more expensive, and folks on the street corners angry.

Schultz didn't rush across the linoleum once he saw me. I figured that meant he hadn't done a thing.

Detective First Class Jay Schultz looked like he combed his hair about every fifteen minutes, and carried a mirror for spot checks. Maybe he used the mirror to see who was gaining on him. He was a test taker, a promotion chaser, a potential captain on the make. Good-looking, if you like the boyish sandy-haired type, which I don't. He gave the impression of a certain coolness, a cultivated so-what. I didn't take a so-what attitude about Wispy Beard. In regard to that situation, I was definitely uncool.

"So," I said, as he guided me to his desk, resting one hand heavily on my shoulder in that proprietary manner I despise, "you know where that bastard I asked you to nail is? Right this very minute?"

"I know he ain't in my jail." Hearty laugh.

"Funny."

"Hey, hey," he said, pointing to a battered chair in his dingy corner. "Cool off. Not for lack of trying."

"Really?" I tried hard to keep the disbelief off my face. Well, not too hard.

"Hey, Carlotta, we busted the creep. Nothing on him."

"Jay, that guy hasn't had nothing on him since the nurse first diapered his ass."

"We thought he had something but he didn't."

"Not in the satchel?"

"No satchel."

"Probably dumped it when he noticed you tailing him."

"Not me personally."

"Of course not, an important guy like you. Jeez, I wouldn't expect anything like that."

"Look, we blew the collar. But we got some interesting stuff."

"Like?"

"Name, date, serial number. Rap sheet, if you're interested, and the creep is into something heavy."

I waited. When they teach cops to interrogate suspects, rule one is never interrupt.

"You know who that bastard called after we charged him? I mean we charged him with some bullshit vagrancy rap, because we didn't have the evidence. Probably should have kicked him loose, but we wanted to see what shook when we rattled his chain. So you know who he called?"

I shrugged my ignorance.

"Wendell Heyer."

Now that was a name to give one pause. Wendell Heyer, a man who did more than his bit to make "lawyer" a four-letter word, emerging from under this particular rock. Word was that when Wendell surfaced, the mob was not far below. Let me tell you, it gave *me* pause.

"Now, look that over for yourself," Jay continued. "You think this freak of yours is an independent, and just happens to have the bucks to retain Wendell, that's your business. But I think we just found the tail end of some big mother, and I'm gonna take some time before I yank it again."

"But you'll let me see the file on this guy. I'm getting tired of calling him by a nickname."

Wispy Beard had his own nickname: Bud. The poor sucker had been named Horace by his adoring mom about thirty-six years back. Horace "Bud" Harold. I could practically hear the schoolyard jeers: "Whore-Ass, Whore-Ass." Destined for a life of crime. Ever notice how all those mean-looking football players are named Lynn and Marion and stuff like that? That's how the best of the weirdly christened turn out. The rest wind up behind bars.

Bud's rap sheet was not quick reading; it was too long for that, but so far it was light. Started boosting cars at eighteen. Either he was pretty good not to get caught until then, or, more likely, he had a sealed juvie record. Nabbed in his nineteenth year for armed robbery. Suspended sentence. Tried it again, seeing as how he got off so easy, and sent a victim to the hospital this time with a chunk of his ear blown away. Four-year sentence at Concord, of which he served a big six months. Just long enough to learn more sophisticated ways to boost. Long enough to hook up with the sort of companions every mom hopes her kid will cultivate.

No drug-related arrests.

Not yet.

"What's the plan?" I asked when I finished reading.

"Wait," he said.

"What do you mean, wait? He's over at the schoolyard now.

"What I said."

"You got an order for a wire? An undercover? What?"

"Look, next week I can put somebody on it. Maybe two weeks. We haven't got enough detectives to cover this right now."

"So I just keep watching the guy."

"Don't spook him."

"Me? You rousted him."

"It's different now."

"Is he dealing crack?"

"Do you know or are you asking?"

"I'm asking."

"I can't say."

"You can't say?"

"Right."

"So tell me," I said to Jay after silently digesting the

127

whole mess, "on a different subject altogether, you got much IRA action going down over here?"

I guess I was just pulling his chain, the way he'd yanked old Horace's. He looked at me as if I'd sprouted horns, and repeated the initials.

"IRA?"

"Yeah? Irish, et cetera, et cetera."

"You kidding? That bunch is out. No more support. No more wicked Noraid collecting money for guns. The government forced Noraid to register as an agent of the IRA, and that was the end of it. It's all respectable these days. The Irish Fund, thank you very much, faith and begorra. Ritzy dinner dances at the Parker House, thousand-dollar-a-plate banquets with Tip O'Neill as emcee. They even made a TV commercial. All the money to the church and charity, and not one penny for the IRA."

"You sure about that?"

"Why?"

Ah, cops. Always a question. "Well, see, on the way over, I met this leprechaun, and he came up to me, and—" I saw the look Jay was giving me, and decided not to ride him. Sometimes cops have bad days. Most of the time, cops have bad days.

"So long, Carlotta."

"Thanks, Jay."

Chapter 22

It's a good thing my Toyota knows the way home. As soon as I got near the car all my volleyball adrenaline and most of my righteous anger leaked out, leaving me deflated and sleepy and kind of ornery. A double-parked patrol car blocked my exit, so I had to clump back up the stairs, and trade insults with the desk sergeant until some jerk grudgingly moved it. I spit on the fender. I'm not proud of it. I just did it.

Roz was in the kitchen, yakking on the phone in her usual position, cross-legged on the countertop. She is a motormouth phone gabber, and it's a miracle anybody ever gets through on my line. Paints, brushes, palette knives, and bottles of oily gook were spread over the kitchen table, and as far as I could tell, she was composing a still life of steel wool pads and a Windex bottle. I always know the cleaning aids I purchase will come in handy.

"Carlotta, great, I've got messages," she said, dropping the phone to one shoulder. "Tequila, how about I call you back? At the Rat? Tonight? Gross. Jeez. Okay. Later." She hung up on Tequila. I wondered if Tequila was a boy or a girl. I knew it wasn't a rat. The Rat is this punk hangout in Kenmore Square. If Mooney got a call to go to the Rat, he'd bring rubber gloves, a chair, and a whip.

I stared blankly at the refrigerator, wondering if anything inside would make me feel human. The clock said three, and the sun was blazing through the window over the sink, so that made it three in the afternoon. Monday afternoon. I felt like it was 3 A.M. on some planet where everything was slightly out of focus. I held open the refrigerator door until it started doubling as an air conditioner. A container of cottage cheese looked vaguely appealing, except I couldn't remember buying cottage cheese, so chances were that if I opened the carton, furry green curds would greet my eyes. I shut the refrigerator door.

"Messages," Roz was saying. "You okay?"

She was wearing this fifties housedress get-up, with lacey white socks and black pointy-toed ankle-high boots. She'd added a purple streak down the left side of her pink hair. Her earrings looked like Coke bottle caps.

"Me?" I said in a dead voice. "I feel great. Absolutely."

"It's the riotous living," Roz said.

Maybe she had eavesdropped on me and Sam. The idea perked me up.

"Carlotta?"

"Yeah?"

"This guy keeps calling. Sam Gianelli."

My face got warm, all of a sudden. I hoped I wasn't blushing. "Yeah?"

"He's phoned like five times. Awesome voice."

"Yeah."

"I told him I didn't know when you'd be back."

He might call Gloria to check when I got off. That would be great. Gloria would razz me for the next hundred years. I stared ruefully at the telephone, picked up the receiver, and slowly replaced it in the cradle. I didn't want to call Sam. I didn't want to see Sam. I didn't want to ask him about Jack Flaherty. Sam's no dummy. He'd know I was investigating at G&W. He'd realize I didn't trust him. And that would be the end. Better leave it for a few days. Then I could say I'd met the guy, and wondered if Sam had ever run into him. Something like that.

I opened the refrigerator again. I had a faint memory of a salami in the meat tray. Three anonymous tinfoil bundles later, I located it. I keep leftovers until they get fuzzy. That way I don't feel guilty about throwing out good food.

"And Mooney's been calling," Roz said. "The cop. Just one message, repeated over and over and over. Call Mooney. Call Mooney. Call Mooney. Capitalized. Underlined. Totally emphatic, with sugar on top."

I shrugged. It took all my concentration to slice three rounds of salami without severing a thumb.

"He got the hots for you, or what?" she asked.

"Didn't he say?"

"He said urgent. Something else, too."

She's like that. Saves up the good parts. Eats her pie starting at the crust end.

"Contest," she said, nodding her head gravely. The bobbing purple streak ruined the solemn effect. "Contest. Urgent, about some contest."

I scooped up the phone so fast I almost dropped the knife on my foot.

And, of course, Mooney was nowhere to be found. I left a message.

Urgent.

"Jeez, that was some mess over in J.P.," Roz said. "Wow. There was this pile of glop in the middle of the kitchen floor you wouldn't believe. Flour and honey and cherry pie filling and oatmeal. Totally gross. Wanna see the pictures?"

"While I'm eating?"

"Lemon wanted to, like, blow the place up or something. He didn't think we could ever get it clean."

"Did you?"

"We had to use boiling water and the ice scraper from the pickup. I'm going back over today to put another coat of wax on the floor."

I excused myself, and dove into the bathroom. T.C.'s cat box looked untouched by other than feline paws. *Leave the money there*, Margaret had said. *I don't want it.* I wondered how long I could live with IRA cash in the bathroom. It generated a bit of tension, like juggling eggs.

Roz was staring critically at the Windex bottle when I got back, edging it a shade to the right of the S.O.S.

131

"You didn't see my old school friend, did you?" I asked. "Uh, Roger Smith or something?"

She cast sheepish eyes at the floor. "Nope, he hasn't been by." She frowned and returned the Windex bottle to its original position. "Unless—"

"Unless?"

She bit down on her tongue, then realized it impeded her speech. "Well, you got one more call, from a weirdo who sounded kind of like Roger Smith. But he said his name was Andrews. From Cedar Wash Condominium Resorts. You're not buying some gross condo, are you?"

"Relax. I'll still be here to collect the rent."

"You like the Windex picture? You think I should put in some fruit? Garlic?" She likes to paint bulbs of garlic. Those I can always find later.

"Lot of potential." That's what I say when I'm baffled by one of Roz's masterpieces. I'm scared she'll explain the deeper meanings.

I ate two slices of salami, called it a balanced meal, and went upstairs.

I didn't call Mooney again. I didn't call Sam. I didn't get back to Andrews at Cedar Wash. I slept six and a half hours, like a rock.

Chapter 23

I didn't like John Flaherty.

It took me two days to cross the guy's path, although we supposedly worked the same shift. The bastard's hours were so irregular Gloria should have given him the boot, except, of course, he'd been personally recommended by her partner—my lover—good old Sam Gianelli.

I finally asked Sam about him, worked it in real casually while we were up in my room, sated and lying back on the bed. Bonnie Raitt crooned "Angel From Montgomery" in the background:

> "I am an old woman, named after my mother.
> My old man is another child that's growin' old.
> If dreams were thunder, and lightnin' was desire,
> This old house would have burnt down
> a long time ago."

I sang along with the first verse. Whenever I hear that song I have to restrain myself from leaping up and grabbing my guitar. It didn't seem appropriate at the moment.

"You know this Jack Flaherty?" I said, running my fingertips down the line of dark curly hair on Sam's chest. "At G and W?"

"Nah." Sam yanked my arm lower, and I couldn't hear any tightness or discomfort in his voice. "You think I know all the drivers?"

"Just the women," I said, to keep it light.

"Oh yeah that Rosie, she's one hot dame."

"Yeah?" The idea cheered me up. I hoped crabby Rosie went home to one steamy romance after another.

"Oh, you got a lot to learn before you're in Rosie's league," he assured me. A pretty good liar, Sam. Papa Gianelli should be proud.

> "Just give me one thing that I can hold on to.
> To believe in this livin' is just a hard way to go."

Raitt gave the song one of her fine wailing finishes. Her voice quieted the other noises in the room, from the ticking clock to T.C. meowing in the corner. He likes to warn me when I pay too much attention to another male.

After that, I didn't feel bad about not telling Sam why I was driving for G&W. I figured we were even, both lying. It might not be the perfect basis for a meaningful relationship, but it was fine for what we had going.

Anyhow, it took me two days to meet this Flaherty, two minutes to decide I'd seen him someplace before, and two seconds to spot him for a jerk. He was a couple years older than me, which made him young by G&W standards, maybe the only Caucasian driver under fifty. He had bad teeth, yellow and crooked. His face was well shaped, but all the features seemed squeezed together in the center. His eyes, nose, and mouth were too small for the flesh surrounding them. He was the kind of guy who gabs with men, but takes a friendly hello from a female as an attempted seduction, so I couldn't get into the kind of conversation that would have naturally led to the questions I longed to ask: So where'd you work before this? How do you know Sam Gianelli? Ever been in Ireland? Collect much money for the IRA last week? Buy any machine guns?

I followed Joe Fergus for half a night, Andy O'Brien the other half. Choosing the guys who'd met at the Rebellion, and giving precedence to Irish-sounding surnames, the next night I followed a Maloney and an O'Keefe. None of them robbed the Bank of Boston. O'Brien made a brief stop at the Rebellion, but I didn't see any other cabs in the parking lot. O'Keefe dropped somebody off at the Yard of Ale. Maloney picked up a fare in front of the All Clear. I tried to make something of it, but taxi drivers get a lot of barroom business these days, what with bartenders worried about getting sued if some drunken patron piles his car into the neighborhood nursery school after tossing back one more for the road.

I listened to radio calls, wrote each one down, but couldn't find a pattern. No calls from a mysterious woman in red at midnight. I was careful to note any woman's name that blared out of the squawkbox, because of what old Pat had said about a woman being involved. But G&W, a small cab company, tried for personalized service. Gloria radioed the name of each caller along with the address: George Burke at 468 Beacon, Mrs. Edelman on Cumberland. Sometimes just a first name, sometimes just a last. I wrote down a lot of women's names.

I was getting nowhere, and Margaret Devens was coming home tomorrow. Not only was Margaret coming home, but I'd called Mr. Andrews and Cedar Wash Condominium Resorts was threatening to revoke my twenty K unless I showed up with my husband, Thomas, within the week. The missing persons report on Eugene Devens had drawn a fat zero. Between Sam and screwed-up biorhythms, I couldn't sleep. I couldn't connect with Mooney on the phone—

As my grandmother used to say: You're such a brain, you can worry more in one minute than other people can in a whole year.

Wednesday night, I decided John Flaherty was the one to tail. I waited until he signed in—late again. He sailed off in cab 442, one of the brand-new ones, which didn't make me like him any better, since I was stuck with another antique. He spoke up maybe ten minutes later, accepting Gloria's offer of a fare in the South End.

Now I know the back roads of Boston. I can beat a civilian to any city location with minutes to spare, but another cabbie, that's a different story. I screeched the tight curves on the Fenway, cut over to Huntington Avenue by the Museum of Fine Arts, and was blessed by the god of traffic lights for once in my life.

A well-dressed young couple promenaded the sidewalk in front of 117 Pembroke Street. The man carried a slim briefcase, and the woman was decked out in Ralph Lauren's version of what Connecticut WASPs wear to the market. I pulled into an unlit sidestreet with a decent view, and waited maybe five seconds for G&W 442 to catch up with me.

Well, we had one exciting night, let me tell you. Cab 442 took the couple as far as the Westin Hotel. I mean, they could practically spit as far as the Westin from Pembroke Street. Walk? At night? God forbid.

442 queued up for the Westin's doorman, and was rewarded with a fare, a lone businessman. From the Westin we journeyed to the Hyatt Regency in Cambridge, tracing Storrow Drive to the Mass. Ave. Bridge, which is a mess of construction lights and battered yellow barrels. Then Memorial Drive up to the Hyatt's front door. Nothing odd in that. I ran my meter just the way Flaherty should have been running his. I'd check the total with Gloria. If I couldn't nab him for anything else, maybe I could get him for embezzlement.

Gloria gave him another fare. Allston, near Boston University. I stayed close around the rotary and across the B.U. Bridge. Whatever else he was, Flaherty was a good driver. Fast. I hoped he didn't keep his eyes glued to his rearview mirror.

So it went. He kept busy. He wasn't dogging it, that's for sure. He grabbed hailers off street corners, worked Kenmore Square cab stands, took his share of radio calls. I was starting to enjoy myself, finally getting accustomed to the time-zone shift, discovering how city nightlife had changed since my last stint as a cabbie. Miniskirts and patterned stockings were back, but with a tough high-heeled edge to them. I saw women wearing black lipstick; men, too. I liked the gritty feel of Kenmore Square. It seemed like a place at home in the dark, pulsing with the restless energy of the red and blue neon Citgo sign. It made me want to smoke cigarettes and listen to funky music, not the bleat of the cab's radio.

At 2:45 A.M. Gloria put out a call to cab 102 to pick up Maudie someplace in Dorchester. 102 started to respond, then Flaherty cut in, and said he'd take it; he was practically next door.

Which was a lie.

I hung way back, over three hundred yards. If I lost him now, it wouldn't be so bad. I could pick him up from the street address. It was after he scored the fare that worried me.

In front of a battered triple-decker, a well-dressed man in

his twenties, with a muscular build and swaggering walk, was escorted to the cab by two young males, big fellows, maybe Hispanic. They looked like the kind of hoods who'd beat up an old lady like Margaret Devens just for the fun of it. The man who got into the cab carried a gym bag. I tailed them toward Franklin Park, keeping well back.

I cut my lights during the race through the park, relying on 442's taillights and the occasional overhead streetlamp. The road felt like it hadn't been repaired in twenty years. If Flaherty didn't actually see me, he could probably hear my car bottoming out in the ravines the Department of Public Works calls potholes. I flicked on my lights at the rotary, followed 442 over the bridge past the Arnold Arboretum and onto the Jamaicaway.

Brake lights flared, too late for me to make an inconspicuous stop. The passenger bailed out on Brookline Ave., in front of Fenway Park. I sailed by, took a left, and three-pointed a turn. By the time I nosed the cab back onto the main street, I could see 442's taillights heading down Brookline to Park Drive.

I would have followed the passenger, except for one thing. The young man had carelessly left his gym bag in the cab.

I prayed for heavier traffic. A nice van to hide behind as we played follow-the-leader over to Commonwealth Ave. No such luck. I pulled in behind a big old dented Pontiac.

I had to squeeze the yellow light at the B.U. Bridge. I'm always surprised when I do that and two cars behind me come barreling through as well.

For a while, I thought Flaherty was homing the gym bag to the cab company, which got me worried. If Sam was there to take possession, I didn't want to be a witness. I breathed easier when 442 passed the shortcut most of the cabbies take home.

442 coasted to a stop on Harvard Street, across the street from the Rebellion. I took a quick turn into an alleyway. Angling my rearview mirror, I could see Flaherty run across

the street, gym bag tucked under his arm. He went to the side door of the bar.

By this time, it was 3:35. Way after closing time. I got my cab turned around, a tight maneuver in the narrow alley. I almost bashed into two parked Green & White cabs. I wrote down their numbers, and started cruising the neighborhood looking for more. I found one right in the Rebellion's parking lot. In a loading zone around the corner, I saw G&W 863, a cab I'd tailed two nights ago. Sean Boyle's cab.

Okay. Something was going down at the Rebellion, something that looked very much like a meeting of the Gaelic Brotherhood Association. Something that could involve the contents of one gym bag picked up at "Maudie's" in Dorchester. I wondered if the contents of the bag came in neatly banded little bundles, like the cash in T.C.'s litter box.

I had options. I could sit here like a dummy. I could find a good location, take photos as each cabbie departed.

The GBA pin I'd found in Eugene's locker seemed suddenly heavy. It weighed my collar down. I touched it. I could just walk in.

Damn. There was the matter of the bartender. If it was the same bartender, old Billy what's-his-face, and if he remembered me, recalled my questions, my license, my card, I'd be sunk.

Maybe I'd have gone in anyway. Maybe I'd have taken some Pulitzer Prize photos, maybe I'd have gotten zip. I'll never know.

Flashing blue lights appeared out of nowhere, racing up behind me.

Shit. I smacked my horn in pure frustration, pulled over. The cops. Always there when you need them.

Chapter 24

"It's her, all right." A huge red-faced cop, the kind they used to call a harness bull, peered in my side window.

"Any problem, Officer?" I said in my sweetest voice. I wondered if the bull was named Doyle or Donahue, if he was employed by the IRA to handle things just in case someone tailed their delivery cab. I thought about the pipe under my seat.

"Carlotta Carlyle?"

"Who wants to know?"

"Lieutenant Mooney wants to talk to you."

"You're kidding."

"Nah, we're supposed to bring you in."

"For questioning," a bright young patrolman added. He was sticking his head in the passenger door.

"You don't have to tell her that," the bull snapped.

"Okay." The young guy backed off.

"Bring me in?" I said incredulously. "Arrest me? Mooney wants to arrest me?"

"He wants to talk to you," the harness bull said, as if that made everything okay.

"This is harassment," I said.

"Harassment," the bull repeated, pawing his book of traffic tickets. "You call this harassment?"

"Look, I didn't do anything—"

"Oh, I thought you might not have signaled back there at the last right turn. Or maybe your high beams aren't working. Or maybe you ran a red."

That, I call harassment.

"So, you want to talk to Lieutenant Mooney, or what?" the bull said.

"What," I answered.

"Good. He's over at Area D. We'll escort you."

Just what I always wanted, a police escort.

At the station, Mooney was tilting back in his swivel chair, big black cop shoes on the desktop, hands clasped behind his head, eyes half closed. He had a dime-sized hole in his left sole, and his right shoe could have used a new heel.

His office was like his shoes. The big walnut desk was scratched and stained. The blotter curled at the edges. Two four-drawer gray filing cabinets overflowed in a corner. No flowers, no plants, no pictures. No wonder Mooney kept his eyes closed.

I knew he wasn't sleeping. I was too damn mad to sit down, so I stood there, arms crossed, fighting off the urge to grab both his heels and teach him to do a somersault. I was probably angrier than I should have been. I tend to get mad when I enter that police station. It's got too many memories for me. Some of them good ones, granted, but mainly it's the bad stuff that lingers. The "partner" who didn't want to let the "girl" drive. The clubby "boys only" atmosphere. The carved-in-granite belief that if I achieved anything it was because I'd slept with the right cop.

I breathed.

Part of it was that when I looked at Mooney, I thought about Sam. And that made me uncomfortable. I mean, why should Mooney remind me of Sam? Why should seeing Mooney's face make me feel guilty? I hate feeling guilty.

"Coffee?" he said.

They have rotten coffee at Area D. They serve it in nasty Styrofoam cups. Instead of milk or cream, there's this big jar of powdered beige gunk.

"Am I under arrest?"

"Coffee?" he repeated. This time his eyes were open.

"Am I under arrest?" I repeated.

"Carlotta, you're gonna thank me for doing this. Why the hell didn't you call? I must have left twenty messages."

"I called. You were out. Am I under arrest, or what? Should I call my lawyer?"

"Christ, I'm sorry I interrupted your life. I was only trying to do you a favor. Forget it. No charges. You can leave anytime."

Now that was infuriating. Mooney knew I'd never leave without finding out what the hell was going on. He turned his attention to a file folder on his desk, and yanked a single sheet of paper, holding it in his right hand. He read a few lines with pretend concentration, shook his head sadly.

"Mooney—"

"Go on. Get lost."

I took the two steps I needed to get close enough, reached over, and jerked the paper out of his grasp. I think he let go on purpose. As I read, I sank into the visitor's chair, a disgusting molded-plastic job.

I hardly noticed the discomfort. What I had in my hand was a criminal record, a rap sheet, for one Thomas Charles Carlyle. And let me tell you, this Thomas Charles Carlyle was one bad boy, a one-man crime spree. Petty Larceny, Grand Larceny: three arrests, two convictions. Illegal Firearms: three violations. Statutory Rape. Rape. Armed Robbery. Et cetera.

There were mug shots attached. No mug shot is great, but these were dreadful, because Thomas Charles Carlyle looked like he'd had a fight with King Kong about an hour before the photographer arrived. His nose was mashed over on one side of his face, his lips were cut and swollen, one eye was puffed shut. He sported a handlebar mustache. If he'd shaved it off, no one could possibly identify him from the photo, what with all the damage to his face. I glanced back at his rap sheet and found a token Resisting Arrest among the offenses.

"Carlotta," Mooney said as soon as I looked up, "there is no condo company at Cedar Wash."

I opened my mouth and shut it again.

"Thomas C. Carlyle," he continued, "*this* Thomas C. Carlyle, the guy with the sheet, is wanted by the FBI. They got a hot tip. They think he's tied to some right-wing radical group in the state, the New Survivalist League, or something."

I'd heard of them. They'd tried to rob an armory someplace in New Hampshire. Shot their guns, made a rumpus, got away with a couple of handguns and a box of grenades. I swallowed and nodded.

"They're using this contest thing to smoke him out," Mooney continued. "They did it in Florida a few years back, tried it out on a few bastards with outstanding arrest warrants. Lots of the creeps showed up for their condo tour, and got slapped in jail instead."

The fluorescent lights in Mooney's office made me blink. "I don't believe this. My cat gets *Mother Jones*. How could they link him to a bunch of right-wingers?"

Mooney's shoes hit the floor with a thud and he stood up. His height was menacing in the small room, and his voice let me know I wasn't the only angry soul around. He spoke softly, aware of the cops on the other side of the glass door pretending to work while they listened. "The Feds are supposed to inform us, not run their own stinking circus. Doing it this way tells me they think the department sucks."

"No twenty thousand," I said. T.C. wasn't going to dine on Fancy Feast and Catviar.

"Not a nickel."

"T.C. was looking forward to it."

"You didn't believe this shit, did you?"

"Of course not," I said. Hell, no. I'd just finished asking Roz if she could fake me a Mass. driver's license. I'd not only called every damn Carlyle in the phone directory, I'd proposed fraud to a cop.

I could tell Mooney was trying to keep a self-satisfied smirk off his face. He shook his head. "Carlotta," he said,

142

"you know why you didn't last as a cop? Your imagination runs away with you."

"Wrong, Mooney. I didn't make it because I didn't brown-nose." There's enough truth in that statement to make it sound good. In spite of the sleaze, and the hostility from the "boys," I might have stayed if I hadn't had to deal with Administration.

"So, you want me to tell the FBI they screwed up?" Mooney asked eagerly.

"No," I said slowly. "Don't say anything. Not yet."

He adjusted to the disappointment. "Yeah, well, okay. Fine. I mean, those FBI bastards, I wouldn't tell 'em if their ass was on fire."

"Yeah."

"Look, keep me informed, will you? If they pull anything really dumb, I want a chance to call the newspapers, and give some reporter a ringside seat, okay?"

Considering how Mooney feels about reporters, he must really despise the FBI. He rocked back on his heels, and looked uncomfortable, and for a moment I thought he was going to ask me out again. But all he said was, "How's that old lady of yours doing? The one who got beat up?"

"Not too bad."

"The case going okay?"

His tone was extra sympathetic. I guess he felt bad about breaking my Cedar Wash bubble. I decided to take advantage of his solicitude.

"Mooney," I said, "You remember the *Valhalla*, that ship that—"

"The IRA gunrunner. You're not hooked up to *that*, are you?"

"Have you heard any gunrunning tales lately, anybody talking IRA revival?"

"Not a thing, Carlotta. Far as I can tell, the only people talking IRA gun deals are FBI, or Alcohol, Tobacco, and Firearms, trying to entrap. Why?"

143

I tried my leprechaun story out on him. He didn't like it any better than Jay Schultz had.

■■■■■■■■■■■■■■■■■■■■■■■■■■■■■■■■■■■■■■■

Chapter 25

I was starting to get a queasy feeling in the pit of my stomach whenever I thought about Eugene Devens.

Screeching the cab into its G&W parking slot dissipated maybe a grain of my foul temper. Gloria pretended not to notice. No doubt she'd given Mooney my cab number. I might have taken exception to her generosity except that all three big brothers, including the former NFL ear-biter, were hanging around the office, glowering on cue.

What I couldn't figure was where Sam Gianelli fit in.

John Flaherty was Jackie, the young Irish firebrand Pat had described. While Mooney was busy mocking my intuitive powers, I'd flashed on the outline of Flaherty's head under the cab's domelight, the set of head on neck, the shape of his ears. I knew where I'd seen him before: reflected in a mirror near a sign proclaiming Michelob Light the preferred weekend brew of every patriotic American. At the Rebellion, the night I'd trailed the three old coots. He was the younger, talkative one. Even though I hadn't seen Flaherty's face that night, on the shape of his ears alone I was ready to label him Irish Jackie, organizer of the GBA revival.

Why Sam had hired Jackie was another matter. I couldn't work Sam into the picture. Like I said, IRA and Gianelli don't exactly mix.

I drove home. The clock said seven-thirty; the sun said morning. I panicked, then remembered this week's Thursday morning volleyball had been postponed due to grievous bodily injuries. My distinctive blend of cab and cop-house smells would never tempt Chanel, so I stripped, tossed my clothes in the hamper, and stood under a stinging shower until the hot water ran cold. I wrapped my hair and the rest of me in matching oversized green towels. My phone's red message light was blipping on and off when I stepped into the bedroom.

"Hey, Carlotta, pretty fancy, answering machine and all, huh? So, uh, this is Detective Schultz calling. Uh, Jay. Um, look, you were right about, uh, the merchandise your, uh, friend is selling, you know. And, uh, if you're taking pictures still, and you should see him passing any vials, well, that would help. Or going into any residences, say. Okay. Uh, good-bye." He'd kept talking as he lowered the receiver, and I could hear him damn all frigging machines. Frigging machines were not properly impressed by boyish good looks and well-groomed hair.

On the whole, I agree. I mean, who wants to talk to machinery? I replayed the message. Translated, it meant Wispy Beard was dealing crack, and the Cambridge cops would appreciate it if I'd continue surveillance, so they could get on with more important things, like citing teenagers for "lewd and lascivious behavior" in Harvard Square.

Speaking of lewd and lascivious, another voice boomed on the tape. Sam's, deep and husky. So sorry, he'd be out of town for the next couple days. Would call me the minute he got back. Shit.

I toweled my hair into a state of tangled semidryness, and slid between the cool sheets. I imagined the FBI arresting my cat. I thought about Wispy Beard, christened Horace. I closed my eyes, and saw Jackie Flaherty's face superimposed on Sam's tanned body. I wondered if Margaret Devens's heart would withstand the shock of coming home to a Roz-and-Lemon-cleaned house. Pretty soon I'd worked myself up to full-blown insomnia. You know, one minute you need toothpicks to prop your eyelids up, the next minute, bingo, wide

145

awake. I get that way sometimes. The best thing I can say for insomnia is it isn't fatal. I've learned when I can't sleep, it's best not to try. So I got up, swore a little, dressed in comfy old jeans and a long cotton knit pullover, ate bacon and eggs for breakfast, or maybe dinner, and piloted my Toyota to Cambridge.

I didn't run into old Horace Wispy Beard right away. Even scumbag druggies take time off. He was not at his usual post near Paolina's front door. I dozed in the car, and woke, with a crick in my neck and a foul taste in my mouth, a little past five in the afternoon. So much for insomnia.

Horace was in place. Motionless, he looked like a monument, the statue of the Unknown Drug Dealer. A pack of cigarettes was rolled into the sleeve of his T-shirt. His skin seemed yellower as the sun sank behind gray clouds. He sat and stared with his blind unfocused gaze. I took his picture. Nobody came near him. A little past eight, he lit a cigarette. The red point of light flared like a beacon, then moved away.

Without much conscious thought, I decided to follow him. I could go straight to G&W afterwards.

If he hopped the subway at Kendall or Central Square, I'd have to let him go. He headed for Central. I followed him. Portland to Main Street to Mass. Ave. Trailing a walker in a car requires patience. I kept my headlights on for a while, flicked them off, then on, pulled ahead of him, parked, turned off his street entirely, and picked him up again at the next corner. He seemed oblivious, possibly toking on something stronger than a Camel.

He passed the subway entrance and crossed Mass. Ave., racing against the light, and nearly getting clipped by a silver Buick. Ran to catch the Dudley bus.

Good thing I'd been hacking the past week. Hanging a U-turn in the middle of Central Square didn't faze me. I sped off after bus 2654, one of the new ones, thank God. I was stiff, my neck hurt, and pretty soon I was going to have to find a bathroom. All I needed was a lung full of bus exhaust.

Horace Wispy Beard slouched in half a double seat near

the rear of the lighted bus. I drove erratically, one eye glued to his back. He stayed on board as the complexions of the passengers slowly changed, and the majority became minority, and the bus headed into Roxbury.

I know Roxbury as well as the next whitey. To tell the truth, I feel more comfortable there than I do in Southie. Don't get me wrong. There are plenty of streets I won't drive in Roxbury. I drew an imaginary boundary line for myself. I was not about to cruise down Sonoma Street into the area cops call "the shooting gallery," both for its heroin and its firearms.

Horace left the bus before I had much time to plan or worry, and set off at a determined pace down Albany Street. He went to the side of a narrow house on Norfolk Street, and knocked at the door. I didn't see him enter, but then I didn't see him come back out either.

Without slowing down, I drove around the block and parked parallel to the Norfolk Street house, in the shadow of the neighborhood's tallest and only tree. Across the street was some two-bit pocket playground. Pairs of sneakers, their laces tied together, decorated the power lines like Christmas lights. The park must have been crowded. I couldn't see much, but I could hear sporadic laughter, the heavy bass beat of a ghetto blaster, and a distant repetitive creak, like someone rocking in a rusty swing.

I wanted the address of that house. I wanted pictures of Wispy Beard entering and leaving. I wanted to weigh his satchel, before and after. I wanted an itemized list of its cargo.

What I could get was another thing.

The area seemed familiar, not because I'd been there before, but because it was like a lot of other crowded urban blocks. A place like this, near a major intersection, with a tiny park, overcrowded flats, slummy-looking row houses, is more active by night than by day. The music in the park blared, suddenly louder.

If I'd tracked Horace to a "crack house," a factory, I could

147

bet a watcher had already noted the red Toyota's passage. My car wouldn't freak anybody. A red Toyota is not a cop car. Even undercover narcs drive American. Still, another loop with the car might cause panic, and then the coke would wind up in the sewer.

The tree blocked my parking spot from any guards stationed on the roof. I hadn't noticed a lookout man on the stoop. So maybe this was Horace's home, a respectable dwelling, for all I knew. I doubled the volume on my radio, and flipped to a hard rock station. It seemed an appropriate neighborhood activity. I started jamming my hair up under my hat, and that was the first I knew of my body's plans to leave the relative safety of the car.

Now darkness can hide a lot of things, but a six-foot-one-inch redhead is not one of them. I wanted to take pictures, but I needed camouflage. Momentarily, I wished Roz was along for the ride, so she could coddle the right high-speed film into the Canon, and do the shoot. Roz provides her own camouflage.

I considered options. I could march up to the front door and ask everybody to say "cheese." I could sneak up on the place from the rear, but the neighbor's scrap-heap yard looked ideal for a nuclear waste dump. I had no desire to get my toes nibbled by rats.

The tree that hid my car so well prevented picture taking. It was what we used to call a nice climbing tree back in Detroit, with a good low split fork, and plenty of heavy branches. Now I haven't climbed a tree in maybe ten years, but the impulse was strong. I overcame it. Trees do not have back doors, and unexpected exits from trees can be both humiliating and painful. I leaned back in the driver's seat.

I was exhausted. Sleep in a car doesn't count like sleep in a bed. I checked my watch. Almost eleven. I took pleasure in imagining the steam rushing from Gloria's ears when I didn't show promptly at G&W. I thought about bathrooms.

Two giggling teenaged girls passed by talking about what Clyde did to Germaine in the back seat of that old Buick.

And what Germaine did to Clyde. And what Howie was gonna do when he found out from Germaine what Clyde did to her. That Germaine would feel the need to confide in Howie was a given.

Lights flared in a house across the street and I slid down in the seat. Slurred voices shouted back and forth, and "never-was-any-fucking-good-Angela" was given the boot for the night.

A clatter of high-heeled shoes and a burst of raucous laughter signaled the arrival of four ladies of the night. I'd worked the Zone long enough to spot the clothes and the walk. Hoots from the park confirmed my judgment. These were not gals returning from a stint at the local convenience mart. Their workday was just beginning.

Now my least favorite cop job was decoy. That's when they'd dress me up as bait, wire me, and see if I could put the fear of God into some john in the market for a quick screw. I mean, I hated it. Not only did it make me feel like a piece of meat, but I always had the sneaking feeling that my backup officers got off on the whole trip.

Ah, the hell with it. All experience comes in useful sooner or later. I yanked off my hat and ran my fingers through my hair. I found a lipstick, but no blusher, in my purse, so Max Factor's Primrose Red had to make due for both. Rearview mirrors are not great for makeup, but I managed an exaggerated mouth, and two slanty cheekbone accents.

My clothes were as wrong as they could be. I checked out the backseat for whatever I'd dumped there. I spend a lot of time in my car, and I'm not neat at heart, so things accumulate. I had my gym stuff: tank top, shorts, sneakers, a terrycloth headband; none too alluring. On the other hand, my sweater was one of those thigh-length numbers.

I wriggled out of my jeans, and tugged at the sweater's neck until it stretched and slipped down over one shoulder. With my bra strap hanging out, the new neckline didn't have much pizazz, so I stuck my arms inside the sleeves, made a temporary tent out of the sweater, reached around, unhooked

149

my bra, and stuffed it in the dash compartment. The new outfit cried for a wide, studded leather belt. What I located was a stingy yard of rope. I tied it around my waist and yanked the sweater up and over, to hide it. The blouson effect wasn't bad, but it made the sweater damn short.

My shoes were disastrous, but that was okay because I have plenty of abandoned shoes in my car. I hate uncomfortable shoes, but since the choice in size 11 is so limited, I often wind up with clunkers I've purchased out of desperation. Shoes that raise blisters generally get kicked off on the way home, because I can't stand driving in them. I found one perfect heeled sandal under the front seat. It must have taken me ten minutes to find the other. I wasn't sure they were a matched set. They pinched like hell. No wonder I'd ditched them.

I bent over at the waist, and gave my head a shake to make the red curls wild. I stepped out of the car whistling, shoulder bag tossed carelessly over my arm, and was rewarded for my efforts by an anonymous wolf whistle from the park across the street. I turned and flashed my unknown admirer a come-hither grin.

Walking the way the pros walk, I joined the gaggle on the corner. My arrival made us a well-integrated group. Two blacks; one Hispanic, who couldn't have been more than sixteen; one washed-out blonde, who looked like an escaped suburban homecoming queen; and Momma's own Jewish princess.

"Hey," I murmured as a low-key greeting. I knew from experience these gals were not much for chatter with strangers.

"Hey," the taller of the black ladies responded, after silently checking with her cohorts to see if anybody knew me. She was wearing a leather miniskirt and a cut-off top that didn't hide the lower curve of her breasts. "Seen Renney tonight?"

I took a while to respond, keeping my eyes half closed, leaning up against a lamppost, and humming a few meandering notes. The streetlight overhead was broken, which was fine because I look too healthy to be a working girl, what with all that volleyball and swimming. "Renney, yeah," I mumbled hazily. "Renney's the man, all right. Ain't nothin' Renney don't know." I slurred the words together in a sing-song chant. I'd seen enough hookers coming down from highs to know the routine. I scratched my arm and yawned. "Jina fixed us up."

There used to be this pimp named Renney who ran a string in the Zone. I hoped he wouldn't pick tonight for a spot check. Jina was a local hooker whose body had been pulled out of a railroad car in South Boston.

I listened to the ladies rap about bullshit arrests, with fifty-buck fines, which don't seem so bad when you make five hundred a night. The older black woman, Estelle, was thinking of ditching the life, spending more time with her kids. The Hispanic lady chuckled and asked her if she knew what they paid an hour at McDonald's. The blonde had a friend who'd gotten AIDS. She'd had herself tested, and was relieved the results were negative. The girls agreed that a checkup every six months was the only way to go. And condoms. And weren't the johns getting freakier, and what the hell did the cops mean, harassing the johns like that?

Cars slowed, honked, stopped. The Hispanic girl went for a ride. The short black lady in the glittery bandeau top and cheeky shorts took a walk in the park, escorted by a gentleman in a leather flight jacket and silver sunglasses. I liked that touch, sunglasses at midnight.

Nothing happened at the house I was watching, but the lights were still blazing, a hopeful sign. I kept my camera ready in my hand, blocked by the shoulder bag. I wasn't sure I could risk walking by the house to get a better shot. And I wasn't going to compromise my cover for any still life. If something didn't happen soon, I was going to have to give up my hooker act, or start a new career.

I wondered how long it would take the gals to get suspicious about my lack of dates. So far, the furthest I'd strayed was the all-night grocery where use of a grimy toilet was available for a buck. Oh, I'd go over to a car and whisper in the guy's ear all right. At first, I priced myself out of the market. Hundred-dollar tricks are not turned on Norfolk Street corners. One guy was so stoned he okayed the hundred. I told him I hoped he had herpes, too. I hardly had time to pull my head out the window before he took off.

A shiny Olds shrieked to a halt right in front of me. The door opened and a new addition to the hooker brigade got out. I pivoted as soon as I saw her face. I knew the lady. God, I'd booked her, what was her name? Marla? Marlene? Hell, I'd booked her so often we were practically best friends.

I backed off, closed my eyes, hunched down, and nodded against the lamppost.

"Babe, you okay?" Marla knelt down next to me. She was the motherly type. Maybe that's why she had six kids, all in state care. I didn't open my eyes. I could hear her breathing, smell her musky scent. "Hey," she said, "hey, don't I know you?"

Adrenaline pumped. I hadn't decided between fight and flight.

"Lemme see now, what's your name, girl?"

I opened my eyes. She stared at me with a puzzled frown, then caught her breath. My legs tensed.

Our eyes locked for a moment that seemed to last a half hour. Then she put her hand to her mouth, giggled, and said, "Bitch, cain't you do nuthin' 'bout that hair?" She slapped me on the shoulder in a friendly fashion, and the other ladies relaxed.

Marla's hair was a different color than it used to be. I think she was wearing a wig. Five years ago, she'd been a looker, high Cherokee cheekbones, and legs that wouldn't quit. She'd put on weight. She had deep carved circles under her eyes, and wore too much makeup to hide them. At the moment, she looked beautiful to me.

"Marla, babe, long time," I said. "Hey, let's walk."

We strolled the block. She asked if she was under arrest,

in the kind of hopeful tone that said she didn't have a place to flop for the night. I said I was no longer a cop, and she shot me a glance of shocked disbelief.

"You ain't hookin'?" she said.

"Look," I said, "you want to make some stand-up money?"

"What I gotta do?" She was in a profession where wariness pays off.

"I want some pictures of a house, and anybody who comes out of it. If we stand right over there, about two feet from that fire hydrant, and gab, and you shield me so they can't see what I'm doing, I'll give you fifty."

"Seventy-five," she said. "I get caught, I can't work this corner no more."

"Sixty-five," I said, because she expected me to bargain.

"You one tight-ass bitch," she said, smiling.

"You doing okay?" I asked.

"Now and then," she said. "The kids are growin' so fast. Where you want me to stand? And how long? Any bad dudes involved, they gonna notice us for sure."

That was true enough, considering my outfit and hers. She made me look downright conservative. Her satin boxer shorts were cut up the thighs, leaving very little to the imagination. She wore a lace-up fake gold-lamé vest, with nothing underneath, and the laces spread wide. I tugged my sweater to get more shoulder exposure. We'd get noticed all right. But noticed as part of the scenery, if we were lucky. We were hiding in plain sight, playing statues.

I decided to give Wispy Beard another hour. My thighs were getting goosebumps, and my self-esteem was suffering, but like I said, I am stubborn.

Sometimes, very rarely, it pays off.

Maybe twenty minutes later, it went down. Probably the last thing I expected.

A cab, a Green & White cab, pulled up in front of the house. The driver didn't sound the horn, just sat there, waiting. I could read the number on the front right fender: 863.

Marla and I had our routine down pretty well by then. We turned together, giggling and chatting like old comrades, and I snapped the camera's shutter. 863 was Sean Boyle's cab, the Old Geezer himself. I caught a glimpse of his white hair.

He waited all of two minutes, then the upstairs lights in the house went out. Fifteen seconds later the front door opened. Three men came out.

The first man seemed in charge. He wore a conservative suit, a white shirt that gleamed in the darkness, and a fashionably narrow tie. His features were shadowed by a dignified fedora. He looked Irish. I'd never seen him before.

The other two walked half a step behind him, like bodyguards. The one on the left had a set of impressive muscles. He carried a gym bag. I'd snapped four pictures before I realized the one on the right was Wispy Beard.

The well-dressed man got into the cab. The gym bag was passed to him. Everybody kept a careful eye on that bag.

I took pictures until the cab disappeared, and Wispy Beard and his friend went back in the house. I gave Marla her sixty-five, plus a ten-dollar bonus of IRA-gotten gains.

Wispy Beard and Sean Boyle. Together.

Faith and begorra.

Or, as my grandmother used to say: All is not butter that comes from a cow.

Chapter 26

As soon as I turned the corner, out of sight of both the hookers and the house on Norfolk Street, I broke into a run and almost killed myself racing to the Toyota in those damn sandals. I kicked them off as soon as I sat down. Then I gunned the motor and took off.

Damn. Damn. Damn. I'd never catch Sean Boyle. If I'd had my cab, the cab I should have picked up two hours ago, I could have flipped on the radio, called Gloria, and found out where Boyle was heading. I screeched a turn, and told myself to cool it. I didn't want to get picked up by the cops; not wearing this classy outfit, I didn't.

I saw a cab's roof lights up ahead, and jammed the accelerator to the floor. It was an innocent Red Cab, idling along, no fare in the backseat.

I braked, hesitated, and decided to head for Green & White. I doubted Gloria would be in a helpful mood, what with my tardiness, but I wasn't about to give up following any guy with a gym bag who took G&W cabs and hung out with scum like Wispy Beard. At the first traffic light, the guy next to me honked, raced his motor, and yelled something out the window. I yanked tissues out of my purse, and managed to smear most of the lipstick off my face. At the second light, I untied the rope around my waist and pulled my sweater down to its full length. I groped in the backseat for my pants, with no luck.

Instead of taking the shortcut, I decided to scoot down Harvard Street. It's not far out of the way, and I wanted to check the Rebellion. John Flaherty had driven his gym bag there like a homing pigeon. Why not Sean Boyle?

Boyle's cab was in the parking lot.

I shot right past, sure my eyes must be deceiving me. Some of the same cabs I'd noted the night before were parked on the street. The bar's neon sign was dead black tubing. The front door was barred, and a steel-mesh curtain shuttered the windows, but something was going on inside. Just like last night. I glanced in my rearview mirror, hoping Mooney hadn't sicced more cops on me. I reviewed last night's thoughts: What next? Wait? Take pictures? Risk entering the bar?

I parked illegally around the corner from the lot. I made

up my mind. I couldn't find my jeans, so I wriggled into my gym shorts. They didn't show under the long sweater, but they made me feel better. So did my bra. I found both my sneakers, but only one sock. I tossed it into the backseat, and laced my shoes onto bare feet.

I have broken into cars before. I have used everything from bent wire coat hangers to your latest high-tech wonder tools, courtesy of a car thief I once arrested, a man eager to prove his superiority to your average car-stealing punk. If he hadn't been absolutely wasted on dope—and hadn't thought himself one of the hunky ladykillers of the world—I doubt he'd have shown off his prize collection of boosters with such pride of ownership. He's doing five at Concord Reformatory, which should curb his desire to impress girls.

Breaking into Sean Boyle's cab was not without challenge. The parking lot was brightly lit, and Harvard Street's a main drag, patrolled by many a police cruiser. Since I hadn't been able to watch last night's gathering of the Gaelic Brotherhood, I had no idea how long tonight's meeting might last. An adrenaline spurt propelled me to the cab faster than my intended casual stroll.

Sean Boyle hadn't bothered to lock the cab, in direct disregard of Gloria's oft-repeated warning. He hadn't been dumb enough to leave the keys in the ignition, which was too bad because "stealing" the cab and searching it at my leisure seemed like a fine idea. I got inside, and quietly pulled the door shut. No need to advertise by leaving the domelight glowing.

I reached under the front seat and found a handful of dirty leaves, got awkwardly down on all fours, and peered under the seat. The rough carpeting scratched my cheek. It smelled of stale cigar ashes and dried mud. I stuck my hands into the cushion cracks and got an assortment of small change, which I pocketed. The dash compartment was locked. I never lock my cab's dash compartment.

Now I can open most locks. Give me time and decent lighting, and I can do the job. It's one of those small hand-coordination things I do well, like picking the guitar. Time was the problem. It seemed like I'd been in cab 863 long enough for Boyle to drink his weight in Guinness. My hands were sweating.

I inhaled deeply, hauled myself up onto the passenger seat, and stuffed my handbag between my legs. I fished out my flashlight on the first plunge, scrounged around for eternity before I located my leather case of metal odds and ends. I jammed the flashlight under my right thigh, aiming its narrow beam as close to the lock as I could manage.

The adrenaline was really pumping now. Slow and easy, I muttered to myself. You can't force a lock. You have to tease it, gentle it along until it's good and ready. Mooney used to make a lot of pointed remarks about my lock-picking skills, but I wish he could have seen me do that lock. If I can't make it as a private investigator, I can always burgle.

I jumped when the light inside the dash compartment lit up. It must have been all of five watts, but it seemed like a wailing burglar alarm. My heart quit leaping around when I saw the package.

It was a four-by-six-by-two box, wrapped in brown mailing paper. No address. Instead of string or tape, it was sealed with ornate green wax seals, initialed GBA. I hefted it. Light. I shook it. Nothing. I smelled it. Not a clue. I figured a gym bag could hold maybe thirty boxes.

I couldn't open the box because of the damn seals, one on each end, two across the main seam of the brown paper. I could steal it, but Boyle would be sure to notice. Not only that, I could see myself explaining to Mooney how I'd come by the damn thing, hear him reciting rules of evidence. Reluctantly, I put it back in the dash compartment, took pictures, hoping the film was fast enough for the available light.

While taking photos, I noticed another item in the dash compartment, a whitish rectangle half hidden under a map of the city. It was a postcard from Ireland, a landscape of green hills and contented sheep. It was signed "Gene."

That puzzled me, so I stole it. I figure people misplace postcards all the time.

Chapter 27

You had to hand it to Margaret Devens. One day removed from her hospital bed, and she was the perfect hostess. Margaret's living room seemed less resilient than the lady herself. Odds and ends of mismatched furniture filled the floor space. Roz and Lemon had hauled an old couch down from the second floor to replace the one the goons had ruined. An armchair wore a temporary splint on one wobbly leg. The rug had been sent to the cleaners. The doors of the curio cabinets were missing, sent to a local repairman. An unbroken vase sat dead center on the mantle, inadequate for such pride of place. It made the absence of other knickknacks more noticeable.

The ''guests'' arrived in straggly groups of twos and threes. They had the pasty faces of men who worked nights, slept days.

They squirmed on the ugly sofa, they teetered on card-table chairs imported for the occasion, the old men of Green & White, the iron core of the Gaelic Brotherhood. Margaret Devens had handpicked the invitees, her brother's friends, ten in all.

If Eugene and Flaherty had been present, we'd have had enough for a jury.

Sean Boyle, looking more sober than usual, was one of the first to arrive. Joe Fergus was grumpy, ready to pick a fight. O'Keefe, O'Callahan, Corcoran followed, Irish every one. All over fifty, some closer to sixty, some older, with glazed, glittery eyes that had seen days when the Irish weren't welcome in Boston, when they were "Micks" and "Harps" and names less specific and less flattering.

The old men stared at the living room's blank walls and unshaded lamps, at the long extension cord looping toward the slide projector. They spoke warily, in low, speculative tones. It reminded me of a wake without a body.

I'd volunteered to start things off, but Margaret had firmly, politely refused. She would handle it, thank you. Her sweet, fussy disguise was gone, maybe for good. No flowered dress, no feathered hat. She wore plain black, buttoned to a high, stiff collar. Her face was pale, her right eye blotched with pale bruises. One knee was bandaged. She didn't smile in welcome as the men trooped dutifully through the foyer. She didn't seem to notice anyone enter the living room.

She took her stand at the entrance to the living room, underneath the archway, and her presence stilled the men's voices. She carried a sheet of paper in her hand. It rustled as she raised it to her eyes.

"No Second Troy," she announced.

The men on the couch gave each other that look, the dotty-old-biddy look, the let's-get-out-of-here look.

Her voice was shaky, not with weakness, but with suppressed emotion. She sounded infinitely old, infinitely weary. "This poem, gentlemen, was found in my brother's room. William Butler Yeats wrote it, about a woman he loved with a hopeless passion. She was a heroine of the Irish Rebellion. Maud was her name, Maud Gonne. And for some reason, my brother, who was no lover of poetry, saw fit to copy it in his own hand. If he could take the time to copy it, surely you can have the courtesy to listen. Possibly, some of you know it already. Please excuse me if I speak too softly—or too slowly."

She didn't say that her mouth and jaw still ached from the beating. She didn't have to.

The old guys settled down, doomed to a long sermon in an uncomfortable pew.

"No Second Troy," Margaret repeated.

"Why should I blame her that she filled my days
With misery, or that she would of late
Have taught to ignorant men most violent ways,
Or hurled the little streets upon the great,
Had they but courage equal to desire?
What could have made her peaceful with a mind
That nobleness made simple as a fire,
With beauty like a tightened bow, a kind
That is not natural in an age like this,
Being high and solitary and most stern?
Why, what could she have done, being what she is?
Was there another Troy for her to burn?"

Silence greeted the ending of the verse. A shrug or two, maybe a few pairs of guarded, narrowed eyes.

Margaret let the paper fall. It drifted into the hallway. She took no notice of it. " *'Taught to ignorant men most violent ways,'* " she repeated. "Now—" She stared at the assembled faces in the room, and seemed to lose the thread of her thoughts. I wondered if she was searching for a face not present. I wondered if she was looking for her brother. She shook her head, and blinked her eyes rapidly. Then she went on. "To the point of our meeting. I hired someone to look into Eugene's disappearance, since none of you gentlemen would tell me where he'd gone. My investigator has some slides to show you. I trust you will find them enlightening." She gave up the floor, and moved, ramrod-stiff, toward the fireplace. Joe Fergus rose as if to offer his seat. She ignored him and passed by.

There was a murmur when I stood up.

"Still a cop," Sean Boyle muttered. "Worse, a spy."

"Shut your trap, Sean Boyle." Margaret Devens wheeled to face him, and snapped out the words with more spark than

I thought she had left. "And don't any of you speak until Miss Carlyle is through. Then you'll get plenty of chance for talk, and I hope you'll take it."

I'd set up the slide projector early that morning, done a dry run with Roz—my darkroom wizard—as audience, because I hate it when my visual aids flop. My first slide was a view of Margaret's living room, post-goon squad.

"You know Miss Devens is upset about her brother's disappearance," I began. "You might think she's angry about what happened to her house, or maybe about the fact that you collect for the IRA."

"IRA" got a couple of guys to sit upright.

"And if they did," Margaret interrupted with a quiet intensity, "it's true they should be ashamed. Big shots, every one of them. They know what IRA money buys. Bombs at holiday resorts to kill hardworking people who've finally saved enough for a trip to the seaside. Plastic explosives in department stores the day before Christmas. Machine guns, maybe, to murder mothers and fathers in front of their children—"

I hadn't had Margaret aboard during the dry run.

"The British have no right—" somebody started to say.

"No right?" Margaret echoed, cutting the protest short. "No right? Who cares who's got rights? Children with their arms blown off, and their legs left bloody stumps? Shut up, you fool. Don't talk to me about rights!"

"Miss Devens," I said. "Should I go on?"

"Oh, yes," she said bitterly. "Let's go on."

Roz, fairly respectable in one of her longer miniskirts, moved a step closer to Margaret, ready to break her fall if she fainted. Roz is good like that.

I flashed a blowup of a police mug shot on the blank white wall. It was greeted by a general mutter of puzzlement.

"This is Horace 'Bud' Harold," I explained. "He has a rap sheet that runs to multiple pages." I hit the button, showed him at the schoolyard, passing something along to a kid. In the blowup, you could see that it wasn't a packet, wasn't the glassine envelope I'd expected. It was a small vial, a fact I was certain would interest my Cambridge cop pal, Jay Schultz. "He is a drug pusher. That vial is full of crack. Cocaine. He sells it to kids."

"So what?" The voice came from the back of the room. I glanced over at Sean Boyle. His red face remained blank. He hadn't recognized his passenger's bodyguard.

"Let me show you a couple more slides," I said. I did them in sequence. First, the mug shot, then the dealing shot, then a good shot of the well-dressed man, in suit and tie, heading down the front walk accompanied by his strong-arm guard.

I used a pencil as a pointer. "This guy look familiar?" I asked, indicating Wispy Beard. Boyle craned his neck for a better view.

"Now watch carefully," I said, and I showed the slides of the well-dressed man boarding Boyle's cab, Horace and the gym-bag-toting goon by his side. The goon passed the gym bag to the passenger. I'd gotten a slice of Marla's thigh in a couple of shots, but they were pretty good photos on the whole.

"A man's got the right to call a cab," Boyle said slowly, "even if he associates with undesirables." You could tell he was thinking hard. "You sure those two are the same man?"

I flashed both pictures of Horace Harold on the wall so he could see for himself. "I tailed him to the house. He brought a satchel with him. It's possible the contents were transferred to a gym bag. I assume your passenger left a gym bag in your cab, as usual, and then you took it over to some bar, maybe the Rebellion, and split up the boxes, and made your deliveries—"

"Wait a minute," Joe Fergus said, rising to his full five six. "We shouldn't say anything. Jackie wouldn't—"

"You're twice-over fools," Margaret said, the words bursting out of her. She couldn't keep them bottled up, and her cold intensity drowned out Fergus's tenor. "Big-deal cab drivers helping out the IRA. Something to brag about at the

162

bars. And all the time, you're running cocaine, and heroin, and God knows what poison around the city like the pack of hoodlums you are.''

"What did she say?''

"Cocaine?''

"What the hell!''

"Drugs? None of us would—''

Shouts, denials, accusations, and general bedlam broke out.

"Hang on,'' I yelled. "Just look at the damn photos.'' I skipped a few slots in the carousel projector because things were moving faster than I'd expected. I hit the button, and John Flaherty's grinning face appeared on the wall.

"Correct me if I'm wrong,'' I said flatly, "but I've heard it from a good authority that you guys have been helping the IRA for a while, in a small way. You picked up change from bar canisters, converted the change to cash, and passed it along to somebody higher up, right?''

"Don't say anything,'' Boyle ordered the troops, which was fine by me.

"Then this man came along. John Flaherty, he calls himself. Jackie.''

"Jackie wouldn't have a thing to do with drugs—''

"Shut up, Corcoran,'' Boyle said. "I, for one, don't believe a word of it. We know Flaherty. It's some trick to get us to admit to helping the Provos. Jackie would never get mixed up with drugs. Cocaine, heroin, where would he get it from, eh?''

"Did Jackie ever tell you where he used to work?'' I asked.

"In the Republic,'' Boyle said proudly. "All over the southern counties. Then in the North. Belfast. Derry. Underground.''

"He's an Irish national, then?''

"Is that a crime?''

"Anybody seen his passport?''

Silence.

"They'd have checked it at the company,'' somebody

piped up. "When they hired him. You've got to do that with foreigners."

In her jerry-rigged basement darkroom, Roz had worked wonders, shooting terrific slides of enlarged B&W negatives of Flaherty's employment application. The slides, rushed through a professional lab that offered six-hour service, were grainy, but legible. Every space remained blank, except for the name slot: "John Flaherty," and the address rectangle, which was filled with a number and street in Dorchester. I'd checked out the address. The Vietnamese couple who'd answered the door of apartment 2A were extremely polite. They smiled and bowed, but spoke little English. The building superintendent had never heard of any John or Jackie Flaherty. I told the old men about the phony address.

"So what?" Fergus shouted. "He's on the run. There are plenty of damned informers, and a lot of Ulster storm troopers who want him dead."

The men, by general murmur, agreed with Fergus.

"If Flaherty was an Irish national, his passport number, his visa status, would have to be on file, right?" I said. "You know how strict Gloria is about that stuff, don't you? Can you think of any reason she might have approved an application like this one, with nothing, no work history, no references?" I had another slide ready for them. A blowup of a second sheet of paper, this one with less information on it. Just a name this time: "John Flaherty." A scrawl occupied the rest of the page. "Hire," it said. It was signed "Sam Gianelli."

The second enlargement wasn't as sharp as the first. I hadn't given Roz much time to work on it. I'd wanted to replace it in Green & White's locked files before Gloria realized it was gone.

"Do you want to ask me again?" I said. "How he might have gotten ahold of drugs? Or have any of you heard of the Gianelli family?"

"Not Sam," somebody murmured. I was glad it wasn't me. I'd been singing that refrain for a day or two now.

164

"Didn't any of you open the parcels you ferried around the city?" I asked.

"They were sealed. For our protection, so the FBI couldn't trace us with fingerprints." The voice was Joe Fergus's, insistent, demanding.

"Listen," I said. "It's no good. I've talked to cops: State, Boston, Cambridge. I've asked around. The word is that nothing, no money, no munitions, is moving out of Massachusetts, except legitimately, through the Ireland Fund. Everything going to Ireland is watched, and counted, and counted again, ever since the *Valhalla* business."

"All that proves is that Jackie and the IRA are smarter than the cops, or the cops are in it with them, and plenty are," came a voice from the back of the room.

"You tell me," I said. "Where are the guns coming from? Armories? Dealers? How are they getting to Ireland? Where are the ships? They're not moving out of Gloucester anymore. Nothing's sailed from the South Shore. Nothing out of Boston. What about the planes? Is Aer Lingus taking off from Logan loaded with guns? Has Jackie found a way to fool the airport metal detectors? Maybe he's using an Air Force base. Are planes taking off from Hanscom Field? For Ireland?" I started at one end of the room and tried to meet each man's eye, to put the questions to each of them. "Nobody here got curious enough to ask? Well, let me tell you this. Irish arms are not circulating in this state. What is moving in Massachusetts is cheap, smokable cocaine—crack—in little vials like the one you saw on the screen. And I think you're moving it, as unpaid, blind couriers. 'Mules,' they call them in the trade."

"I don't believe a word," Sean Boyle said.

I had an answer. In the form of a slide. A copy of an old mug shot, granted, but Roz does good work, and the resemblance was clear.

"Your precious John Flaherty has a record," I said. "A friend of mine ran the name for me, and came up with a drug bust and conviction back in 'seventy-nine. Three months in

165

the Concord Reformatory. He was not an Irish national in 'seventy-nine.''

He hadn't even used an alias for his operation at Green & White. How dumb can you get?

The old guys didn't say anything. They stared at young Jackie Flaherty with numbers across his chest and a defiant glare in his eyes. His hair was longer, tousled. I expected somebody to protest. I mean, a record isn't everything. There are felons who go straight. I didn't think our Jackie was one of them.

"Somebody here is FBI," one of the men in the back declared, a loyalist to the core. "As soon as we admit to anything, we're all in the slammer.''

Margaret Devens drew herself up to her full height. "You have my word, Dan O'Keefe, and you have no reason to doubt my word. No one here has any authority to keep you. Leave if you like. If it were up to me, I'd arrest the whole lot of you, for what you tried to do, and for what you did. God knows which is a worse sin, but evil is evil, and either way, it's a burden you'll carry forever on your soul.''

Nobody said anything for a full minute, maybe two. I could hear the dining room clock ticking away.

"Well," I said, "I've shown you that one of your 'IRA' couriers hangs out with a known drug dealer. I've given you a source of the drugs, the Gianellis. Maybe I've even shaken your faith in Jackie. Here's your chance to prove me wrong, to say, 'I opened that parcel, and it contained one automatic pistol with a green ribbon tied around the barrel.' "

Nobody said a word.

"How about you, Boyle? You want to tell me that the courier in the photo didn't use the name 'Maud' when he called G and W?''

Silence.

"So none of you got curious enough to open a package," I said.

"My brother Eugene was an inquiring man all his life,''

said Margaret Devens, softly. "A curious man, not one to take things on faith."

"Oh, my God." The words punched the wind out of Sean Boyle, and he sat heavily on the couch.

I said, "Tell us where Eugene went."

"Well, he's in Ireland," Joe Fergus said petulantly. "In Ireland."

"Dear Lord," Margaret whispered, "the man still believes."

"Boyle had a postcard," Fergus insisted.

While Boyle was patting his jacket pockets, I held it up. "Never mind where I got it," I said. "Is this the one?"

Boyle grabbed it, checked both sides, nodded.

"Tell them what you told me, Margaret," I said.

"It's not his handwriting," she said. "Not even close."

Roz had enlarged the smeared postmark. I didn't have the heart to tell them the card had been sent from Dublin, New Hampshire.

"My God, if this is true," Sean Boyle said slowly, "then Eugene's not—maybe not in Ireland at all. Margaret, believe me, we thought he was on his way with a shipment of arms. It was his dream."

Right out of his boys' adventure novels.

"Where's Eugene, then?" Boyle murmured. Elbows on knees, he cupped his palms, and let his head sink into his hands.

Margaret Devens knew the answer to that one. You could read it in her face.

"Margaret," Sean Boyle said, "I just don't know . . . I don't know what to say to you."

"The whole lot of you should go to prison for what you've done—"

"Margaret," I interrupted. We'd been over that ground.

"All you can say, Boyle," she continued bitterly, "is nothing. And all you can do is pay attention to this red-haired woman. You do exactly what she says, and maybe you won't see the inside of a cell for years to come."

I cleared my throat, to give the men time to think about what they'd heard, and because it was hard to watch Margaret and not get caught up in her pain. "I know something about the distribution plan," I said. "I know it has to do with the cab radios, and with the code name 'Maud,' from the poem." I gave a silent thank you to Pat, who'd put me on the right track. A woman's name. Something poetic.

I thought about Jackie Flaherty with reluctant admiration. True, he was too dumb to change his name, but he was smart enough to find a secret organization in place, a band of men well known in the community, with access to all neighborhoods, a reliable communication network—a group ripe for co-opting. Talk about a respectable cover—God, half of them must have cousins on the force. A whole fleet of unpaid, dependable mules, dreaming outdated dreams of glory. An unquestioning army brimming with unexploited loyalty.

If felons were smart all the time, cops would go out of business. I wondered if the setup had been Flaherty's idea from the start. Or if it had come from the top.

"Maud," Sean Boyle began slowly, looking at Margaret, but speaking to me. "Maud or Maudie, that was the signal. And it was always a woman's voice that made the call, so Gloria wouldn't get suspicious, and the calls were made none too often, and never from the same place twice."

Chapter 28

At home the next morning, Red Emma was in a feisty mood, digging her claws into my index finger and pecking away at the kitchen phone. I held her farther off so she wouldn't disturb the cute little bugging mechanism I'd discovered inside the speaker.

"Budgies of the world, unite!" I intoned at the bird. "Read my lips, kid."

Muzak oozed from the receiver. I held it a good six inches from my ear.

"How about 'Better red than dead'?" I asked. Red Emma was not interested. She wanted to peck my nose off. "Better green than dead?"

"What did you say?" The voice was female and accusing. I almost dropped both the receiver and the budgie.

"I'm trying to reach Mr. Andrews," I said politely. "It's important. Urgent, you might say."

Muzak gushed.

I can always tell Red Emma's mood by her degree of fluffiness. On those rare occasions when she is cheerful, she puffs up into a green featherball. When she's pissed, she gets so skinny you can barely see her. She dug her talons into my finger, and looked positively anorexic. Not without difficulty, I waved her off. She contentedly dive-bombed my head.

"Mrs. Carlyle." The welcoming bass was that of "our Mr. Andrews" all right. Thanks to Mooney, I knew who he really was. I kept my knowledge out of my voice.

"Great news, Mr. Andrews," I said eagerly. "I got in touch with Thomas. Is there any chance you can wait till the end of the week for us to visit Cedar Wash? He'll be home by then, and I'm sure he'll want to—"

The bastard tripped over his own words in his eagerness. "Where did you say he was now? Did he call?"

If he'd called, you'd have heard every word, Mr. FBI man, I thought.

"He called a friend, a business partner, and the, uh, friend got in touch with me. But the important thing is that Tom will be home by, oh, Friday, at the latest. So, do you think you can stretch the contest rules for us? We can visit Cedar Wash as soon as he gets home."

"Just a minute," Andrews said. He put me on hold. I

169

imagined him chortling on the other end of the line, informing his colleagues that he'd hooked a big one.

"Well," he said, returning after a suspenseful pause, "since we've come this far, I suppose we might as well go all the way. Cedar Wash is run by a group of caring individuals. We pride ourselves on that."

I almost choked.

"So," Mr. Andrews said contentedly, "as soon as your husband gets home, be sure to give us a call."

Right.

Believe me, the days never zipped by faster. Friday, which had seemed a distant prospect when I'd contacted Mr. Andrews, was looming closer. The clocks speeded up. The Old Geezers were strung tight. If things didn't start moving soon, one of them, probably hot-tempered Joe Fergus, would snap, storm up to Jackie Flaherty, and punch his lights out. Or else the Cambridge cops would wake up, bust Wispy Beard, plea-bargain him till he talked, and arrest everybody at G&W.

I was glad I had so much to do. Activity kept me from brooding over possible points of disaster.

I couldn't use my phone because of the bug. I dropped a lot of change in pay-phone slots.

Headquarters was Margaret Devens's house. Roz and Lemon moved in with her for the duration—for protection, and as an auxiliary work force. It took them a whole day to record the addresses of all "Maud" or "Maudie" pickups and deliveries.

I let Sean Boyle split up the list because he kept hounding me for something to do. He used my old police area map as a guide. All Area A addresses went on one sheet of paper, all Area B locations on a second, all Area C—and so forth. Joe Fergus xeroxed copies at a self-service machine in Harvard Square.

The main thing the cabbies had to do, the main thing I hoped they could do, was shut up and play along, not give Flaherty any cause for suspicion. They also served as on-the-spot observers, with Boyle as their captain. He divided them into three squadrons of three cabbies each. Fergus, O'Keefe, and Corcoran were his lieutenants. Flaherty's every move was reported, charted, analyzed. Timing was everything. No way was he going to take delivery of a single new shipment of dope. I was willing to keep the cops out as long as no more cocaine traveled the route. But as soon as the coke came in, the cops came in. That was the deal. I owed it to the kids at the schoolyard, to Paolina.

I gave Gloria the bare bones of the story. I didn't mention Gianelli. I felt lousy about it, but I didn't know what else to do.

"What?" She slammed an unfinished Mars Bar down on her desk, glared at me, and repeated herself an octave higher. "What?"

"I thought your boys were IRA collectors, right?"

"Right. I got that part."

"Sometime last year, around the time Pat left, they let a new member into the Gaelic Brotherhood Association—that's what GBA stands for, by the way. This new brother outdid all the rest when it came to blarney. Instead of passing the money along to the IRA, he bought cocaine with it—maybe not a huge amount at first, but business expanded. And he fed your cabbies a tale about bigger deals with the IRA, and pretty soon he got them picking up cash, and scooting drugs around the city, and feeling proud of themselves to boot."

I outlined the mechanics of Flaherty's plan. When I got to the part about her own unwitting involvement through the "Maudie" calls, she did something I'd never seen her do before. She tossed the unfinished Mars Bar in the trash can.

"Mules," she muttered sadly. She hit her broad forehead with the flat of her palm. "I've got a stable full of fucking mules. No way you can keep cops out of this, Carlotta."

I felt terrible. I wanted to retrieve the Mars Bar. "You're right, Glory," I said gently. "But maybe G and W can stay in the background."

"Hah. Right. Background." Gloria's brief peal of laughter had no humor in it.

"The Old Geezers didn't know what they were doing—and I, for one, don't think they should go to jail for being half-assed romantic jerks who live in a time warp."

"Well, I don't want to go to jail either, Carlotta. The food would sure as hell kill me."

"There might be a way out."

"Oh, Christ, Carlotta, is this the lead-up to one of your cockeyed schemes? I'm starting to sweat."

"It's your choice, Gloria. You can call the cops now, and put them all behind bars."

"And probably go with them. What the hell kind of choice is that?"

"Then play along," I said. "Your part is small, but crucial, Glory. Your chance to be a star."

"Star, hell," she muttered. "Don't give me any of that beat star shit. Next thing you'll tell me not to worry."

"Calm down, Gloria."

"What I want to know is, will your plan keep my ass out of jail?"

"I think so. I hope so."

She glanced around for her Mars Bar, shook her head despondently when she couldn't locate it. "Wait till I tell my brothers," she said.

I could wait. I'd deliberately picked a time when none of the bruisers were around. I didn't want them asking me why I was hassling their sister.

"If you need more muscle," Gloria said, "you let me know. I'm sure my brothers could help."

I swallowed. "Keep them in reserve, okay, Gloria? The fewer people who know about this the better."

"This new GBA member," she said, "is he one of my drivers? Say, somebody who came on about the time old Pat left?"

So much for keeping things from Gloria.

I swallowed. "I'd rather not say."

"Oh, shit," she said. "I've gotta tell my brothers."

"Okay. If you think your brothers are big on self-control,

you just go ahead and tell them. But if they move before I'm ready, they'll screw the entire plan. And I don't think the guards allow any junk-food care packages at Framingham State.''

As I walked out the door, she unwrapped a fresh Mars Bar, and gobbled it in two huge bites, as though it might be her last.

Chapter 29

Among the calls I made from pay phones was one to my lawyer, just in case. Whenever I left the house, I dialed home religiously, every half hour. Roz was staying at Margaret's most of the time. She had strict instructions not to answer my phone when she dropped by for a change of clothes or a meal of peanut butter. I used my remote beeper to check calls received. I heard from a manufacturer of vinyl siding, and a woman doing a toothpaste survey.

From my home phone, I made no calls, with the exception of one preplanned session with Roz, stationed at a pay phone in a Jamaica Plain diner. We chatted about how pleased I was that Tom was finally coming home.

I didn't let the Devens case totally rule my life. I ate. I slept. I played volleyball. I told myself it would all be over by Friday. Nothing would interfere with Paolina's Saturday band concert. I had plenty of time. Instead of picking her up for our regular noon rendezvous, I was expected in the school auditorium at 7 P.M. sharp. I look forward to band concerts with mixed emotions. My ears wince, my heart smiles.

I called Mooney from Dunkin' Donuts, after a strenuous

morning at the Y. I'd intended to visit him, but I changed my mind after dueling a tough squad from the East Boston Y. Near the end of the game, I blocked a spiked ball with the heel of my palm so hard the return practically shot to the ceiling. My team made the point, but we lost. I hoped it wasn't an omen. My hand ached.

That really doesn't explain why I was not in a mood to confront Mooney. Let's just say that he always had a way of punching holes in my cases when I was a cop. Besides, I like his voice on the phone. It's low and gruff and rumbly. He'd have made a good blues singer.

I asked if the door to his office was closed.

"Nope."

"Could you close it?"

"Now?"

"Yeah."

"People will think I'm getting a personal phone call."

I could picture the wide grin on his face. "You are," I said. "Personal and business-related and important."

I heard the receiver thump against his wooden desktop, the slam of his office door.

"What's all this?" he asked.

"Mooney," I said. "Would you say you still owed me a favor, or what?"

He considered it for a while. "I'd say we're pretty even."

"Then how's my credit?"

"Depends."

"Mooney, how'd you like to help your career, and give the FBI a gorgeous black eye at the same time? Would you be remotely interested?"

"I could be," he said cautiously.

"Look, I don't need any credit for this. I'm not saying I'd mind seeing my name in the papers. It might be good for business. But I'll leave that up to you. What I want is cooperation."

"What kind of cooperation, Carlotta? I can't break the law."

"Don't tell me what cops can do, Moon. I know what you can do. You can make plans based on the word of a reliable informant. You can make judgment calls."

"Go on."

"Mooney, I've never been more certain of anything in my life. This will all go down by Friday, or else I'll turn it over to you. Completely. The whole thing. You've got my word."

Silence.

"I can do it without you, Mooney. I just thought you might like to be there for the finale, make the FBI look dumb."

"What's my end of the deal? What do I have to guarantee?"

"First, that you won't jump the gun. Even if you decide to pass on it, you'll give me until Friday, free and clear."

"This Friday?"

"Make it Saturday morning. Eight A.M."

"Is it about T.C.?"

"Sort of."

"Would it require a lot of work?"

"I'd leave that up to you, Mooney. I trust you. You've got to trust me. No more Twenty Questions."

I could hear him breathing. "Deal," he said.

We talked.

Mooney, being Mooney and Irish to the core, could see my point. He felt a sneaking sympathy for the Old Geezers. He didn't want to arrest a whole bunch of cops' elderly uncles and fathers-in-law. Nor did he wish to arrest a fat black woman in a wheelchair, especially one with three hulking brothers. I admit I played fast and loose with Gloria. She would have despised my romantic version of her plight. I didn't let that stop me. I was convincing as hell. Once I even had to lower my voice because the Dunkin' Donuts waitress was taking an interest in my performance.

There were parts of it Mooney didn't like. I'd expected that. He said I was relying too heavily on cops taking informants seriously. I agreed with him completely, a technique that leaves him speechless. I told him he could make it work by

175

letting me know which officers would be likely to move fast on drug arrests, which cops were busting ass for promotion.

"This is going to be a lot of work," he grumbled.

He agreed to get the warrants ready. He agreed to stand by. He wanted to tap my telephone.

I had to remind him that it was already bugged.

"I'll call you," I said. "Don't call me."

I've always wanted to say that.

He was still blitzing questions when I bade him a firm good-bye, and hung up.

Rude, I know. But Mooney's never satisfied.

Chapter 30

was so busy juggling half a dozen mental balls that, when the doorbell buzzed, it never occurred to me that Sam Gianelli would be on the stoop. If it had, I wouldn't have answered the door.

Wearing a cotton plaid shirt—beige with a navy stripe—and khaki slacks, he looked cool, relaxed, and casual. He carried flowers. Purple iris.

I must have opened the door, because somehow he was in the foyer. I guess I spoke to him, uttered polite, inane sentences, thanked him for the flowers, but my mind had gone profoundly blank.

I am no Mata Hari. There is no way I could play a bedroom scene with a man I intended to screw in an entirely different sense of the word. I mean, I hadn't thought much about Sam the past few days, what with all the frenzied planning. I'd just hoped he'd stay the hell out of town.

And here he was, with flowers in his hand, and a warm smile on his face, inquiring whether I'd missed him while he was gone.

T.C. rubbed against my leg, immediately and instinctively jealous. I knelt down and fussed over him. My uncharacteristic behavior must have shocked the cat, but it gave me something to do while I pulled myself together.

It was early Wednesday afternoon. Three days had passed since the meeting at Margaret Devens's house. Things were heating up. All the arrangements, the signals, the codes, had been set. We were waiting for one particular phone call—from "Maud."

I'd rather do anything than wait. My personal hell will be a dentist's lobby, filled with ancient, thumbed copies of *Glamour*. To avoid reverting to chain-smoking or nail-biting, I was cooking—for me a rare occupation. Paolina's class was having a bake sale, and she'd asked me to contribute these weird confections my mom used to make. They went over big with the Girl Scouts, and now I'm doomed to bake them for all eternity. Not that I mind, for Paolina.

I was wearing white painter's pants, streaked with egg yolk, and an electric blue T-shirt, similarly stained. I don't own an apron, and I'm not overly neat with an eggbeater. I'm sure I had dabs of batter on my face. Neither my outer nor inner self was prepared for Sam's company.

"I'm, uh, cooking," I said, less than brilliantly.

"You?"

"Yeah. I'm making these chocolate chip meringue things. Paolina wants them colored, green and pink. Class colors. The food coloring doesn't make them taste any different, but they look kind of gross."

I led him into the kitchen. I had the FM radio tuned to a local blues station. I turned the volume down. I found a vase, and snipped the ends of the iris stems at an angle. I arranged the flowers. I felt like a robot.

"How was the trip?" I asked.

"So-so."

Score any cocaine? I wondered.

He asked for a glass of water, admitted orange juice would be better, agreed that a little vodka wouldn't hurt the taste. I poured a large swig of Smirnoff's into mine. The kitchen timer gave a ding that sounded like the starting bell for Round One of the Middleweight Boxing Championship, and I yanked a tray of meringues out of the oven, burning myself as usual. For me, they ought to make pot holder mitts that reach clear to the shoulder.

"Smells good," Sam said, staring dubiously at the neat rows of pink blobs.

"Help yourself. I couldn't remember if I doubled the recipe last time or tripled it, so this time I tripled it. I may have made enough of these suckers to go into business for myself."

"Then you can stop driving a hack. You enjoying it?"

"No sweat," I lied.

"Bring the extras over to Gloria. She can eat maybe three dozen," Sam said. "Look, were you expecting anybody?"

"No."

"Do you mind my coming by? I should have called, I guess."

I took another pull on my vodka-laced orange juice.

"This is nice," Sam said, gazing around the kitchen.

"What?" My kitchen is never going to be featured in *Better Homes and Gardens*. Dirty dishes were piled in the sink. I missed Roz.

"Domestic interior," he said, smiling wickedly. "Woman baking, man appreciatively sampling the goods. I should have married you years ago, when you didn't know any better. You'd have straightened me out."

I stole a glance at him out of the corner of my eye. Yeah. More likely, we'd have warped together.

"These things aren't bad." He spoke through a mouthful of chips and meringue.

"You get one. The rest are for Paolina."

178

"She sounds like quite a kid," he said. "I'll have to meet her."

Never, I thought.

"You really think of her as your sister?"

"She's all the family I've got."

He grimaced and said, "Sometimes I wish I didn't have any family."

I whisked together egg whites and sugar, and added two drops of green food coloring for the final batch. The drops produced a pale grayish tint. I decided another drop couldn't hurt, tilted the bottle again. I must have shaken it pretty hard. Eight, maybe nine drops of the stuff hit the meringue. I wondered if anyone would eat loden green chocolate chip meringues.

The silence was stretching uncomfortably long, so I asked Sam how he was getting on with the rest of the Gianellis. It was social chat. I didn't really want to know. I wanted him to leave.

"Hell, I don't even see them, except for my sister."

"I didn't know you had a sister."

"Older than me, the second oldest. She married an outsider."

"An outsider?"

"Not an Italian—not, you know—" He waved his arms around and did a Godfather imitation. "Not a Gianelli Sicilian Italian." He winked, dropped the act, and smiled. His teeth were white and even.

I added chocolate chips to the batter, studied it, tossed in a few more. "Your family didn't like that?"

"Are you kidding? It was like a mortal sin. The guy's Irish, for Christ's sake. Working class. And my sister chose him herself, which made it worse. My father hit the ceiling. He's from the old school. I guess he thought he'd give his only daughter as a reward to one of his faithful retainers. On a silver platter."

I scooped weird greenish batter, mixed with lumps of dark chocolate, into small mounds on a baking sheet. I couldn't remember if I'd buttered the tray or not. I'd scoured the damn thing for half an hour after locating it down in Roz's darkroom filled with murky fluid. I devoutly hoped I was not about to poison the entire fifth grade.

"God are these sweet," Sam said.

"You're not eating another one are you?"

"You know," he went on, "the day Gina married Martin, my mom dressed in black. She didn't go to the wedding, but she put on this black dress, and she walked around the North End, so everybody would know she was in mourning. Didn't speak to Gina for years, until the grandchildren started coming. She sees them occasionally, but she almost never speaks to Flaherty. If he answers when she phones, she hangs up. So sometimes I think you're lucky, choosing your family like that."

My spoon hung in the air, drooling meringue.

"Flaherty," I repeated. "Not—"

"Look, don't mention this at the garage, okay?" Sam said, coming up behind me. He wrapped his arms around my rib cage. I could feel his breath on my neck, his smoothly shaven cheek against mine. "That driver you mentioned—Flaherty—he's Gina's kid."

Oh, God. No wonder he couldn't use an alias at the cab company.

"John's been nothing but trouble for her," Sam went on, "so she asked me to give him a job, see if he straightens out. What he really wanted was to go into the—you know, my dad's business. And that would kill Gina. She steered clear of that bunch, made a pretty decent life for herself. But I don't know. I don't think John likes hacking much. I don't think he likes me."

He nuzzled my neck, and turned me around. My face felt like it was frozen.

"Hey." Sam tilted my chin up with his index finger, forced my eyes to meet his. "John hasn't been coming on to you, has he?"

I kissed him, to stop his words. The kiss lingered. He

twined his fingers in my hair, and pushed me back against the countertop. I got chocolate chip mush on my white pants. I was breathing too heavily to care.

I know what I said about Mata Hari. But what followed wasn't cool or calculated. Part of it was relief. Part of it was pure longing.

"Your clothes are dirty," Sam said after a while. "Let's take them off."

"Not in the kitchen. I have a tenant."

"We can't do it on the kitchen table?"

We steamed up the shower instead, playing with the soap, and with each other, almost losing our balance on the slippery tile. We washed each other's hair with huge handfuls of lather. Sam scrunched his eyes shut to avoid any wayward soap. Rinsed, we toweled off and got into my bed. I hit the button on the tape deck, and Bonnie Raitt sang "That Song About the Midway." Her aching, soaring voice sounded lonely and lost:

"Well, I met you on a midway at a fair last year,
And you stood out like a ruby in a black man's ear.
 You were playing on horses, playing on guitar
strings,
 You were playing like a devil wearing wings."

We moved to the music like familiar lovers, timing our thrusts for mutual pleasure, but our thoughts couldn't have been more separate. Our lovemaking was gentle and slow. Intense. The afternoon light slanted in through the blinds. Tangles of his dark hair tickled my face.

I don't know what Sam was thinking. How do you ever know what another soul is thinking? Me, I guess I was saying good-bye.

Maybe if I had warned him then, it would have turned out differently. But the wheels were in motion. It was too late.

Chapter 31

The call came late Thursday night. Early Friday morning, really. Fifteen minutes past midnight.

"Maudie" needed a cab at the Trailways Terminal.

According to Sean Boyle, Flaherty handled bus depot and train station runs personally. Any member of the GBA could cover a "Maud" call at a residential address, do routine pickup and delivery work, but only Flaherty answered the bus or train station calls. The stations must be where he did business, trading cash for drugs. That was smart, using buses and trains. What with all the baggage checks at airports these days, a lot of federal agents were locating dope instead of terrorists.

Flaherty wasn't dealing in Gianelli channels. He must have made his own connection, which wouldn't have been too hard. A river of dope flows from New York to Boston. Maybe Flaherty saw the whole Green & White scam as some kind of apprenticeship. Maybe he thought after he earned his rep as an independent, he could go to Papa Gianelli and request his rightful place in the family business.

Eugene Devens must have suspected, must have followed him on one of his station runs. How Eugene had lifted the cash, I didn't know. Why he hadn't passed it on to the IRA—whom he considered its true owner—I did know. He hadn't passed it on because he was dead. And whoever had killed him had been dumb enough to do it before he told them where the money was.

I got the call from Gloria at sixteen minutes past midnight.

I recognized her voice immediately. She apologized for dialing the wrong number. That was the signal. She'd stalled "Maudie" as agreed, told the woman it would be half an hour or more before a cab could get loose. In half an hour Gloria would put the call on the airwaves.

Unless she heard from me that something had gone drastically wrong.

I dialed the Harvard Square pay phone where Lemon had been staked out for so many nights I was afraid he'd called it quits. But the patience he'd developed from playing statue—plus the salary I was paying him from T.C.'s hoard—kept him faithful. He picked up on the second ring.

"Tom," I said, as soon as I heard his voice. "Tom, honey, how was the trip?"

"It's great to be home," Lemon said. "I missed you, babe."

Don't schmaltz it up, kid, I thought.

"I missed you, too," I said. "How about if I pick you up at the Trailways Terminal? In half an hour? Is that okay? I can't wait to see you."

"Me, neither, babe. Look, don't be late. I don't want anybody to notice me hanging around."

"And you'll go along with this contest thing?" I asked.

"Look, Carlotta," he said impatiently, "we've been through this. I'm not going on any wild-goose chases with you. I'll be at the bus station in half an hour, and then I don't know. I might be moving out again tonight."

"Tonight," I wailed. "But we won't have any time."

"Shut up," he said roughly. I'd described the real Thomas Carlyle to Lemon in enough detail for him to embellish his role. "Just meet me at the Trailways Terminal."

"The new one," I said. "On Atlantic Avenue. In half an hour," I repeated, just in case.

"I'll be there," Lemon said. He added as an afterthought, "Love 'ya."

I cradled the receiver carefully. Now it was up to Lemon

and Roz to make the other calls, the cabbies to make speedy deliveries, the cops to act.

T.C. does not like to travel except when he likes to travel. I hadn't had him in the Toyota since the last time he threw up on the dashboard.

Mooney had insisted.

I grabbed the cat and wrestled a leash attachment onto his collar. He glared at me with wide-eyed disbelief, and exercised his claws. I kept a grip on him, and pretty soon he calmed down.

I took my gun out of my shoulder bag. I thought about leaving it home. I thought about Wispy Beard. I thought about the two thugs who'd roughed up Margaret. I jammed it into the waistband of my jeans, at the small of my back. It was uncomfortable.

Just as well. When a gun starts feeling comfortable, I'll know it's time to quit.

Chapter 32

I know my way around the old Greyhound Terminal in Park Square. It used to be a highlight of my beat, a dimly lit trough stinking of urine and rancid grease, a magnet for pimps. There they'd lurk, night after night, meeting those buses from Peoria, greeting those lost, young, hungry-eyed runaways. The Greyhound pimps were something else—bizarre, perverted Welcome Wagon hosts with a set line of patter, a memorized, routine rap: "Hey, girl, you lookin' good. You look like you could use a meal. You got a place to stay? You want a little reefer? A little coke?"

Park Square got urban-renewed with a vengeance. They tore down practically every building in sight, but left the Greyhound Terminal, a monument to sleaze. I don't understand why, since they promptly built a shiny new bus depot near South Station. The Trailways Terminal.

I zipped up Storrow Drive to the Southeast Expressway, my eyes peeled for traffic cops, although getting nailed for speeding is no real threat in Boston. I hit seventy. That's when my Toyota starts to shimmy. I slowed to sixty-eight. Two dark cars followed me, so I politely used my blinkers to signal lane changes and turns. My shadows moved with me, no signals. I took the High Street exit, a left on Congress, a right on Atlantic Ave. I hung an illegal U into the Trailways parking lot, and sandwiched the Toyota between an old VW bus and a tiny Escort. I glanced at my watch. Gloria's call should have gone out two minutes ago. From here on in, the timing depended on Flaherty.

T.C. and I stared at each other in the dark. After yowling along with the radio for a few ear-shattering moments, he'd settled into one of his silent, accusing modes. Hell, I agreed with him. I should have left him home. I cracked my window open an inch. He could stay in the car and sulk.

There was a cab stand smack in front of the futuristic glass-and-steel structure. Flaherty wouldn't even have to hunt for a parking space. Green & White number 442 was nowhere in sight. Yet.

I was relieved not to see any other G&W cabs nearby. I'd had trouble keeping the Old Geezers under wraps the past few days, especially Boyle and Fergus. They wanted Flaherty for breakfast. They tossed around words like ''tar'' and ''feathers.'' Hanging was too good for the bastard.

The bastard. Sam's nephew. His only sister's only son.

I swallowed, gulped salty air, and stomped on the rubber mat that opened the sliding door. I focused straight ahead, so I wouldn't seem to notice the men behind me. I could feel their eyes on the back of my neck.

The station was like an airplane hangar, with steel overhead beams, soaring escalators, and narrow catwalks over an enormous central lobby. I buttoned my jacket against the air-conditioned chill. The air smelled wrong—canned and recycled to a metallic breeze. All that glass, and not a single window that opened.

I shook my head as I looked around. Spiffy new building, same pimps, same winos, same runaways. On one bench an exhausted young woman in a denim jumper held a baby on her lap, and scolded a toddler to stay close. I didn't recognize anyone right off, but I wasn't trying to recognize anyone. I just wanted to know who was where, check the pieces on the board. A quick scan of the waiting room showed only pawns—pawns, and the well-dressed, elaborately casual men I wasn't supposed to notice.

I checked the schedule board posted over the Trailways counter, did the same at Peter Pan, then at Continental. Buses had come in from New York on two of the three bus lines within the hour. I didn't have to know which bus interested Flaherty. He would show me. I hoped.

I hadn't glanced at my watch more than, say, forty times, when he strode through the sliding glass doors twenty-two minutes later. He'd brought two goons along. My heart almost dropped out the bottom of my sneakers when I saw they weren't carrying anything.

They didn't notice me. I was wearing baggy faded jeans, a blah T-shirt, a shapeless jacket. I'd tucked every strand of red hair out of sight under a beige scarf. I wore glasses so lightly tinted they were useless in the sun. None of the pimps or the winos or the ticket-counter people had given me a second glance. I was flattered by their lack of regard. I felt close to invisible.

Engrossed in a flyer selling Trailways' cross-country tours, I pretended not to notice Flaherty and his colleagues. They walked by, eyeing the winos and the pimps and the late-night, weary travelers. I dropped a quarter into a slot and bought a news-box copy of the *Globe*. Then I followed them, hanging back, keeping out of sight. They made their way

186

down a staircase. I took the escalator, which was broken or stopped for the night. My sneakers were silent on the metal treads.

Lockers lined one wall. Some were large enough to stow a steamer trunk, others too small for my shoulder bag. Red-tagged keys flagged the unused lockers. Maybe Eugene had stolen—I'm sure he would have said "reclaimed"—the loot in T.C.'s cat box from one of these lockers, once he'd figured the scam. Any fool could jimmy a bus station locker.

I made tracks for a nearby ladies' room, because the two guards were doing their stuff, watching all the traffic while Flaherty worked the lock. I held the door open an inch, and saw Flaherty remove a briefcase, leaving the key in the lock. A good trick, never using the same locker twice. Flaherty was almost smart.

He'd just underestimated Eugene Devens. And his sister.

Flaherty and the goons filed back upstairs, crossing the vast lobby. I trailed them in fits and starts. I was aware of men following me.

I love a parade.

Damn. I hoped the deal wouldn't go down in the men's room. I hadn't thought of that. Christ, you can't think of everything.

The terminal was laid out like a spider. The lobby was the body. Long, angled walkway legs led to the loading docks. Flaherty and his companions marched down one of the corridors. A red sign overhead said Continental. Gates 3-7. They were alert now, poised for trouble. You could see it in the set of their shoulders.

They walked for what seemed forever, Flaherty front and center, the others half a step behind, darting glances right and left.

Three figures, almost a mirror image of Flaherty and company, came out of the shadows to meet them. One carried a gym bag. The other two flanked him. One was a woman, not much more than a teenager. They'd need a woman's voice for "Maudie." And traveling with a female was less suspicious. You could always cuddle up and pretend to be newlyweds anticipating the honeymoon. This gal didn't look cuddly. She wasn't tall, not more than five five, but she was broad through the shoulders. A scar cut her forehead, and she didn't comb any of her lank hair forward to hide it.

The walkway was deserted. The Continental bus had arrived at eleven forty-five. "Maudie" must have waited until the passengers dispersed before calling G&W.

Now I waited—hardly breathing, a beige nobody hunched against a cinderblock wall—while the swap took place. I wanted my targets relaxed. I wanted it clear that everything was business as usual. I watched shoulders, arms, hands. Four of the six held themselves like they were carrying.

I felt my own .38 pressing against the small of my back. A bead of sweat trickled down my neck.

The briefcase was swapped for the gym bag.

Time.

I breathed.

I stepped away from the wall. Not too far out, because I didn't intend to place myself in any firing line. I spoke as loudly as I could, directly to Jackie Flaherty. I hoped "Mr. Andrews" of Cedar Wash Condominiums could tell which man I'd targeted, but it really didn't make much difference.

"Tommy," I yelled. My voice sounded hollow, rusty. I'd stored up too much tension in my throat, and my vocal cords almost refused to cooperate. I willed enthusiasm and strength into them. "Tommy, darling, it's so good to see you again."

Maybe one of the guys was actually named Tommy, because Flaherty's right-hand bodyguard turned toward me with a questioning look on his face. The others shrugged. The girl glanced behind her, to see if this dame's Tommy was racing up the hall.

"Drop the suitcases." The voice belonged to "Mr. Andrews" of Cedar Wash, but it was amplified and distorted. It seemed to come from everywhere at once, swelling out of the floorboards, bouncing off the walls. "Get your hands up. You are under arrest."

188

The six swiveled in various directions, confused by the nondirectional, godlike quality of the voice. Two made half-hearted moves toward less than immediately accessible fire-arms, then froze when they saw what they were up against. They were sloppy. They'd played this game too often without a hitch. In sharp contrast, the FBI men were anything but lax. There must have been eight of them, with artillery in plain sight.

There was a moment of silent standoff. I tried to join the wall, pushed myself flat against it. I was impressed. I mean, for a downtown drug bust, you'd be lucky to get two halfway interested cops these days. They've lost their enthusiasm, and in some ways I can see their point. It wears you down, ar-resting the same creeps over and over.

The FBI looked sharp. I mean, they had us surrounded. They must have flashed those badges and gotten instant ac-cess. Impressed as I was, I hoped no nervous junior G-man would pull the trigger by mistake.

None of the drug dealers drew a weapon. Twelve hands eased themselves over six sullen heads. Mine had shot up the minute the FBI requested it. I was pleased. It seemed nobody wanted to bleed on the shiny linoleum.

I breathed again.

See, I thought the bad part was over.

Chapter 33

It wasn't Mooney's fault.

There were too many cops and too many crooks.

I first caught sight of him on a catwalk overhead, and I

wondered how long he'd been in position, whether he'd appreciated the FBI's neatness, or whether he was still too pissed at them to let admiration temper his anger. He rocked back and forth on his heels, ready to pounce. He waited patiently while the FBI disarmed and handcuffed the six. I'd been right. Four carried pieces. The FBI leader—"Andrews," or "George Robinson," or my old school chum, "Roger Smith"—ordered me to step aside and stay put, and warned me that I'd be charged as an accessory. Nobody searched me or the scar-faced woman, probably because they hadn't brought a female officer, and didn't want to risk a lawsuit. That was legit, but nobody cuffed us either, which was totally dumb. What do they think, men are the only jerks with guns?

I didn't see how Mooney got down from his perch. All I know is that he was downstairs and approaching fast, with a sea of blue uniforms around him. They halted ten feet away, and he stepped forward, grinning broadly. He'd brought more than blues. He'd enlisted a Deputy Superintendent, probably to handle the press. He'd shanghaied a bruiser I remembered from the Narcotics Division.

He said, "Thank you. 'Mr. Robinson,' isn't it? Or is it 'Andrews'?" He flashed his tin and continued, "Boston Police. Possibly you've heard of us. We'll take over now." He nodded to the narcotics officer. "Hey, Joe, you wanna read these jerks their rights?"

"Andrews" hardly looked at him. "Lose yourself," he said. "These people are in federal custody. I have a warrant for the arrest of Thomas C. Carlyle. We've just cracked the New Survivalist League wide open."

The flash of relief on Flaherty's face was instantaneous. "But I'm not—we're not. Look, somebody's made a big mistake here."

"Yeah," Mooney agreed, "and you're it." He turned back to "Andrews." "And you can use that warrant for toilet paper, because none of these bastards is any Thomas C. Carlyle. You've just assisted on a local drug bust. We appre-

190

ciate it. We thank you for all your help. We know how big you are on cooperating with your local police force, but now you can waltz on out the door. I've got warrants, too, with the right names.''

"Look here, mister—"

"Don't 'mister' me. Lieutenant Mooney. Of the Boston Police, an outfit you're supposed to cooperate with. Remember?'' Mooney spotted me standing against the wall. "Carlotta?''

I whipped off the turban and glasses, and he looked relieved. I guess he thought I'd shaved my head. "Hey, Carlotta, you bring T.C. along like I asked?''

"Andrews's '' jaw dropped.

"I left him in the car. He's in no mood to be bothered."

Gloria and Roz were right. "Andrews" was definitely cute, especially when he was angry. Mooney said, "You'll find the real Thomas C. Carlyle in a red Toyota in the parking lot. The same car you followed over here. Don't worry. He's unarmed.''

"But not declawed," I offered.

"He is a cat," Mooney said. "You went after a cat. Send one of your men out to read him his rights, somebody who doesn't mind getting scratched.''

One of the FBI team moved off at a curt nod from his superior. I was glad I'd left my car doors locked. I didn't think the FBI would break into my car, but I had Mooney send along a uniform to make sure.

"Andrews" stepped closer to Mooney. So did I. I didn't want to miss anything.

"You mean you knew about this whole—this whole charade?" he said quietly. There was so much anger in his voice that he had to speak softly to keep it from cracking.

"Charade?" Mooney said loudly, loving every minute. "You mean like a phony contest?''

I didn't like the way Flaherty was staring at me. His face was white and pinched, his small, mean features drawn together. Sweat was pouring down his forehead, but his eyes measured distances, and his arms strained against the cuffs. His eyes looked like holes cut in a cardboard mask. The others seemed more relaxed. One guy was bobbing his head, and I wondered if he was high.

Heated words were exchanged about which agency was going to take charge of the evidence. The Deputy Superintendent stood to one side and let Mooney do the talking, but you could see he was delighted. The press was mentioned. It seemed a local columnist was right outside, a guy who loved to skewer public agencies. A few of the FBI men lowered their guns and murmured among themselves.

I sneaked another glance at Flaherty. He had Sam's build, Sam's shoulders. I wanted him in a cop car, out of here, behind bars.

"Look," Mooney's voice drowned out "Andrews." "Forget it. You did the bust, but we've got the paper. We've got a tie-in to a likely homicide."

The FBI commando who'd been dispatched to my car returned. He said, "It's a goddamned cat all right."

"Arrest it, why don't you?" Mooney said. "You've got a warrant for that cat."

Common sense tells you the bad guys give up when they're disarmed and outnumbered and cuffed. Common sense has nothing to do with it.

Flaherty started it. He broke away, twisting and turning and hollering, and the whole group flew apart. Shouts rang out, but no fire. There were too damn many cops—uniforms, brass, suited FBI. Nobody wants to risk shooting another cop. Nobody wants to shoot a cuffed suspect either, not even the FBI, and worse, the prisoners were heading for the lobby, for the shelter of the pimps, travelers, and runaways.

I started after Flaherty. It was a gut reaction. I stopped. I thought about Sam. I chased another guy instead, the goon who'd grabbed the gym bag. None of that stuff was going to make it to Paolina's housing project.

He could run, I'll give him that. But in that bright open lobby, there was no place to hide. He leaped over counters, but he couldn't use his hands to break a fall. He dropped the gym bag. We danced around a bench. I could have ended it with my gun, but the woman with the two children was clutching them both on her lap, praying at top volume, and ignoring all my pleas to hit the floor. I could hear other people screaming, shouting.

I brought the bastard down with a flying volleyball lunge that stung my knees. His head smacked a bench with a satisfactory thud. I jumped to my feet, out of his reach. He lay there, winded. I checked to make sure he was breathing, then I pulled my gun, and let him know that prone was the preferred position.

The woman with the two kids was well into her seventeenth Hail Mary. She hadn't moved. Her eyes were closed tight.

Flaherty was directly in front of me. An empty handcuff loop dangled like a huge earring from his left wrist. Maybe some FBI jerk hadn't cuffed him properly. Maybe he'd socked a cop, gotten the key, given it to the woman. Maybe she'd unlocked his cuffs. I don't know. It didn't matter. His jacket pocket was torn. His forehead was smeared with grime or blood or both. He had a gun pointed at my head.

I raised my arms until I had a gun pointed at his.

He said, "You're my ticket out."

I don't know how long we stared each other down. My hands were damp. My finger felt like it was glued to the trigger. Eleven pounds of pressure to pull that trigger. The universe condensed to that necessary tug. I studied Jackie Flaherty's face. I didn't think he'd fire. I think he wanted me to kill him.

I almost did. I almost squeezed the trigger. I would have squeezed it. I would have. Sam or no Sam. This had nothing to do with Sam. This was him or me, and that's one thing I learned when I was a cop. If it's him or me—it's me, every time.

"Down, Carlotta!" I know Mooney's voice like I know my own, and I dove for the floor like it was an Olympic pool.

One elbow hit hard. A pinwheel of light blinded me, and then I was deafened by the crack of revolver fire. There were two quick shots, then silence. I wondered if I'd been hit.

I lifted my face. Over Flaherty's body, maybe thirty feet away, I saw the outline of his killer, high boots first, then muscled thighs in camouflage fatigues. Because I was flat on the ground, the man seemed larger than life. My eyes traveled up—belt, shirt—and I clamped my mouth shut to force back a scream. Flaherty's killer had no face, only a black hood with slitholes for eyes.

I never found out which of the Old Geezers contacted the real IRA. And I'm not saying the police were in on it.

But somehow, in the confusion, in spite of all the cops, Jackie Flaherty's executioner melted into the crowd and got away.

Chapter 34

Hours ticked by. I told the same edited story to an endless parade of increasingly high-ranking cops, then to two Assistant District Attorneys, then to a full-fledged DA who looked about twelve years old, and finally to a comfortably graying Deputy Superintendent. I drank vile coffee. I ate two mysterious sandwiches that could have been tuna fish or chicken salad, but were mainly mayonnaise. After my chat with the Deputy Super, I expected release, but two more cops came in and started the whole show over again. Then two more. My mouth felt numb. Everything I said started to sound wrong. I sat and stared at cracked walls and peeling paint, concentrating on them with grim single-mindedness because the ugliness of the interrogation room beat the pictures in my imagination.

Over and over and over. The core of my story was that I'd uncovered a drug ring while observing and tailing Wispy Beard. I had no client. The drug dealer's location had posed a threat to my little sister. Check it out with Officer Jay Schultz of the Cambridge force if you don't believe me. Since I was an ex-Boston cop, I'd brought my discovery of an upcoming deal to the attention of my former superior. He'd made the bust, but things had gone wrong due to the wholly unexpected interference of the FBI. What were those guys doing there anyway? Who was this Thomas C. Carlyle?

I didn't think "Andrews" would be eager to discuss the tap on my phone.

As to who killed the drug dealer—Flaherty, was that his name? I didn't know. I really didn't. Sometimes I sound more convincing when I'm lying than when I'm telling the truth.

Not a word about the cab company.

It was such a simple story you'd think they'd have gotten it straight the first time, but no, I had to recite the bilge for anyone who had a spare half hour. It was a good thing I'd been on the other side of police interrogations, or I'd have gotten nervous, what with all the comings and goings, and pointless, repeated questions.

Mooney was with me the first time—taking mental notes, I hoped—so he could make his version jibe with mine. Flaherty was dead. What would it hurt to keep the Old Geezers out of it? Not that they deserved protection, the damned fools. But Gloria did. And Sam.

I wondered who'd tell John Flaherty's mother that her son was dead. Who'd tell Sam?

I got increasingly nervous as the hours wore on, not because I really thought they'd hold me, but because I didn't want to disappoint Paolina. Word started filtering in about a number of other drug busts. Wasn't it odd, cop after cop asked, that informants had been so considerate on this night of all nights? Yes, I enthused, wasn't the Mayor's Drop a Dime/Stop a Crime program wonderful? I stared at my watch. I listened to my stomach rumble.

At five past five, I cornered Mooney and told him I absolutely had to leave.

At half past six, he breezed into Interrogation and interrupted two new-minted detectives with the news that he was to escort Miss Carlyle over to Area B. I didn't say anything until we were safely out of the building. Then I remembered the cat.

"Don't worry. Your tenant came and rescued him."

"You see her?"

He nodded. "Pink hair, purple streak. You can pick 'em."

"Do I have to go over to B?"

"Nah. Those guys were just questioning you for practice. I'm taking you home."

"My car—"

"Impounded. You can probably get it back tomorrow. I'll see what I can do."

"Thanks." My mouth was so dry I could hardly get words out.

Mooney's car was parked about two feet from the curb in a No Parking zone. He's got an old, dented, gas-guzzling Buick whose passenger door opens only from the inside. I slid in from the driver's side.

"How are you?" Mooney said, once we were settled. In all the hours since Flaherty's death, nobody had asked that one.

I swallowed and grimaced. "Okay. You?"

"Okay." He lit a cigarette, and shook his head the way he always does when he realizes he hasn't given up smoking yet. "You lie pretty well."

"I guess you do, too, or we'd be sharing a cell."

"I might have to name the cab company. If we can't squeeze Devens's murder out of one of the punks."

"Okay," I said. I didn't care anymore. That's how the cops get most of their confessions. You just don't care about anything after fifteen hours of looking at the same brown walls and hearing the same questions and breathing the same stale air.

"What's so important tonight? Heavy date?"

I explained about Paolina.

"You want to go straight to the concert?"

I glanced down at my sloppy jeans and worn jacket. "I have to change—"

"I'll wait for you."

"I can call a cab."

"I'd like to wait."

Mooney has infinite patience, which is one of the things that makes him such a good cop. I zipped upstairs, yanked on a green dress, brushed my hair, and was back in eight minutes flat. The bed called to me, but I knew if I lay down for a second I wouldn't get up for nine hours. And Paolina expected me.

Bypassing Harvard Square, we dodged the Broadway potholes into East Cambridge. We didn't talk or listen to the radio, but the silence was warm and easy. Battered cars crowded the small parking lot near Paolina's school.

"Thanks, Mooney." I said, getting ready to open the car door.

"Hang on. I'll find a space."

"I can get out here."

"Look," he said. "Do you mind if I tag along?"

"Mooney, it's a kid's band concert. Do your ears a favor."

"I like band concerts," he said stubbornly. "I'd like to see Paolina."

Paolina has met Mooney three times. The first time, he was wearing his full-dress uniform, and he awed her into scared silence. The second time, he spent about an hour blowing soap bubbles with her on the front steps of the station house. The third time, they were old friends. His presence would more than make up for my lateness.

"Okay," I said.

He parked illegally, and left his Officer-On-Duty card displayed prominently on the windshield. We went inside.

All grammar schools are exactly the same, the way all hospitals and all airports are. Rows of lockers, long tiled hallways, a smell that comes from the union of chalk and blackboards. For me, that particular aroma always evokes shrill cries of "Single file in the hallways, line up according to height, please." Which used to mean that all the little girls lined up first, and then all the little boys, and then yours truly at the back of the pack.

We didn't need directions to the auditorium. The noise—I hesitate to say music—guided us toward double doors on the left. We crept in like the shamefaced latecomers we were, and fumbled for seats in the dark. I saw two on the aisle way back on the right, and tugged at Mooney's hand until he saw them too.

The stage was a raised wooden platform, so high that the folks in the front row got a good view of forty little pairs of feet. They do that deliberately in schools, to give speakers more authority. It does nothing for acoustics. The lighting was a matter of on or off, and the front of the stage remained in twilight, which didn't bother me because Paolina was near the back.

The imitation-leather seats might have been roomy for ten-year-olds. I felt as if my knees were kissing my chin, and I regarded Mooney's struggle to find a halfway comfortable position with sympathy.

Normally I can turn my mind off with music, quiet the incessant murmur of my brain. Marching-band tunes performed by an elementary school ensemble do not do the trick.

I have perfect pitch. Usually I consider it a blessing. I'm not sure if my perfect pitch is absolute or relative. I carry around a middle C in my head, and I do the rest of the scale based on that one note. Tonight the gift was not a blessing. One of the flute players should have been muffled. A couple of violins weren't even close. The entire brass section should have been locked in a room way down the hall, preferably soundproofed.

Mooney patted his knee in time to the music.

People hear music differently. For me, it's a thumping bass line that I love, and voices twining in close harmony. Paolina doesn't sing very well. Paolina hears the beat.

She plays percussion, and I think she's terrific, but then I would. In a white blouse and a dark pleated skirt exactly like the blouses and skirts worn by all the other girls in the band, she stood out as if a spotlight were focused on her. She sported two bright red plastic clips in her hair, one over each ear. She spent most of the time waiting for her cues. She seemed to vibrate with the music, her face taut with the excitement of the count, the unbearable tension of the moment before the cymbals or the snare drum or the triangle was sounded. She told me once that she hears music as a series of counts, like footsteps. That's why she was so delighted with the ballet. She never hesitates about whether something is three-quarter or four-quarter time, much less more complicated rhythms. It's her gift, one of many.

I wondered if Jackie Flaherty had played an instrument in his grammar school band. I felt the first tear slide down my cheek.

Of forty-seven people arrested on drug possession charges in Boston and Cambridge that night, one was my pal "Bud" Harold, aka Wispy Beard. With his record, another arrest might mean Walpole, the state penitentiary they call something else these days—Woodsy Glen or Meadow Marsh or some such name—to distinguish it from the fair town of Walpole. No more lazy drug-pushing days on Paolina's stoop for him. I watched my little sister, poised for a cymbal strike, cheeks glowing, eyes intense, hearing the beat so clearly that it pulsed inside her—and I knew there would always be another drug dealer.

I mumbled an excuse to Mooney and left the auditorium. I couldn't find the ladies' room. All I could find were doors marked Boys and Girls, and I finally entered the girls' room closest to the auditorium. The place was impossibly small. It had four skinny stalls with graffiti-covered wooden doors that topped off at four feet. The mirror reflected my breasts on down, and the sink was so low I'd have to get on my knees to wash my face. I felt like Alice after she'd eaten the mushroom, and that made me cry harder.

When I'm hot I sweat, and when I'm sad I cry. Neither is socially acceptable, and you might just as well tell me to stop sweating as to stop crying. When I say sweat, I mean *sweat*, not "mist" or "dew" or any attractively feminine version of sweat. And I don't weep into any dainty handkerchief either. I wail. I howl. I gulp and hiccup and blow my nose.

I knelt on the cement floor, and turned the cold tap on full. A discouragingly thin stream trickled into the yellowed basin.

I heard somebody rap on the door.

"Carlotta?"

"Go away."

"Are you all right?" Mooney asked.

"Yeah."

He pushed the door open. The room halved in size. His shoulders almost hit the door frame.

"Are you okay?"

"I'm fine, Mooney. Do you mind?"

"Can I help?"

"Go away."

He just stood there.

I never cried when I was a cop. It was a point of honor. If the "boys" took it as weakness, I wouldn't be weak. I'd show them. And after a while I lost the knack, and things just welled up inside, and hardened into a constant nagging ache.

As a private operative, I'd made peace with my tears.

"Look, Mooney, I'm fine. I just feel bad when I see somebody die. That's all."

He didn't say anything.

"Mooney, you saw me at the bus station. Was I good?"

200

"Yeah."

"Was I a good cop?"

"Yeah."

"Then what I do afterwards, if I scream or faint or froth at the mouth or throw things, that's my own business, okay?"

I cupped my hands in the sink, and submerged my face in the water. Mooney had a stack of rough paper towels waiting. While my eyes were covered, he put his hands on my shoulders.

"Mooney," I said. "I appreciate it, but I don't need a man to lean on. I don't burst into tears in the hope one will come along."

His face got red, and he yanked his hands off my shoulders as if they were on fire. "For Christ's sweet sake, Carlotta, will you stop treating me like some goddamned representative male! It's because I'm a cop, right? Just because I'm a cop doesn't mean I'm some kind of fascist macho asshole. I see rooms full of women in tears every week, and I don't want to comfort them. I want to comfort you. *You*, Carlotta. I don't mean it as an insult, dammit. I saw the bastard die too, goddammit, and it would comfort me to hold you."

He stopped dead. His voice echoed off the walls. I could hear a distant trombone, wailing off-key.

"Jesus Christ," he said quietly, "I guess I yell when I see somebody die. Sorry."

"It's okay," I said, standing.

There was hardly room for both of us. The walls pushed us together, and we stood in the little girls' john, hugging. Friends—and maybe more. He kissed my hair, my forehead, my cheek. I think he would have gotten around to my mouth.

The door squeaked. A small child in a flowered pinafore entered, dragging her black-garbed grandmother by the hand. The little girl paused openmouthed, made a noise like the door squeak, and retreated fast. Mooney's back was to the door, so he didn't see the mask of scandalized outrage freeze across the woman's bony face. She raised her furled umbrella high. She looked just like my third grade teacher, and I felt

201

trapped in a manic flashback—ten years old, hiding in the girls' room, caught without my math homework.

"I don't know what you think you're up to, young man," she screeched.

It must have been a while since anyone had called Mooney "young man" in that tone of voice. I could feel him jump. He glanced around. His face flamed as he became fully aware of his surroundings.

He pivoted to face his accuser "It's okay, lady," he said quickly. "I'm a cop."

I was laughing so hard I had to sit down on the floor.

Chapter 35

I made it home before midnight, and spent some time sitting cross-legged on my unmade bed, chewing my fingernails. Then I got resolutely to my feet, and walked across the room to the telephone. The journey seemed like a long one. I didn't think I'd wake Sam. He's a night owl; used to be, anyway. The phone rang and rang; ten, twelve, fourteen times. The answering machine never answered. I thought I might have dialed the wrong number, so I tried again, and kept on trying until 2 A.M.—playing guitar, dialing, wondering where he was, dialing. Pretty soon I knew his number by heart.

The next morning, when the receiver clicked and I heard his voice, I started talking before I realized it was a recording. He must have come home, flipped on the machine, and left again, unless he was using the damn thing to monitor calls. The phone beeped in my ear. I panicked and hung up, unprepared for my allotted thirty seconds. What the hell could I say in thirty seconds? I dialed again, left my name, asked him to return my call. I sounded cool and impersonal, even to myself. He didn't call back.

I read about the funeral in the *Globe*. Not a detailed obituary, just one of those small alphabetized notices, listing the funeral home—a place I'd never heard of in the North End—and visiting hours: Wednesday 2-4. In other notices, husbads, wives, children were named as chief mourners. This one began: "Grandson of Anthony Gianelli." Then it listed his mother's name, then his father's. It said: "Relatives only." No funeral mass. No place to send donations in lieu of flowers.

I bought flowers at a shop on Huron Avenue, purple iris that wilted in the unseasonable heat. My gray wool skirt clung to my thighs. It was too hot for wool, but I didn't own any summer mourning. By the time I got to Park Street Station, I was sweating and sorry I'd chosen the airless Red Line train instead of my Toyota. I once made a vow never to drive into the North End. The streets are so narrow, and parking is impossible.

The North End is no place for an Irish funeral. It's Italian, densely populated, sliced off from the rest of Boston by the Central Artery. The streets are edged with strips of uneven sidewalk that directly abut the narrow three-story row houses. No lawns, no trees. But the buildings are surprisingly well maintained, clean and freshly painted. Pots of geraniums brighten window boxes and iron fire escapes. Old men sit on the front stoops reading the papers, passing the time. Espresso shops and bakeries scent the air. Sheets of cream-filled canolli sit in the bakery windows.

The funeral home was unusual, set back from the street, a squat brick house with three steps up to a pillared portico, separated from its neighbors by foot-wide walkways. A hearse was parked at the curb, followed by three black limos. They turned the two-way street into a one-lane battle zone. Six Boston cops added to the confusion.

A steady stream of people flowed up the front walk, the

women subdued, the men in dark suits, white shirts, dark ties. Most were elderly. As they entered, the door swung wide, and I could see a dim foyer where two men in black suits flanked an inner double doorway.

Cars honked. Adding to the traffic jam was a gas company van, parked across the street, two wheels up on the sidewalk, yellow lights flashing. It had tinted-glass side windows. The FBI likes to film Cosa Nostra funerals. I wondered why they hadn't just planted the camera in plain sight.

I gulped a deep breath, and started up the front walk. I'd walked over a mile already, from Park Street Station. My shoes pinched. My skirt felt heavy. My stockings chafed. I should have worn a hat. My hair looks out of place at funerals. Most of the old ladies had their heads covered with black lace mantillas.

The air in the foyer was pleasantly cool. I felt the slightest pressure tugging my right elbow. Then my left elbow was gently pushed and I was shunted neatly aside, one large goon at each side.

Tweedledee said, "Family only, miss."

Tweedledum said, "We'll express your condolences."

I tried to shake them off. They held on. I said, "Yeah. What name'll you give?"

The grip on my arms tightened. I dropped my bouquet. I hoped one of them would reach for it, but they were professionals. They left it lying on the tile, one droopy iris bent double.

The inner doors were half glass. Through them I could see a narrow reception hall with deep red flocked wallpaper, oak wainscoting, a crystal chandelier. A gilded mirror over a fireplace reflected marble statues and groups of softly chatting mourners. An ornate sideboard held a cut-glass vase of lilies. I thought I could see the back of Sam's head. He'd gotten a haircut. The back of his neck was pale.

"Tell Sam Gianelli—" I began.

"Family only, miss," Tweedledee said firmly. "You don't want to make a scene."

204

"Big family," I muttered.

The tall man turned his head. It was Sam, his face as fixed as the marble bust on the mantelpiece. Through the glass door, he looked as if he existed in a different world, a sad, formal place where no one smiled. A portly man patted his shoulder, shook his hand. Sam stared at me over the fat man's head. He couldn't have missed me. His lips parted slightly, then pressed themselves together in a thin line. He swallowed. He didn't look away. He didn't look down. He looked right through me.

I closed my eyes, just for an instant. When I opened them he was gone.

I turned to the goon on my right. "Will you give Mrs. Flaherty the flowers?" I asked. My voice was shaky, but I think he heard me.

A third man elbowed his way out of the reception hall, grabbed the bouquet, and shoved it in my arms. They turned me around, and gave me a dignified version of the bum's rush out the door.

I stood blinking on the portico, one hand touching a cool pillar, more for reassurance than support. I was aware of a low rumble of voices, raised eyebrows.

I left the damn flowers on the hearse.

Chapter 36

The hurly-burly died down after a while, in spite of *Herald* headlines the likes of BLACK MASK KILLER ON THE LOOSE. About a week after Flaherty's funeral, somebody got a hot tip, and came around to question Gloria. She says her largest brother answered the doorbell chewing on a hunk of raw meat. I don't believe a word of it, but whatever happened, nothing ever got into print concerning the Old Geezers' conspiracy.

I talked to reporters at first, on the grounds that publicity couldn't hurt business. I got tired of the game before the press did. After a while I started letting the parakeet answer the phone.

First, I took the bug out of the receiver. I gave it to Mooney as a keepsake of his encounter with the FBI. Mooney didn't do too badly in the papers either, and the Deputy Superintendent declared himself indebted for the entertainment value of the early part of the evening. And while the unexpected killing may have given Mooney a couple of sleepless nights, it didn't bother the department as a whole. I mean, what's one more drug pusher? Flaherty's death was back-page news, except for the spectacular manner of his going. Nobody mourns a dead drug pusher long—except his family.

Six days after the bus station fiasco, the earthly remains of Eugene Devens were pulled from the harbor, near the spot where they'd found his cab abandoned, not far from the bus terminal. One of the local goons talked.

All the Old Geezers came to his funeral. And a lot of unknown men paid their respects as well. At the wake, I kept wondering: Which one killed Jackie Flaherty? Which of the faces crowded into O'Brien's Funeral Home had I last seen masked by a black hood?

About the money . . . Margaret Devens was not only serious about not wanting it back, she was even more determined that the Old Geezers and the IRA should never know it existed. She didn't want to donate it to the church. There was no charity she wished to endow in Eugene's memory. She wanted to forget about it.

T.C. waltzed off with the loot after all.

I made Margaret take the difference between the insurance settlement and the damage to her house, and enough to cover Eugene's burial. She couldn't have been left too hard up because she bought one of Roz's tamer paintings for two hundred bucks.

To celebrate, Roz dyed her hair fright-wig white.

After figuring my time and expenses, I deposited my fee, plus a bonus, in my checking account. I made a donation to the Animal Rescue League in T.C.'s name. I treated myself to two sets of GHS guitar strings, a new Chris Smither album, and an old Lightnin' Hopkins one. I gave a goodly sum to the YWCA, anonymously. Otherwise, they hound you for life.

I consider the rest Paolina's college fund.

I hope "Mr. Andrews" is still out there somewhere, searching for Thomas C. Carlyle.

About the Author

Linda Barnes is an award-winning author whose "Michael Spraggue mysteries" include BLOOD WILL HAVE BLOOD, BITTER FINISH, DEAD HEAT, and CITIES OF THE DEAD, all published by Fawcett.

Ms. Barnes lives with her husband in Brookline, Massachusetts.